Praise for
CHARLAINE HARRIS
and her Sookie Stackhouse novels

"It's the kind of book you look forward to reading before you go to bed, thinking you're only going to read one chapter, and then you end up reading seven."
—Alan Ball on *Dead Until Dark*

"Vivid, subtle, and funny in her portrayal of southern life."
—*Entertainment Weekly*

"Charlaine Harris has vividly imagined telepathic barmaid Sookie Stackhouse and her small-town Louisiana milieu, where humans, vampires, shapeshifters, and other sentient critters live . . . Her mash-up of genres is delightful, taking elements from mysteries, horror stories, and romances."
—*Milwaukee Journal Sentinel*

"Blending action, romance, and comedy, Harris has created a fully functioning world so very close to our own, except, of course, for the vamps and other supernatural creatures."
—*The Toronto Star*

"[An] entertaining series . . . It['s] easy to understand why these oddly charming books have become so popular."
—*The New Orleans Times-Picayune*

"[A] light, fun series."
—*Los Angeles Times*

"It's a bit hard to imagine having vampires and werewolves lurking around every corner, but Harris has a way of making the reader buy it hook, line, and sinker."
—*The Monroe (LA) News-Star*

"I love the imaginative, creative world of Charlaine Harris!"
—Christine Feehan, #1 *New York Times* bestselling author

continued . . .

DEAD AND GONE

Charlaine Harris

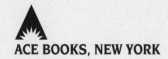

ACE BOOKS, NEW YORK

THE BERKLEY PUBLISHING GROUP
Published by the Penguin Group
Penguin Group (USA) Inc.
375 Hudson Street, New York, New York 10014, USA
Penguin Group (Canada), 90 Eglinton Avenue East, Suite 700, Toronto, Ontario M4P 2Y3, Canada
(a division of Pearson Penguin Canada Inc.)
Penguin Books Ltd., 80 Strand, London WC2R 0RL, England
Penguin Group Ireland, 25 St. Stephen's Green, Dublin 2, Ireland (a division of Penguin Books Ltd.)
Penguin Group (Australia), 250 Camberwell Road, Camberwell, Victoria 3124, Australia
(a division of Pearson Australia Group Pty. Ltd.)
Penguin Books India Pvt. Ltd., 11 Community Centre, Panchsheel Park, New Delhi—110 017, India
Penguin Group (NZ), 67 Apollo Drive, Rosedale, Auckland 0632, New Zealand
(a division of Pearson New Zealand Ltd.)
Penguin Books (South Africa) (Pty.) Ltd., 24 Sturdee Avenue, Rosebank, Johannesburg 2196,
South Africa

Penguin Books Ltd., Registered Offices: 80 Strand, London WC2R 0RL, England

This is a work of fiction. Names, characters, places, and incidents either are the product of the author's imagination or are used fictitiously, and any resemblance to actual persons, living or dead, business establishments, events, or locales is entirely coincidental. The publisher does not have any control over and does not assume any responsibility for author or third-party websites or their content.

PRINTING HISTORY
Ace hardcover edition / May 2009
Ace mass-market edition / April 2010
Ace trade paperback edition / April 2011

Ace trade paperback ISBN: 978-0-441-01921-2

The Library of Congress has cataloged the Ace hardcover edition as follows:

Harris, Charlaine.
    Dead and gone / Charlaine Harris.—1st ed.
    p. cm.
    ISBN 978-0-441-01715-7
    1. Vampires—Fiction. 2. Werewolves—Fiction. I. Title.

PS3558.A6427D4 2009
813'.54—dc22

2009001834

PRINTED IN THE UNITED STATES OF AMERICA

10   9   8   7   6   5   4   3   2   1

ACKNOWLEDGMENTS

There are lots of people who've helped me along the way, and that help has put me where I am today. I want to give thanks to just a few. The current moderators of my website (Katie, Michele, MariCarmen, Victoria, and Kerri) make my life so much easier, and the moderators emeriti (Beverly and Debi) deserve a tip of the hat, too. The readers who visit www.charlaineharris .com to offer their comments, theories, and pats on the back are always a source of encouragement.

Backed by a cast of thousands—okay, four—Toni Kelner and Dana Cameron are a constant source of support, encouragement, commiseration, and enthusiasm. I wouldn't know what to do without them.

DEAD AND GONE

Chapter 1

"Caucasian vampires should never wear white," the television announcer intoned. "We've been secretly filming Devon Dawn, who's been a vampire for only a decade, as she gets dressed for a night on the town. Look at that outfit! It's all wrong for her!"

"What was she thinking?" said an acidic female voice. "Talk about stuck in the nineties! Look at that blouse, if that's what you call it. Her skin just cries out for contrasting color, and what is she putting on? Ivory! It makes her skin look like a Hefty bag."

I paused in the act of tying my shoe to watch what happened next as the two vampire fashionistas burst in on the hapless victim—oh, excuse me, the lucky vampire—who was about to get an unsolicited makeover. She'd have the additional pleasure of realizing her friends had turned her in to the fashion police.

"I don't think this is going to end well," Octavia Fant

said. Though my housemate Amelia Broadway had sort of
slid Octavia into my house—based on a casual invitation I'd
issued in a weak moment—the arrangement was working out
okay.

"Devon Dawn, here's Bev Leveto from *The Best Dressed
Vamp*, and I'm Todd Seabrook. Your friend Tessa called to tell
us you needed fashion help! We've been secretly filming you
for the past two nights, and— *AAACKK!*" A white hand
flashed at Todd's throat, which vanished, leaving a gaping
reddish hole. The camera lingered, fascinated, as Todd crumpled to the floor, before it rose to follow the fight between
Devon Dawn and Bev.

"Gosh," said Amelia. "Looks like Bev's gonna win."

"Better strategic sense," I said. "Did you notice she let
Todd go through the door first?"

"I've got her pinned," Bev said triumphantly on the screen.
"Devon Dawn, while Todd recovers his speech, we're going to
go through your closet. A girl who's going to live for eternity
can't afford to be tacky. Vampires can't get stuck in their
pasts. We've got to be fashion forward!"

Devon Dawn whimpered, "But I like my clothes! They're
part of who I am! You've broken my arm."

"It'll heal. Listen, you don't want to be known as the little
vampire who couldn't, do you? You don't want to have *your*
head stuck in the past!"

"Well, I guess not . . ."

"Good! I'll let you up now. And I can tell from the coughing that Todd's feeling better."

I switched off the television and tied my other shoe, shaking my head at America's new addiction to vampire "reality"
shows. I got my red coat out of the closet. The sight of it

reminded me that I myself had some absolutely real problems with a vampire; in the two and a half months since the takeover of the Louisiana vampire kingdom by the vampires of Nevada, Eric Northman had been fully occupied with consolidating his position within the new regime and evaluating what was left of the old.

We were way overdue for a chitchat about Eric's newly recovered memories of our strange and intense time together when he'd temporarily misplaced his memory due to a spell.

"What are you going to do tonight while I'm at work?" I asked Amelia and Octavia, since I didn't need to go another round of imaginary conversations. I pulled on the coat. Northern Louisiana doesn't get the horrific temperatures of the *real* north, but it was in the forties tonight and would be colder when I got off work.

"My niece and her kids are taking me out to dinner," Octavia said.

Amelia and I gave each other surprised looks while the older woman's head was bent over the blouse she was mending. It was the first time Octavia had seen her niece since she'd moved from the niece's house to mine.

"I think Tray and I are coming to the bar tonight," Amelia said hastily, to cover the little pause.

"So I'll see you at Merlotte's." I'd been a barmaid there for years.

Octavia said, "Oh, I've got the wrong color thread," and went down the hall to her room.

"I guess you aren't seeing Pam anymore?" I asked Amelia. "You and Tray are getting to be a regular thing." I tucked my white T-shirt into my black pants more securely. I glanced in the old mirror over the mantel. My hair was pulled up into its usual ponytail for work. I spotted a stray long blond hair against the red of the coat, and I plucked it off.

"Pam was just a wild hair, and I'm sure she felt the same way about me. I *really* like Tray," Amelia was saying. "He doesn't seem to care about Daddy's money, and he's not worried about me being a witch. And he can rock my world in the bedroom. So we're getting along great." Amelia gave me a cat-eating-the-canary grin. She might look like a well-toned soccer mom—short, gleaming hair, beautiful white smile, clear eyes—but she was very interested in sex and (by my standards) diverse in those interests.

"He's a good guy," I said. "Have you seen him as a wolf yet?"

"Nope. But I'm looking forward to it."

I picked up something from Amelia's transparent head that startled me. "It's soon? The revelation?"

"Would you *not do* that?" Amelia was normally matter-of-fact about my mind-reading ability, but not today. "I've got to keep other people's secrets, you know!"

"Sorry," I said. And I was, but at the same time I was mildly aggrieved. You'd think that I could relax in my own house and loosen the tight wrappings I tried to keep on my ability. After all, I had to struggle every single day at work.

Amelia said instantly, "I'm sorry, too. Listen, I've got to go get ready. See you later." She went lightly up the stairs to the second floor, which had been largely unused until she'd come back from New Orleans with me a few months before. She'd missed Katrina, unlike poor Octavia.

"Good-bye, Octavia. Have a good time!" I called, and went out the back door to my car.

As I steered down the long driveway that led through the

woods to Hummingbird Road, I wondered about the chances of Amelia and Tray Dawson sticking together. Tray, a werewolf, worked as a motorcycle repairman and as muscle for hire. Amelia was an up-and-coming witch, and her dad was immensely wealthy, even after Katrina. The hurricane had spared most of the materials at his contracting warehouse and provided him with enough work to last for decades.

According to Amelia's brain, tonight was the night—not the night Tray asked Amelia to marry him, but the night Tray came out. Tray's dual nature was a plus to my roommate, who was attracted by the exotic.

I went in the employee entrance and right to Sam's office. "Hey, boss," I said when I saw him behind his desk. Sam hated to work on the books, but that was what he was doing. Maybe it was providing a needed distraction. Sam looked worried. His hair was even more tangled than usual, its strawberry waves standing out in a halo around his narrow face.

"Brace yourself. Tonight's the night," he said.

I was so proud he'd told me, and he'd echoed my own thoughts so closely, I couldn't help but smile. "I'm ready. I'll be right here." I dropped my purse in the deep drawer in his desk and went to tie on my apron. I was relieving Holly, but after I'd had a talk with her about the customers at our tables, I said, "You oughta stick around tonight."

She looked at me sharply. Holly had recently been letting her hair grow out, so the dyed black ends looked like they'd been dipped in tar. Her natural color, now showing about an inch at the roots, turned out to be a pleasant light brown. She'd colored it for so long that I'd clean forgotten. "This going to be good enough for me to keep Hoyt waiting?" she asked. "Him and Cody get along like a house on fire, but I am Cody's mama." Hoyt, my brother Jason's best buddy, had been co-opted by Holly. Now he was *her* follower.

"You should stay awhile." I gave her a significant lift of my eyebrows.

Holly said, "The weres?" I nodded, and her face brightened with a grin. "Oh, boy! Arlene's going to have a shit fit."

Arlene, our coworker and former friend, had become politically sensitized a few months before by one of her string of man friends. Now she was somewhere to the right of Attila the Hun, especially on vampire issues. She'd even joined the Fellowship of the Sun, a church in all but name. She was standing at one of her tables now, having a serious conversation with her man, Whit Spradlin, a FotS official of some sort who had a day job at one of the Shreveport Home Depots. He had a sizeable bald patch and a little paunch, but that didn't make any nevermind to me. His politics did. He had a buddy with him, of course. The FotS people seemed to run in packs—just like another minority group they were about to meet.

My brother, Jason, was at a table, too, with Mel Hart. Mel worked at Bon Temps Auto Parts, and he was about Jason's age, maybe thirty-one. Slim and hard-bodied, Mel had longish light brown hair, a mustache and beard, and a pleasant face. I'd been seeing Jason with Mel a lot lately. Jason had had to fill the gap Hoyt had left, I assumed. Jason wasn't happy without a sidekick. Tonight both men had dates. Mel was divorced, but Jason was still nominally married, so he had no business being out in public with another woman. Not that anyone here would blame him. Jason's wife, Crystal, had been caught cheating with a local guy.

I'd heard Crystal had moved her pregnant self back to the

little community of Hotshot to stay with relatives. (She could find a room in any house in Hotshot and be with relatives. It's that kind of place.) Mel Hart had been born in Hotshot, too, but he was the rare member of the tribe who'd chosen to live elsewhere.

To my surprise Bill, my ex-boyfriend, was sitting with another vampire, named Clancy. Clancy wasn't my favorite guy regardless of his nonliving status. They both had bottles of TrueBlood on the table in front of them. I didn't think Clancy had ever dropped in to Merlotte's for a casual drink before, and certainly never with Bill.

"Hey, guys, need a refill?" I asked, smiling for all I was worth. I'm a little nervous around Bill.

"Please," Bill said politely, and Clancy shoved his empty bottle toward me.

I stepped behind the bar to get two more TrueBloods out of the refrigerator, and I uncapped them and popped them in the microwave. (Fifteen seconds works best.) I shook the bottles gently and put the warm drinks on the tray with some fresh napkins. Bill's cold hand touched mine as I placed his drink in front of him.

He said, "If you need any help at your place, please call me."

I knew he meant it kindly, but it sort of emphasized my current manless status. Bill's house was right across the cemetery from mine, and the way he roamed around at night, I figured he was well aware I wasn't entertaining company.

"Thanks, Bill," I said, making myself smile at him. Clancy just sneered.

Tray and Amelia came in, and after depositing Amelia at a table, Tray went up to the bar, greeting everyone in the place along the way. Sam came out of his office to join the burly man, who was at least five inches taller than my boss and almost twice as big around. They grinned at each other. Bill and Clancy went on alert.

The televisions mounted at intervals around the room cut away from the sports event they'd been showing. A series of beeps alerted the bar patrons to the fact that something was happening on-screen. The bar gradually hushed to a few scattered conversations. "Special Report" flashed on the screen, superimposed on a newscaster with clipped, gelled hair and a sternly serious face. In solemn tones he said, "I'm Matthew Harrow. Tonight we bring you a special report. Like newsrooms all across the country, here in Shreveport we have a visitor in the studio."

The camera moved away to broaden the picture, and a pretty woman came into view. Her face was slightly familiar. She gave the camera a practiced little wave. She was wearing a sort of muumuu, an odd choice for a television appearance.

"This is Patricia Crimmins, who moved to Shreveport a few weeks ago. Patty—may I call you Patty?"

"Actually, it's Patricia," the brunette said. She was one of the members of the pack that had been absorbed by Alcide's, I remembered. She was pretty as a picture, and the part of her not swathed in the muumuu looked fit and toned. She smiled at Matthew Harrow. "I'm here tonight as the representative of a people who have lived among you for many years. Since the vampires have been so successful out in the open, we've decided the time's come for us to tell you about ourselves. After all, vampires are dead. They're not even human. But we're regular people just like you-all, with a difference." Sam turned the volume up. People in the bar began to swivel in their seats to see what was happening.

The newsman's smile had gotten as rigid as a smile could be, and he was visibly nervous. "How interesting, Patricia! What—what are you?"

"Thanks for asking, Matthew! I'm a werewolf." Patricia had her hands clasped around her knee. Her legs were crossed. She looked perky enough to sell used cars. Alcide had made a good choice. Plus, if someone killed her right away, well . . . she was the new girl.

By now Merlotte's was silent as the word went from table to table. Bill and Clancy had risen to stand by the bar. I realized now that they were there to keep the peace if they were needed; Sam must have asked them to come in. Tray began unbuttoning his shirt. Sam was wearing a long-sleeved T-shirt, and he pulled it over his head.

"You're saying you turn into a wolf at the full moon?" Matthew Harrow quavered, trying hard to keep his smile level and his face simply interested. He didn't succeed very well.

"And at other times," Patricia explained. "During the full moon, most of us *have* to turn, but if we're pure-blooded wereanimals, we can change at other times as well. There are many kinds of wereanimals, but I turn into a wolf. We're the more numerous of all the two-natured. Now I'm going to show you-all what an amazing process this is. Don't be scared. I'll be fine." She shucked her shoes, but not the muu-muu. I suddenly understood she'd worn it so she wouldn't have to undress on camera. Patricia knelt on the floor, smiled at the camera one last time, and began to contort. The air around her shivered with the magic of it, and everyone in Merlotte's went *"Ooooooo"* in unison.

Right after Patricia committed herself to the change on

the television screen, Sam and Tray did, too, right then and there. They'd worn underthings they didn't mind ripping to shreds. Everyone in Merlotte's was torn between watching the pretty woman change into a creature with long white teeth, and the spectacle of two people they knew doing the same. There were exclamations all over the bar, most of them not repeatable in polite society. Jason's date, Michele Schubert, actually stood up to get a better view.

I was so proud of Sam. This took a lot of courage, since he had a business that depended to some extent on his likability.

In another minute, it was all over. Sam, a rare pure shape-shifter, turned into his most familiar form, that of a collie. He went to sit in front of me and gave a happy yip. I bent over to pat his head. His tongue lolled out, and he grinned at me. Tray's animal manifestation was much more dramatic. Huge wolves are not often seen in rural northern Louisiana; let's face it, they're scary. People shifted uneasily and might have gotten up to flee from the building if Amelia hadn't squatted by Tray and put her arm around his neck.

"He knows what you're saying," she told the people at the nearest table encouragingly. Amelia had a great smile, big and genuine. "Hey, Tray, take them this coaster." She handed him one of the bar coasters, and Tray Dawson, one of the most implacable fighters both in and out of his wolf form, trotted over to lay the coaster on the lap of the female customer. She blinked, wavered, and finally came down on the side of laughing.

Sam licked my hand.

"Oh, my lord Jesus," Arlene exclaimed loudly. Whit Spradlin and his buddy were on their feet. But though a few other patrons looked nervous, none of them had such a violent reaction.

Bill and Clancy watched with expressionless faces. They were obviously ready to handle trouble, but all seemed to be going well at the Great Reveal. The vampires' Great Revelation night hadn't gone so smoothly, because it was the first in the series of shocks mainstream society would feel in the years to come. Gradually vampires had come to be a recognized part of America, though their citizenship still had certain limitations.

Sam and Tray wandered among the regulars, allowing themselves to be petted as if they were regular tame animals. While they were doing that, the newscaster on television was visibly trembling as he faced the beautiful white wolf Patricia had become.

"Look, he so scared, he shaking!" D'Eriq, the busboy and kitchen helper, said. He laughed out loud. The drinkers in Merlotte's relaxed enough to feel superior. After all, they'd handled this with aplomb.

Jason's new buddy Mel said, "Ain't nobody got to be scared of a lady that pretty, even if she does shed some," and the laughter and relaxation in the bar spread. I was relieved, though I thought it was a little ironic that people might not be so quick to laugh if Jason and Mel had changed; they were werepanthers, though Jason couldn't change completely.

But after the laughter, I felt that everything was going to be all right. Bill and Clancy, after a careful look around, went back to their table.

Whit and Arlene, surrounded by citizens taking a huge chunk of knowledge in their stride, looked stunned. I could hear Arlene being extra confused about how to react. After all, Sam had been our boss for a good many years. Unless she wanted to lose her job, she couldn't cut up. But I could also read her fear and the mounting anger that followed close behind. Whit had one reaction, always, to anything he didn't understand. He hated it, and hate is infectious. He looked at his drinking companion, and they exchanged dark looks.

Thoughts were churning around in Arlene's brain like lottery balls in the popper. It was hard to tell which one would surface first.

"Jesus, strike him dead!" said Arlene, boiling over. The hate ball had landed on top.

A few people said, "Oh, Arlene!" . . . but they were all listening.

"This goes against God and nature," Arlene said in a loud, angry voice. Her dyed red hair shook with her vehemence. "You-all want your kids around this kind of thing?"

"Our kids have always been around this kind of thing," Holly said equally loudly. "We just didn't know it. And they ain't come to any harm." She rose to her feet, too.

"God will *get us* if we don't strike them down," Arlene said, pointing to Tray dramatically. By now, her face was almost as red as her hair. Whit was looking at her approvingly. "You don't understand! We're all going to hell if we don't take the world back from them! Look who they got standing there to keep us humans in line!" Her finger swung around to indicate Bill and Clancy, though since they'd resumed their chairs she lost a few points.

I set my tray on the bar and took a step away, my hands clenched in fists. "We all get along here in Bon Temps," I said, keeping my voice calm and level. "You seem to be the only one upset, Arlene."

She glared around the bar, trying to catch the eyes of various patrons. She knew every one of them. Arlene was genuinely shocked to realize more people weren't sharing her reaction. Sam came to sit in front of her. He looked up at her face with his beautiful doggy eyes.

I took another step closer to Whit, just in case. Whit was deciding what to do, considering jumping Sam. But who would join him in beating up a collie? Even Whit could see the absurdity, and that made him hate Sam all the more.

"How could you?" Arlene screamed at Sam. "You been lying to me all these years! I thought you were human, not a damn supe!"

"He is human," I said. "He's just got another face, is all."

"And you," she said, spitting out the words. "You're the weirdest, the most inhuman, of them all."

"Hey, now," Jason said. He leaped to his feet, and after a moment's hesitation, Mel joined him. His date looked alarmed, though Jason's lady friend just smiled. "You leave my sister alone. She babysat your kids and she cleaned your trailer and she put up with your shit for years. What kind of friend are you?"

Jason didn't look at me. I was frozen in astonishment. This was a very un-Jason gesture. Could he have grown up a little bit?

"The kind that don't want to hang around with unnatural creatures like your sister," Arlene said. She tore off her apron, said, "I quit this place!" to the collie, and stomped back to Sam's office to retrieve her purse. Maybe a fourth of the people in the bar looked alarmed and upset. Half of them were fascinated with the drama. That left a quarter on the fence. Sam whined like a sad dog and put his nose between his paws. After that got a big laugh, the discomfort of the moment passed. I watched Whit and his buddy ease out the front door, and I relaxed when they were gone.

Just on the off chance Whit might be fetching a rifle from his truck, I glanced over at Bill, who glided out the door after him. In a moment he was back, nodding at me to indicate the FotS guys had driven away.

Once the back door thunked closed behind Arlene, the rest of the evening went pretty well. Sam and Tray retired to Sam's office to change back and get dressed. Sam returned to his place behind the bar afterward as if nothing had happened, and Tray went to sit at the table with Amelia, who kissed him. For a while, people steered a little clear of them, and there were lots of surreptitious glances; but after an hour, the atmosphere of Merlotte's seemed just about back to normal. I pitched in to serve Arlene's tables, and I made sure to be especially nice to the people still undecided about the night's events.

People seemed to drink heartily that night. Maybe they had misgivings about Sam's other persona, but they didn't have any problem adding to his profits. Bill caught my eye and raised his hand in good-bye. He and Clancy drifted out of the bar.

Jason tried to get my attention once or twice, and his buddy Mel sent big smiles my way. Mel was taller and thinner than my brother, but they both had that bright, eager look of unthinking men who operate on their instincts. In his favor, Mel didn't seem to agree with everything Jason said, not the way Hoyt always had. Mel seemed to be an okay guy, at least from our brief acquaintance; that he was one of the few werepanthers who didn't live in Hotshot was also a fact in his favor, and it may even have been why he and Jason were such big buddies. They were like other werepanthers, but separate, too.

If I ever began speaking to Jason again, I had a question for him. On this major evening for all Weres and shifters, how come he hadn't taken the chance to grab a little of the spotlight for himself? Jason was very full of his altered status as a werepanther. He'd been bitten, not born. That is, he'd contracted the virus (or whatever it was) by being bitten by another werepanther, rather than being born with the ability to change as Mel had been. Jason's changed form was man-like, with hair all over and a pantherish face and claws: really scary, he'd told me. But he wasn't a beautiful animal, and that griped my brother. Mel was a purebred, and he would be gorgeous and frightening when he transformed.

Maybe the werepanthers had been asked to lie low because panthers were simply *too* scary. If something as big and lethal as a panther had appeared in the bar, the reaction of the patrons almost certainly would have been a lot more hysterical. Though wereanimal brains are very difficult to read, I could sense the disappointment the two panthers were sharing. I was sure the decision had been Calvin Norris's, as the panther leader. *Good move, Calvin,* I thought.

After I'd helped close down the bar, I gave Sam a hug when I stopped by his office to pick up my purse. He was looking tired but happy.

"You feeling as good as you look?" I asked.

"Yep. My true nature's out in the open now. It's liberating. My mom swore she was going to tell my stepdad tonight. I'm waiting to hear from her."

Right on cue, the phone rang. Sam picked it up, still smiling. "Mom?" he said. Then his face changed as if a hand had wiped off the previous expression. "Don? What have you done?"

I sank into the chair by the desk and waited. Tray had come to have a last word with Sam, and Amelia was with him. They both stood stiffly in the doorway, anxious to hear what had happened.

"Oh, my God," Sam said. "I'll come as soon as I can. I'll get on the road tonight." He hung up the phone very gently. "Don shot my mom," he said. "When she changed, he shot her." I'd never seen Sam look so upset.

"Is she dead?" I asked, fearing the answer.

"No," he said. "No, but she's in the hospital with a shattered collarbone and a gunshot wound to her upper left shoulder. He almost killed her. If she hadn't jumped . . ."

"I'm so sorry," Amelia said.

"What can I do to help?" I asked.

"Keep the bar open while I'm gone," he said, shaking off the shock. "Call Terry. Terry and Tray can work out a bartending schedule between them. Tray, you know I'll pay you when I get back. Sookie, the waitress schedule is on the wall behind the bar. Find someone to cover Arlene's shifts, please."

"Sure, Sam," I said. "You need any help packing? Can I gas up your truck or something?"

"Nope, I'm good. You've got the key to my trailer, so can you water my plants? I don't think I'll be gone but a couple of days, but you never know."

"Of course, Sam. Don't worry. Keep us posted."

We all cleared out so Sam could get over to his trailer to pack. It was in the lot right behind the bar, so at least he could get everything ready in a hurry.

As I drove home, I tried to imagine how Sam's stepdad had come to do such a thing. Had he been so horrified at the discovery of his wife's second life that he'd flipped? Had she changed out of his sight and walked up to him and startled him? I simply couldn't believe you could shoot someone you loved, someone you lived with, just because they had more to them than you'd thought. Maybe Don had seen her second self as a betrayal. Or maybe it was the fact that she'd concealed it. I could kind of understand his reaction, if I looked at it that way.

People all had secrets, and I was in a position to know most of them. Being a telepath is not any fun. You hear the tawdry, the sad, the disgusting, the petty . . . the things we all want to keep hidden from our fellow humans, so they'll keep their image of us intact.

The secrets I know least about are my own.

The one I was thinking of tonight was the unusual genetic inheritance my brother and I share, which had come through my father. My father had never known that his mother, Adele, had had a whopper of a secret, one disclosed to me only the past October. My grandmother's two children—my dad and his sister, Linda—were not the products of her long marriage with my grandfather.

Both had been conceived through her liaison with a half fairy, half human named Fintan. According to Fintan's father, Niall, the fairy part of my dad's genetic heritage had been responsible for my mother's infatuation with him, an infatuation that had excluded her children from all but the fringes of her attention and affection. This genetic legacy hadn't seemed to change anything for my dad's sister, Linda; it certainly hadn't helped her dodge the cancer bullet that had ended her life or kept her husband on-site, much less infatuated. However, Linda's grandson Hunter was a telepath like me.

I still struggled with parts of this story. I believed the history Niall had related to be true, but I couldn't understand my grandmother's desire for children being strong enough to lead her to cheat on my grandfather. That simply didn't jibe with her character, and I couldn't understand why I hadn't read it in her brain during all the years that we'd lived together. She must have thought about the circumstances of her children's conceptions from time to time. There was just no way she could've packed those events away for good in some attic of her mind.

But my grandmother had been dead for over a year now, and I'd never be able to ask her about it. Her husband had passed away years before. Niall had told me that my biological grandfather Fintan, too, was dead and gone. It had crossed my mind to go through my grandmother's things in search of some clue to her thinking, to her reaction to this extraordinary passage in her life, and then I would think . . . *Why bother?*

I had to deal with the consequences here and now.

The trace of fairy blood I carried made me more attractive to supes, at least to some vampires. Not all of them could detect the little trace of fairy in my genes, but they tended to at least be interested in me, though occasionally that had negative results. Or maybe this fairy-blood thing was bull, and vampires were interested in any fairly attractive young woman who would treat them with respect and tolerance.

As to the relationship between the telepathy and the fairy blood, who knew? It wasn't like I had a lot of people to ask or any literature to check, or like I could ask a lab to test for it. Maybe little Hunter and I had both developed the condition through a coincidence—yeah, right. Maybe the trait was genetic but separate from the fairy genes.

Maybe I'd just gotten lucky.

Chapter 2

I went into Merlotte's early in the morning—for me, that means eight thirty—to check the bar situation, and I remained to cover Arlene's shift. I'd have to work a double. Thankfully, the lunch crowd was light. I didn't know if that was a result of Sam's announcement or just the normal course of things. At least I was able to make a few phone calls while Terry Bellefleur (who made ends meet with several part-time jobs) covered the bar. Terry was in a good mood, or what passed for a good mood for him; he was a Vietnam vet who'd had a very bad war. At heart he was a good guy, and we'd always gotten along. He was really fascinated by the weres' revelation; since the war, Terry had done better with animals than people.

"I bet that's why I've always liked to work for Sam," Terry said, and I smiled at him.

"I like to work for him, too," I said.

While Terry kept the beers coming and kept an eye on

Jane Bodehouse, one of our alcoholics, I started phoning to find a replacement barmaid. Amelia had told me she would help a little but only at night, because she now had a temporary day job covering the maternity leave of a clerk at the insurance agency.

First I phoned Charlsie Tooten. Charlsie, though sympathetic, told me she had the full care of her granddaughter while her daughter worked, so she was too tired to come in. I called another former Merlotte's employee, but she'd started work at another bar. Holly had said she could double up once but didn't want to do it more than that because of her little boy. Danielle, the other full-time server, had said the same. (In Danielle's case she had twice the excuse because she had two children.)

So, finally, with a huge sigh to let Sam's empty office know how put-upon I was, I called one of my least favorite people— Tanya Grissom, werefox and former saboteur. It took me a while to track her down, but by calling a couple of people out in Hotshot, I was finally able to reach her at Calvin's house. Tanya had been dating him for a while. I liked the man myself, but when I thought of that cluster of little houses at the ancient crossroads, I shuddered.

"Tanya, how you doing? This is Sookie Stackhouse."

"Really. Hmmm. Hello."

I didn't blame her for being cautious.

"One of Sam's barmaids quit—you remember Arlene? She freaked about the were thing and walked out. I was wondering if you could take over a couple of her shifts, just for a while."

"You Sam's partner now?"

She wasn't going to make this easy. "No, I'm just doing the looking for him. He got called away on a family emergency."

"I was probably on the bottom of your list."

My brief silence spoke for itself.

"I figure we can work together," I said, because I had to say something.

"I got a day job now, but I can help a couple of evenings until you find someone permanent," Tanya said. It was hard to read anything from her voice.

"Thanks." That gave me two temporaries, Amelia and Tanya, and I could take any hours they couldn't. This wouldn't be hard on anyone. "Can you come in tomorrow for the evening shift? If you could be here about five, five thirty, one of us can show you the ropes again, and then you'll be working until the bar closes."

There was a short silence. "I'll be there," Tanya said. "I got some black pants. You got a T-shirt I can wear?"

"Yep. Medium?"

"That'll do me."

She hung up.

Well, I could hardly expect to find her happy to hear from me or delighted to oblige since we'd never been fans of each other. In fact, though I didn't believe she remembered, I'd had her bewitched by Amelia and Amelia's mentor, Octavia. I still squirmed when I thought of how I'd altered Tanya's life, but I didn't think I'd had a lot of choices there. Sometimes you just have to regret things and move on.

Sam called while Terry and I were closing the bar. I was so tired. My head was heavy, and my feet were aching.

"How are things going there?" Sam asked. His voice was rough with exhaustion.

"We're coping," I said, trying to sound perky and carefree. "How's your mom?"

"She's still alive," he said. "She's talking and breathing on her own. The doctor says he thinks she'll recover just fine. My stepfather is under arrest."

"What a mess," I said, genuinely distressed on Sam's behalf.

"Mom says she should have told him beforehand," he told me. "She was just scared to."

"Well . . . rightly so, huh? As it turns out."

He snorted. "She figures if she'd had a long talk with him, then let him see her change after he'd watched the change on TV, he would've been okay."

I'd been so busy with the bar I hadn't had a chance to absorb the television reports of the reactions around the world to this second Great Revelation. I wondered how it was going in Montana, Indiana, Florida? I wondered if any of the famous actors in Hollywood had admitted to being were-wolves. What if Ryan Seacrest was fuzzy every full moon? Or Jennifer Love Hewitt or Russell Crowe? (Which I thought was more than likely.) That would make a huge difference in public acceptance.

"Have you seen your stepfather or talked to him?"

"No, not yet. I can't make myself. My brother went by. He said Don started crying. It was bad."

"Is your sister there?"

"Well, she's on her way. She had a hard time arranging child care." He sounded a little hesitant.

"She knew about your mom, right?" I tried to keep the incredulity out of my voice.

"No," he said. "Real often, were parents don't tell the kids who aren't affected. My sibs didn't know about me, either, since they didn't know about Mom."

"I'm sorry," I said, which stood for a lot of things.

"I wish you were here," Sam said, taking me by surprise.

"I wish I could be more help," I said. "If you can think of anything else I can do, you call me at any hour."

"You're keeping the business running. That counts for a lot," he said. "I better go get some sleep."

"Okay, Sam. Talk to you tomorrow, okay?"

"Sure," he said. He sounded so worn-out and sad it was hard not to cry.

I felt relieved that I'd put my personal feelings aside to call Tanya, after that conversation. It had been the right thing to do. Sam's mother being shot for what she was—well, that just put my dislike of Tanya Grissom into perspective.

I fell into bed that night, and I don't think I even twitched after that.

I'd been sure the warm glow generated by Sam's call would carry me through the next day, but the morning started badly.

Sam always ordered the supplies and kept up with the inventory, naturally. Also, naturally, he'd forgotten to remind me that he had some cases of beer coming in. I got a phone call from the truck driver, Duff, and I had to leap out of bed and hurry to Merlotte's. On my way out the door, I glimpsed the blinking light on my answering machine, which I'd been too tired to check the night before. But I didn't have time to worry about missed messages now. I was simply relieved Duff had thought of calling me when he got no answer at Sam's.

I opened the back door of Merlotte's, and Duff wheeled the cases in and put them where they were supposed to go. Somewhat nervously, I signed for Sam. By the time that was done and the truck had pulled out of the parking lot, Sarah Jen, the mail carrier, came by with the bar mail and Sam's personal mail. I accepted both. Sarah Jen had her talking shoes on. She'd heard (already) that Sam's mom was in the hospital, but I didn't feel I had to enlighten her about the circumstances. That was Sam's business. Sarah Jen also wanted to tell me how she wasn't astonished at all that Sam was a wereanimal, because she'd always thought there was something strange about him.

"He's a nice guy," Sarah Jen admitted. "I'm not saying he's not. Just . . . something odd there. I wasn't a bit surprised."

"Really? He's sure said such nice things about you," I said sweetly, looking down so the line would be a throwaway. I could see the delight flooding Sarah Jen's head as clearly as if she'd drawn me a picture.

"He's always been real polite," she said, suddenly seeing Sam in the light of a most perceptive man. "Well, I better be going. I got to finish the route. If you talk to Sam, tell him I'm thinking of his mom."

After I carried the mail to Sam's desk, Amelia called from the insurance agency to tell me that Octavia had called her to ask if either of us could take her to Wal-Mart. Octavia, who'd lost most of her stuff in Katrina, was stuck out at the house without a car.

"You'll have to take her on your lunch hour," I said, barely managing not to snap at Amelia. "I got a full plate today. And here comes more trouble," I said as a car pulled up beside mine in the employee parking lot. "Here's Eric's daytime guy, Bobby Burnham."

"Oh, I meant to tell you. Octavia said Eric tried to call you at home twice. So she finally told Bobby where you were this morning," Amelia said. "She figured it might be important. Lucky you. Okay, I'll take care of Octavia. Somehow."

"Good," I said, trying not to sound as brusque as I felt. "Talk to you later."

Bobby Burnham got out of his Impala and strode up to me. His boss, Eric, was bound to me in a complicated relationship that was based not only on our past history but also on the fact that we'd swapped blood several times.

This hadn't been an informed decision on my part.

Bobby Burnham was an asshole. Maybe Eric had gotten him on sale?

"Miss Stackhouse," he said, laying the courtliness on thick. "My master asks that you come to Fangtasia tonight for a sit-down with the new king's lieutenant."

This was not the summons I'd expected or the kind of conversation I'd foreseen with the vampire sheriff of Area Five. Given the fact that we had some personal issues to discuss, I'd imagined Eric would call me when things had settled down with the new regime, and we'd make some kind of appointment—or date—to talk about the several items on our mutual plate. I wasn't pleased by this impersonal summons by a flunky.

"You ever hear of a phone?" I said.

"He left you messages last night. He told me to talk to you today, without fail. I'm just following orders."

"Eric told you to spend your time driving over here and asking me to come to his bar tonight." Even to my own ears, I sounded unbelieving.

"Yes. He said, 'Track her down, deliver the message in person, and be polite.' Here I am. Being polite."

He was telling me the truth, and it was just killing him. That was almost enough to make me smile. Bobby really didn't like me. The closest I could come to defining why was that Bobby didn't think I was worthy of Eric's notice. He didn't like my less-than-reverent attitude toward Eric, and he couldn't understand why Pam, Eric's right-hand vampire, was fond of me, when she wouldn't give Bobby the time of day.

There was nothing I could do to change this, even if Bobby's dislike had worried me . . . and it didn't. But Eric worried me plenty. I had to talk to him, and I might as well get it over with. It had been late October when I'd last seen him, and it was now mid-January. "It'll have to be when I get off here. I'm temporarily in charge," I said, sounding neither pleased nor gracious.

"What time? He wants you there at seven. Victor will be there then."

Victor Madden was the representative of the new king, Felipe de Castro. It had been a bloody takeover, and Eric was the only sheriff of the old regime still standing. Staying in the good graces of the new regime was important to Eric, obviously. I wasn't yet sure how much of that was my problem. But I was thumbs-up with Felipe de Castro by a happy accident, and I wanted to keep it that way.

"I might be able to get there by seven," I said after some inner computation. I tried not to think about how much it would please me to lay eyes on Eric. At least ten times in the past few weeks, I'd caught myself before I'd gotten in my car to drive over to see him. But I'd successfully resisted the impulses, because I'd been able to *tell* that he was struggling to maintain his position under the new king. "I've got to brief the new gal. . . . Yeah, seven is just about doable."

"He'll be so relieved," Bobby said, managing to work in a sneer.

Keep it up, asshole, I thought. And possibly the way I was looking at him conveyed that thought, because Bobby said, "Really, he will be," in as sincere a tone as he could manage.

"Okay, message delivered," I said. "I got to get back to work."

"Where's your boss?"

"He had a family problem in Texas."

"Oh, I thought maybe the dogcatcher got him."

What a howl. "Good-bye, Bobby," I said, and turned my back on him to go in the back door.

"Here," he said, and I turned around, irritated. "Eric said you would need this." He handed me a bundle wrapped in black velvet. Vampires couldn't give you anything in a Wal-Mart bag or wrapped in Hallmark paper, oh, no. Black velvet. The bundle was secured with a gold tasseled cord, like you'd use to tie back a curtain.

Just holding it gave me a bad feeling. "And what would this be?"

"I don't know. I wasn't tasked with opening it."

I *hate* the word "tasked," with "gifted" running close behind. "What am I supposed to do with this?" I said.

"Eric said, 'Tell her to give it to me tonight, in front of Victor.'"

Eric did nothing without a reason. "All right," I said reluctantly. "Consider me *messaged*."

I got through the next shift okay. Everyone was pitching in to help, and that was pleasing. The cook had been working hard all day; this was maybe the fifteenth short-order cook we'd had since I'd begun working at Merlotte's. We'd had every variation on a human being you could imagine: black, white, male, female, old, young, dead (yes, a vampire cook), lycanthropically inclined (a werewolf), and probably one or two I'd completely forgotten. This cook, Antoine Lebrun, was real nice. He'd come to us out of Katrina. He'd outstayed most of the other refugees, who'd moved back to the Gulf Coast or moved on.

Antoine was in his fifties, his curly hair showing a strand or two of gray. He'd worked concessions at the Superdome, he'd told me the day he got hired, and we'd both shuddered. Antoine got along great with D'Eriq, the busboy who doubled as his assistant.

When I went in the kitchen to make sure he had everything he needed, Antoine told me he was really proud to be working for a shapeshifter, and D'Eriq wanted to go over and over his reaction to Sam's and Tray's transformations. After he'd left work, D'Eriq had gotten a phone call from his cousin in Monroe, and now D'Eriq wanted to tell us all about his cousin's wife being a werewolf.

D'Eriq's reaction was what I hoped was typical. Two nights before, many people had discovered that someone they knew personally was a were of some kind. Hopefully, if the were had never shown signs of insanity or violence, these people would be willing to accept that shape-changing was an unthreatening addition to their knowledge of the world. It was even exciting.

I hadn't had time to check reactions around the world, but at least as far as local stuff went, the revelation seemed to be going smoothly. I didn't get the feeling anyone was going to be firebombing Merlotte's because of Sam's dual nature, and I thought Tray's motorcycle repair business was safe.

Tanya was twenty minutes early, which raised her up in my estimation, and I gave her a genuine smile. After we ran over a few of the basics like hours, pay, and Sam's house rules, I said, "You like being out there in Hotshot?"

"Yeah, I do," she said, sounding a little surprised. "The families out in Hotshot, they really get along well. If something goes wrong, they have a meeting and discuss it. Those that don't like the life, they leave, like Mel Hart did." Almost everyone in Hotshot was either a Hart or a Norris.

"He's really taken up with my brother lately," I said, because I was a little curious about Jason's new friend.

"Yeah, that's what I hear. Everyone's glad he's found someone to hang with after being on his own so long."

"Why didn't he fit in out there?" I asked directly.

Tanya said, "I understand Mel doesn't like to share, like you have to if you live in a little community like that. He's real . . . 'What's mine is mine.'" She shrugged. "At least, that's what they say."

"Jason's like that, too," I said. I couldn't read Tanya's mind too clearly because of her double nature, but I could read the mood and intent of it, and I understood the other panthers worried about Mel Hart.

They were concerned about Mel making it in the big world of Bon Temps, I guessed. Hotshot was its own little universe.

I was feeling a bit lighter of heart by the time I'd finished briefing Tanya (who had definitely had experience) and hung up my apron. I gathered my purse and Bobby Burnham's bundle, and I hurried out the employee door to drive to Shreveport.

I started to listen to the news as I drove, but I was tired of grim reality. Instead, I listened to a Mariah Carey CD, and I felt the better for it. I can't sing worth a damn, but I love to belt out the lyrics to a song when I'm driving. The tensions of the day began to drain away, replaced by an optimistic mood.

Sam would come back, his mother having recovered, and her husband having made amends and having pledged he'd love her forever. The world would *oooh* and *aaah* about werewolves and other shifters for a while, then all would be normal again.

Isn't it always a bad idea, thinking things like that?

Chapter 3

The closer I got to the vampire bar, the more my pulse picked up; this was the downside to the blood bond I had with Eric Northman. I knew I was going to see him, and I was simply *happy* about it. I should have been worried, I should have been apprehensive about what he wanted, I should have asked a million questions about the velvet-wrapped bundle, but I just drove with a smile on my face.

Though I couldn't help how I felt, I could control my actions. Out of sheer perversity, since no one had told me to come around to the employees' entrance, I entered through the main door. It was a busy night at Fangtasia, and there was a crowd waiting on benches inside the first set of doors. Pam was at the hostess podium. She smiled at me broadly, showing a little fang. (The crowd was delighted.)

I'd known Pam for a while now, and she was as close to a friend as I had among the vampires. Tonight the blond vampire was wearing the obligatory filmy black dress, and she'd camped it up with a long, sheer black veil. Her fingernails were polished scarlet.

"My friend," Pam said, and came out from behind the podium to hug me. I was surprised but pleased and gladly hugged her back. She'd spritzed on a little perfume to eclipse the faint, rather dry smell of vampire. "Have you got it?" she whispered in my ear.

"Oh, the bundle? It's in my purse." I lifted my big brown shoulder bag by its straps.

Pam gave me a look I couldn't interpret through the veil. It appeared to be an expression that compounded exasperation and affection. "You didn't even look inside?"

"I haven't had time," I said. It wasn't that I hadn't been curious. I simply hadn't had the leisure to think about it. "Sam had to leave because his mom got shot by his stepdad, and I've been managing the bar."

Pam gave me a long look of appraisal. "Go back to Eric's office and hand him the bundle," she said. "Leave it wrapped. No matter who's there. And don't handle it like it was a garden tool he left outside, either."

I gave her the look right back. "What am I doing, Pam?" I asked, jumping on the cautious train way too late.

"You're protecting your own skin," Pam said. "Never doubt it. Now, go." She gave me a get-along pat on the back and turned to answer a tourist's question about how often vampires needed to get their teeth cleaned.

"Would you like to come very close and look at mine?" Pam asked in a sultry voice, and the woman shrieked with delighted fear. That was why the humans came to vampire bars, and vampire comedy clubs, and vampire dry cleaners, and vampire casinos . . . to flirt with danger.

Every now and then, flirtation became the real thing.

I made my way between the tables and across the dance floor to the rear of the bar. Felicia, the bartender, looked unhappy when she saw me. She found something to do that involved crouching down out of my sight. I had an unfortunate history with the bartenders of Fangtasia.

There were a few vampires seated throughout the bar area, strewn among the gawking tourists, the costumed vampire wannabes, and the humans who had business dealings with the vamps. Over in the little souvenir shop, one of the New Orleans vampire refugees from Katrina was selling a Fangtasia T-shirt to a pair of giggling girls.

Tiny Thalia, paler than bleached cotton and with a profile from an ancient coin, was sitting by herself at a small table. Thalia was actually tracked by fans who had devoted a website to her, though she would not have cared if they'd all burst into flames. A drunken serviceman from Barksdale Air Force Base knelt before her as I watched, and as Thalia turned her dark eyes on him, his prearranged speech died in his throat. Turning rather pale himself, the strapping young man backed away from the vampire half his size, and though his friends jeered as he returned to his table, I knew he wouldn't approach her again.

After this little slice of bar life, I was glad to knock on Eric's door. I heard his voice inside, telling me to come in. I stepped inside and shut the door behind me. "Hi, Eric," I said, and was almost rendered mute by the surge of happiness that swept through me whenever I saw him. His long blond hair was braided tonight, and he was wearing his favorite jeans-and-a-tee combo. The T-shirt tonight was bright green, making him look whiter than ever.

The wave of delight wasn't necessarily related to Eric's gorgeousness or the fact that we'd bumped pelvises, though. The blood bond was responsible. Maybe. I had to fight the feeling. For sure.

Victor Madden, representative of the new king, Felipe de Castro, stood and inclined his curly dark head. Victor, short and compact, was always polite and always well-dressed. This evening he was especially resplendent in an olive suit and brown striped tie. I smiled at him and was just about to tell him I was glad to see him again when I noticed that Eric was eyeing me expectantly. Oh, right.

I shucked off my coat and extracted the velvet bundle from my purse. I dropped the purse and coat in an empty chair, and walked over to Eric's desk with the bundle extended in both hands. This was making as much of the moment as I could, short of getting on my knees and crawling over to him, which I would do when hell froze over.

I laid the bundle in front of him, inclined my own head in what I hoped was a ceremonious manner, and sat down in the other guest chair.

"What has our fair-haired friend brought you, Eric?" Victor asked in the cheerful voice that he affected most of the time. Maybe he was actually that happy, or maybe his mama had taught him (a few centuries ago) that you catch more flies with honey than you do with vinegar.

With a certain sense of theater, Eric untied the golden cord and silently unfolded the velvet. Sparkling like a jewel on the dark material was the ceremonial knife I'd last seen in the city of Rhodes. Eric had used it when he officiated at the marriage of two vampire kings, and he'd used it to nick himself later when he'd taken blood from me and given me blood in return: the final exchange, the one that (from my point of view) had caused all the trouble. Now Eric lifted the shining blade to his lips and kissed it.

After Victor recognized the knife, there was no trace of a smile remaining on his face. He and Eric regarded each other steadily.

"Very interesting," Victor said finally.

Once again, I had that feeling of drowning when I hadn't even known I was in the pool. I started to speak, but I could feel Eric's will pressing on me, urging me to be silent. In vampire matters, it was smart to take Eric's advice.

"Then I'll take the tiger's request off the table," Victor said. "My master was unhappy about the tiger wanting to leave, anyway. And of course, I'll inform my master about your prior claim. We acknowledge your formal attachment to this one."

From the inclination of Victor's head in my direction, I knew I was "this one." And I knew only one male weretiger. "What are you talking about?" I asked bluntly.

"Quinn requested a private meeting with you," Victor said. "But he can't come back to Eric's area without Eric's permission now. It's one of the terms we negotiated when we . . . when Eric became our new associate."

That was a nice way to say, *When we killed all the other vampires in Louisiana except for Eric and his followers. When you saved our king from death.*

I wished I had a moment to think, far away from this room where two vampires were staring at me.

"Does this new rule apply only to Quinn or to all wereanimals who want to come into Louisiana? How could you boss the weres? And when did you put that rule into effect?" I said to Eric, trying to buy some time while I collected myself. I wanted Victor to explain the last part of his little speech, too, that bit about the formal attachment, but I decided to tackle one question at a time.

"Three weeks ago," Eric said, answering the last question first. His face was calm; his voice was uninflected. "And the 'new rule' applies only to wereanimals who are associated with us in a business way." Quinn worked for E(E)E, which I suspected was at least partially vampire owned, since Quinn's job was not putting on the weddings and bar mitzvahs the company's human branch dealt with. Quinn's job was staging supernatural events. "The tiger got his dismissal from you. I heard it from his own lips. Why should he return?" Eric shrugged.

At least he didn't try to sugarcoat it by saying, "I thought he might bother you" or "I did it for your own good." No matter how bonded we were—and I was actually struggling against the temptation to smile at him—I felt the hair on the back of my neck rising at Eric managing my life like this.

"Now that you and Eric are openly pledged," Victor said in a silky voice, "you certainly won't want to see Quinn, and I'll tell him so."

"We're *what*?" I glared at Eric, who was looking at me with an expression I can only describe as bland.

"The knife," Victor said, sounding even happier. "That's its significance. It's a ritual knife handed down over the centuries and used in important ceremonies and sacrifices. It's not the only one of its kind, of course, but it's rare. Now it's only used in marriage rituals. I'm not sure how Eric came to have possession of it, but its presentation from you to Eric, and his acceptance, can only mean that you and Eric are pledged to each other."

"Let's all step back and take a deep breath," I said, though

I was the only person in the room who was breathing. I held up my hand as though they'd been advancing on me and my "halt" gesture would stop them. "Eric?" I tried to pack everything into my voice, but one word can't carry that much baggage.

"This is for your protection, dear heart," he said. He was trying to be serene so that some of that serenity would run through our bond and drown my agitation.

But a few gallons of serenity wouldn't calm me down. "This is so arrogant," I said in a choked voice. "This is sheer gall. How could you do this without talking to me about it? How could you think I would let you commit me to something without talking about it first? We haven't even seen each other in months."

"I've been a little busy here. I'd hoped your sense of self-preservation would kick in," Eric said, which was honest, if not tactful. "Can you doubt that I want what's best for you?"

"I don't doubt that you want what *you think* is best for me," I said. "And I don't doubt that that marches right along with what you think is good for *you*."

Victor laughed. "She knows you well, Eric," he said, and we both glared at him. "Oops," he said, and pretended to zip his mouth shut.

"Eric, I'm going home. We'll talk about this soon, but I don't know when. I'm running the bar while Sam's gone. There's trouble in his family."

"But Clancy said the announcement went well in Bon Temps."

"Yes, it did, but at Sam's own family home in Texas, it didn't go so well."

Eric looked disgusted. "I did my best to help. I sent at least one of my people around to every public venue. I went to watch Alcide himself shift at the Shamrock Casino."

"That went okay?" I asked, temporarily sidetracked.

"Yes, only a few drunkards acted up. They were quelled quite easily. One woman even offered herself to Alcide in his wolf form."

"Ewww," I said, and got up, grabbing my purse. He'd distracted me long enough.

Eric rose and vaulted over the desk in a movement that was as startling as it was impressive. Suddenly he was right in front of me, and his arms went around me, and he held me to him. It took everything I had to keep my back stiff, to keep from relaxing against him. It's hard to explain how the bond made me feel. No matter how furious I got with Eric, I was happier when I was with him. It wasn't that I yearned for him uncontrollably when we were separated; it was just that I was aware of him. All the time. I wondered if it was the same for him.

"Tomorrow night?" he said, releasing me.

"If I can get away. We have a lot to talk about." I gave Victor a stiff nod, and I left. I glanced back once to see the knife shining against the black velvet as it lay on Eric's desk.

I knew how Eric had gotten the knife. He'd simply kept it rather than returning it to Quinn, who'd been in charge of the wedding ritual between two vampires, a ceremony I'd witnessed in Rhodes. Eric, who was some kind of mail-order priest, had officiated at the service, and afterward, he'd evidently kept the knife just on the chance it would come in handy. How he'd retrieved it from the wreck of the hotel, I didn't know. Maybe he'd gone back during the night, after the daytime explosion. Maybe he'd sent Pam. But he'd gotten it, and now he'd used it to pledge me to him.

And thanks to my own dazed affection . . . or warmth . . . or infatuation . . . for the Viking vampire, I had done exactly what he'd asked without consulting my common sense.

I didn't know who I was angrier with—myself, or Eric.

Chapter 4

I spent a restless night. I would think of Eric and feel the warm rush of joy, and then think of Eric and want to punch him in the face. I thought of Bill, the first man I'd ever dated more than once, the first man I'd ever gone to bed with; when I remembered his cool voice and body, his contained calm, and contrasted it with Eric, I couldn't believe I had fallen for two such different males, especially when my all-too-brief episode with Quinn was factored in. Quinn had been warm-blooded in every respect, and impulsive, and kind to me, and yet so scarred by his past, he hadn't shared it with me—which, in my view, had led to our relationship being ruined. I'd dated Alcide Herveaux, packleader, too, but it had never gone further.

Sookie Stackhouse's All-Male Revue.

Don't you just hate nights like that, when you think over every mistake you've made, every hurt you've received, every bit of meanness you've dealt out? There's no profit in it, no point to it, and you need sleep. But that night, men were on my mind, and not in a happy way.

When I'd exhausted the topic of my problems with the male sex, I launched into worrying about the responsibility of the bar. I finally got three hours' sleep after I made myself admit that there was no way I could run Sam's business into the ground in a few days.

Sam called the next morning while I was still at home to tell me his mother was better and was definitely going to recover. His brother and sister were now dealing with the family revelations in a much calmer way. Don, of course, was still in jail.

"If she keeps improving, I may be able to start back in a couple of days," he said. "Or even sooner. Of course, the doctors keep telling us they can't believe how fast she's healing." He sighed. "At least we don't have to conceal that now."

"How's your mom handling the emotional part?" I asked.

"She's quit insisting they should release him. And since she had a frank talk with the three of us, she's admitting she and Don might have to get a divorce," he said. "She's not happy about the idea, but I don't know if you can completely reconcile with someone who's shot you."

Though I'd answered the phone by my bed and was still comfortably prone, I found it impossible to go back to sleep after we'd hung up. I'd hated to hear the pain in Sam's voice. Sam had enough to fret about without troubling him with my problems, so I hadn't even seriously considered bringing up the knife incident, though I would have been relieved to share my worries with Sam.

I was up and dressed by eight o'clock, early for me. Though I was moving and thinking, I felt as rumpled and wrinkled as my bedsheets. I wished someone could yank me smooth and orderly, the way I yanked the sheets. Amelia was home (I checked to see if her car was parked out back when I made the coffee) and I'd glimpsed Octavia shuffling into the hall bathroom, so it was shaping up to be a typical morning, as mornings went nowadays at my house.

The pattern was broken by a knocking at the front door. Usually I'm warned by the crunching of the gravel driveway, but in my heavier-than-usual morning fog, I'd missed it.

I looked through the peephole to see a man and a woman, both dressed in proper business suits. They didn't look like Jehovah's Witnesses or home invaders. I reached out to them mentally and found no hostility or anger, only curiosity.

I opened the door. I smiled brilliantly. "Can I help you?" I said. The cold air gusted around my bare feet.

The woman, who was probably in her early forties, smiled back. Her brown hair had a little gray in it and was cut in a simple chin-length style. She'd parted it very precisely. Her pantsuit was charcoal with a black sweater underneath, and her shoes were black. She carried a black bag, which wasn't exactly like a purse, more like a laptop case.

She held out her hand to shake, and when I touched her, I knew more. It was hard to keep the shock off my face. "I'm from the New Orleans office of the FBI," she said, which is a bombshell of an opener for your average conversation. "I'm Agent Sara Weiss. This is Special Agent Tom Lattesta from our Rhodes office."

"You're here about . . . ?" I kept my face pleasantly blank.

"May we come in? Tom's come all the way from Rhodes to talk to you, and we're letting all your warm air out."

"Sure," I said, though I was far from sure. I was trying hard to get a fix on their intent, but it wasn't easy. I could only tell they weren't there to arrest me or anything drastic like that.

"Is this a convenient time?" Agent Weiss asked. She implied she'd be delighted to come back later, though I knew that wasn't true.

"This is as good as any," I said. My grandmother would have given me a sharp look for my ungraciousness, but then, Gran had never been questioned by the FBI. This was not exactly a social call. "I do have to leave for work pretty soon," I added to give myself an escape hatch.

"That's bad news, about your boss's mother," Lattesta said. "Did the big announcement go well at your bar?" From his accent, I could tell he'd been born north of the Mason-Dixon Line, and from his knowledge of Sam's whereabouts and identity, he'd done his homework, down to investigating the place I worked.

The sick feeling that had started up in my stomach intensified. I had a moment of wanting Eric there so badly it made me a little dizzy, and then I looked out the window at the sunshine and felt only anger at my own longing. *This is what you get,* I told myself.

"Having werewolves around makes the world more interesting, doesn't it?" I said. The smile popped onto my face, the smile that said I was really strained. "I'll take your coats. Please, have a seat." I indicated the couch, and they settled on it. "Can I get you some coffee or some iced tea?" I said, thanking Gran's training for keeping the words flowing.

"Oh," Weiss said. "Some iced tea would be wonderful. I

know it's cold outside, but I drink it year-round. I'm a south-ern woman born and bred."

And laying it on a little too thick, in my opinion. I didn't think Weiss would become my best friend, and I didn't plan to swap any recipes. "You?" I looked at Lattesta.

"Sure, great," he said.

"Sweet or unsweet?" Lattesta thought it would be fun to have the famous southern sweet tea, and Weiss accepted sweet as a matter of bonding. "Let me tell my roommates we have company," I said, and I called up the stairs, "Amelia! The FBI is here!"

"I'll be down in a minute," she called back, not sounding surprised at all. I knew she'd been standing at the top of the stairs listening to every word.

And here came Octavia in her favorite green pants and striped long-sleeved shirt, looking as dignified and sweet as an elderly white-haired black woman can look. Ruby Dee has nothing on Octavia.

"Hello," she said, beaming. Though she looked like every-one's favorite granny, Octavia was a powerful witch who could cast spells with almost surgical precision. She'd had a lifetime of practice in concealing her ability. "Sookie didn't tell us she was expecting company, or we would have cleaned up the house." Octavia beamed some more. She swept a hand to indicate the spotless living room. It would never be fea-tured in *Southern Living*, but it was clean, by golly.

"Looks great to me," Weiss said respectfully. "I wish my house looked this neat." She was telling the truth. Weiss had two teenagers and a husband and three dogs. I felt a lot of sympathy—and maybe some envy—for Agent Weiss.

"Sookie, I'll bring tea for your guests while you talk," Octavia said in her sweetest voice. "You just sit down and

visit a spell." The agents were settled on the couch and looking around the shabby living room with interest when she
returned with napkins and two glasses of sweet tea, ice rat-
tling in a pleasant way. I rose from the chair opposite the
couch to put napkins in front of them, and Octavia placed
the glasses on the napkins. Lattesta took a large swallow. The
corner of Octavia's mouth twitched just a little when he made
a startled face and then did his best to amend his expression
to pleased surprise.

"What did you-all want to ask me?" Time to get down to
brass tacks. I smiled at them brightly, my hands folded in my
lap, my feet parallel, and my knees clamped together.

Lattesta had brought in a briefcase, and now he put it on
the coffee table and opened it. He extracted a picture and
handed it to me. It had been taken in the middle of the afternoon in the city of Rhodes a few months before. The picture
was clear enough, though the air around the people in it was
blighted with the clouds of dust that had billowed up from
the collapsed Pyramid of Gizeh.

I kept my eyes on the picture, I kept my face smiling, but
I couldn't stop my heart from sinking into my feet.

In the picture, Barry the Bellboy and I were standing
together in the rubble of the Pyramid, the vampire hotel that
a splinter Fellowship group had blown up the previous October. I was somewhat more recognizable than my companion,
because Barry was standing in profile. I was facing the camera, unaware of it, my eyes on Barry's face. We were both
covered in dirt and blood, ash and dust.

"That's you, Miss Stackhouse," Lattesta said.

"Yes, it is." Pointless to deny the woman in the picture was
me, but I sure would have loved to have done so. Looking at

the picture made me feel sick because it forced me to remember that day all too clearly.

"So you were staying at the Pyramid at the time of the explosion?"

"Yes, I was."

"You were there in the employ of Sophie-Anne Leclerq, a vampire businesswoman. The so-called Queen of Louisiana."

I started to tell him there had been no "so-called" about it, but discretion blocked those words. "I flew up there with her," I said instead.

"And Sophie-Anne Leclerq sustained severe injuries in the blast?"

"I understand she did."

"You didn't see her after the explosion?"

"No."

"Who is this man standing with you in the picture?"

Lattesta hadn't identified Barry. I had to keep my shoulders stiff so they wouldn't sag with relief. I shrugged. "He came up to me after the blast," I said. "We were in better shape than most, so we helped search for survivors." Truth, but not the whole truth. I'd known Barry for months before I'd encountered him at the convention at the Pyramid. He'd been there in the service of the King of Texas. I wondered how much about the vamp hierarchy the FBI actually knew.

"How did the two of you search for survivors?" Lattesta asked.

That was a very tricky question. At that time, Barry was the only other telepath I'd ever met. We'd experimented by holding hands to increase our "wattage," and we'd looked for brain signatures in the piles of debris. I took a deep breath. "I'm good at finding things," I said. "It seemed important to help. So many people hurt so bad."

"The fire chief on-site said you seemed to have some psychic ability," Lattesta said. Weiss looked down at her tea glass to hide her expression.

"I'm not a psychic," I said truthfully, and Weiss immediately felt disappointed. She felt she could be in the presence of a poseur or a nut job, but she had hoped I'd admit I was the real thing.

"Chief Trochek said you told them where to find survivors. He said you actually steered the rescue crews to the living."

Amelia came down the stairs then, looking very respectable in a bright red sweater and designer jeans. I met her eyes, hoping she'd see I was silently asking for help. I hadn't been able to turn my back on a situation where I could actually save lives. When I'd realized I could find people—that teaming up with Barry would result in saving lives—I couldn't turn away from the task, though I was scared of being exposed to the world as a freak.

It's hard to explain what I see. I guess it's like looking through infrared goggles or something. I see the heat of the brain; I can count the living people in a building, if I have time. Vampire brains leave a hole, a negative spot; I can usually count those, too. Plain old dead people don't register with me at all. That day when Barry and I had held hands, the joining had magnified our abilities. We could find the living, and we could hear the last thoughts of the dying. I wouldn't wish that on anyone. And I didn't want to experience it again, ever.

"We just had good luck," I said. That wouldn't convince a toad to hop.

Amelia came forward with her hand extended. "I'm Amelia Broadway," she said, as if she expected them to know who she was.

They did.

"You're Copley's daughter, right?" Weiss asked. "I met him a couple of weeks ago in connection with a community program."

"He's so involved in the city," Amelia said with a dazzling smile. "He's got his fingers in a dozen pies, I guess. Dad's real fond of the Sook, here." Not so subtle, but hopefully effective. *Leave my roommate alone. My father's powerful.*

Weiss nodded pleasantly. "How'd you end up here in Bon Temps, Ms. Broadway?" she asked. "It must seem real quiet here, after New Orleans." *What's a rich bitch like you doing in this backwater? By the way, your dad's not around to run interference for you.*

"My house got damaged during Katrina," Amelia said. She left it at that. She didn't tell them that she'd been in Bon Temps already when Katrina happened.

"And you, Ms. Fant?" Lattesta asked. "Were you an evacuee also?" He'd by no means abandoned the subject of my ability, but he was willing to go along with the social flow.

"Yes," Octavia said. "I was living with my niece under cramped circumstances, and Sookie very kindly offered me her spare bedroom."

"How'd you know each other?" Weiss asked, as if she was expecting to hear a delightful story.

"Through Amelia," I said, smiling just as happily back at her.

"And you and Amelia met——?"

"In New Orleans," Amelia said, firmly cutting off that line of questioning.

"Did you want some more iced tea?" Octavia asked Lattesta.

"No, thank you," he said, almost shuddering. It had been Octavia's turn to make the tea, and she did have a heavy hand with the sugar. "Ms. Stackhouse, you don't have any idea how to contact this young man?" He indicated the picture.

I shrugged. "We both helped to look for bodies," I said. "It was a terrible day. I don't remember what name he gave."

"That seems strange," Lattesta said, and I thought, *Oh, shit.* "Since someone answering your description and a young man answering his description checked into a motel some distance from the explosion that night and shared a room."

"Well, you don't have to know someone's name to spend the night with them," Amelia said reasonably.

I shrugged and tried to look embarrassed, which wasn't too hard. I'd rather they think me sexually easy than decide I was worthy of more attention. "We'd shared a horrible, stressful event. Afterward, we felt really close. That's the way we reacted." Actually, Barry had collapsed in sleep almost instantly, and I had followed soon afterward. Hanky-panky had been the furthest thing from our minds.

The two agents stared at me doubtfully. Weiss was thinking I was lying for sure, and Lattesta suspected it. He thought I knew Barry very well.

The phone rang, and Amelia hurried to the kitchen to answer it. She came back looking green.

"Sookie, that was Antoine on his cell phone. They need you at the bar," she said. And then she turned to the FBI agents. "Probably you should go with her."

"Why?" Weiss asked. "What's up?" She was already on her feet. Lattesta was stuffing the picture back into his briefcase.

"A body," Amelia said. "A woman's been crucified behind the bar."

Chapter 5

The agents followed me to Merlotte's. There were five or six cars parked across the spot where the front parking lot ended and the back parking began, effectively blocking access to the back. But I leaped out of my car and picked a path between them, and the FBI agents were right on my heels.

I had hardly been able to believe it, but it was true. There was a traditional cross erected in the employee parking lot, back by the trees where the gravel gave way to dirt. A body was nailed to it. My eyes scanned it, took in the distorted body, the streaks of dried blood, came back up to the face.

"Oh, no," I said, and my knees folded.

Antoine, the cook, and D'Eriq, the busboy, were suddenly on either side of me, pulling me up. D'Eriq's face was tearstained, and Antoine looked grim, but the cook had his head together. He'd been in Iraq and in New Orleans during Katrina. He'd seen things that were worse.

"I'm sorry, Sookie," he said.

Andy Bellefleur was there, and Sheriff Dearborn. They walked over to me, looking bigger and bulkier in their water-proof quilted coats. Their faces were hard with suppressed shock.

"Sorry about your sister-in-law," Bud Dearborn said, but I could barely pay attention to the words.

"She was pregnant," I said. "She was pregnant." That was all I could think about. I wasn't amazed that someone would want to kill Crystal, but I was really horrified about the baby.

I took a deep breath and managed to look again. Crystal's bloody hands were panther paws. The lower part of her legs had changed, too. The effect was even more shocking and grotesque than the crucifixion of a regular human woman and, if possible, more pitiful.

Thoughts raced through my head with no logical sequence. I thought of who needed to know that Crystal had died. Calvin, not only head of her clan but also her uncle. Crystal's husband, my brother. Why was Crystal left here, of all places? Who could have done this?

"Have you called Jason yet?" I said through numb lips. I tried to blame that on the cold, but I knew it was shock. "He would be at work this time of day."

Bud Dearborn said, "We called him."

"Please don't make him look at her," I said. There was a bloody mess trailing down the wood of the cross to the ground at its base. I gagged, got myself under control.

"I understand she cheated on him, and that their breakup was pretty public." Bud was trying to be dispassionate, but the effort was costing him. Rage was in the back of his eyes.

"You can ask Dove Beck about that," I said, instantly on the defensive. Alcee Beck was a detective for the Bon Temps police department, and the man Crystal had chosen to cheat with was Alcee's cousin Dove. "Yeah, Crystal and Jason had separated. But he would never do anything to his baby." I knew Jason would not have done such a horrific thing to Crystal no matter what the provocation, but I didn't expect anyone else to believe me.

Lattesta walked over to us, Agent Weiss following close behind. She looked a little white around the mouth, but her voice was steady. "From the condition of the body, I believe this woman was a . . . werepanther." She said the word as if it was hard to get it through her lips.

I nodded. "Yes, ma'am, she was." I was still fighting to gain control of my stomach.

"Then this could be a hate crime," Lattesta said. His face was locked down tight, and his thoughts were orderly. He was composing a mental list of phone calls he should make, and he was trying to figure out if there was any way he could take charge of the case. If the murder had been a hate crime, he had a good shot at being in on the investigation.

"And who might you be?" Bud Dearborn asked. He had his hands on his belt, and he was looking at Weiss and Lattesta as if they were pre-need burial plot salesmen.

While the law enforcement types were all introducing themselves and saying profound things about the crime scene, Antoine said, "I'm sorry, Sookie. We had to call 'em. But we called your house right after."

"Of course you had to call them," I said. "I just wish Sam was here." Oh, gosh. I pulled my cell phone out of my pocket and pressed his speed-dial number.

"Sam," I said when he picked up. "Can you talk?"

"Yes," he said, sounding apprehensive. He could already tell something was wrong.

"Where are you?"

"I'm in my car."

"I have bad news."

"What's happened? Did the bar burn down?"

"No, but Crystal's been murdered in the parking lot. Out back by your trailer."

"Oh, shit. Where's Jason?"

"He's on his way here, near as I can find out."

"I'm sorry, Sookie." He sounded exhausted. "This is going to be bad."

"The FBI is here. They're thinking it might be a hate crime." I skipped the explanation of why they'd happened to be in Bon Temps.

"Well, a lot of people didn't like Crystal," Sam said cautiously, surprise in his voice.

"She was crucified."

"Dammit to *hell*." A long pause. "Sook, if my mom is still stable and nothing's happening legally with my stepfather, I'll start back later today or early tomorrow."

"Good." I couldn't begin to pack enough relief into that one word. And it was no use pretending I had everything under control.

"I'm sorry, *cher*," he said again. "Sorry you're having to handle it, sorry Jason will be suspected, sorry about the whole thing. Sorry for Crystal, too."

"I'll be glad to see you," I said, and my voice was shaky with incipient tears.

"I'll be there." And he hung up.

Lattesta said, "Ms. Stackhouse, are these men other bar employees?"

I introduced Antoine and D'Eriq to Lattesta. Antoine's

expression didn't change, but D'Eriq was completely impressed that he'd met an FBI agent.

"Both of you knew this Crystal Norris, right?" Lattesta said mildly.

Antoine said, "Just by sight. She come in the bar some."

D'Eriq nodded.

"Crystal Norris Stackhouse," I said. "She's my sister-in-law. The sheriff's called my brother. But you need to call her uncle, Calvin Norris. He works at Norcross."

"He her nearest living relative? Besides the husband?"

"She's got a sister. But Calvin's the leader of—" I stopped, not sure if Calvin had endorsed the Great Reveal. "He raised her," I said. Close enough.

Lattesta and Weiss huddled with Bud Dearborn. They were deep in conversation, probably about Calvin and the tiny community out at the bleak crossroads. Hotshot was a group of small houses containing lots of secrets. Crystal had wanted to escape from Hotshot, but she also felt most secure there.

My eyes returned to the tortured figure on the cross. Crystal was dressed, but her clothes had ripped when her arms and legs had changed to panther limbs, and there was blood everywhere. Her hands and feet, impaled with nails, were crusted with it. Ropes did the work of holding her to the crossbar, kept the flesh from ripping free of the nails.

I'd seen a lot of awful things, but this was maybe the most pathetic. "Poor Crystal," I said, and found tears were rolling down my cheeks.

"You didn't like her," Andy Bellefleur said. I wondered how long he'd been out here, looking at the ruin of what had once been a living, breathing, healthy woman. Andy's cheeks were patched with stubble, and his nose was red. Andy had a cold. He sneezed and excused himself to use a handkerchief.

D'Eriq and Antoine were talking to Alcee Beck. Alcee was the other Bon Temps police detective, and that didn't make the investigation look too promising. He wouldn't be too regretful about Crystal's death.

Andy faced me again after he'd stuffed his handkerchief in his pocket. I looked at his weary, broad face. I knew he'd do his best to find out who'd done this. I trusted Andy. Square-built Andy, some years my senior, had never been a smiley kind of guy. He was serious and suspicious. I didn't know if he'd chosen his occupation because it suited him, or if his character had altered in response to his occupation.

"I hear she and Jason had split," he said.

"Yes. She cheated on him." This was common knowledge. I wasn't going to pretend otherwise.

"Pregnant and all, like she was?" Andy shook his head.

"Yeah." I spread my hands. *That was the way she was.*

"That's sick," Andy said.

"Yeah, it is. Cheating with your husband's baby in your stomach between you . . . that's just specially icky." It was a thought I'd had but never voiced.

"So, who was the other man?" Andy asked casually. "Or men?"

"You're the only guy in Bon Temps who doesn't know she was screwing Dove Beck," I said.

This time it registered. Andy glanced over at Alcee Beck and back to me. "I know now," he said. "Who hated her that much, Sookie?"

"If you're thinking Jason, you can just think again. He would never do that to his baby."

"If she was so free with herself, maybe it wasn't his baby," Andy said. "Maybe he found that out."

"It was his," I said with a firmness I wasn't sure I felt. "But even if it wasn't, if some blood test says it wasn't, he wouldn't kill anybody's baby. Anyway, they weren't living together. She'd moved back in with her sister. Why would he even go to the trouble?"

"Why were the FBI at your house?"

Okay, so this questioning thing was going to go one way. "Some questions about the explosion in Rhodes," I said. "I found out about Crystal while they were there. They came along out of professional curiosity, I guess. Lattesta, the guy, thinks this might be a hate crime."

"That's an interesting idea," he said. "This is undoubtedly a hate crime, but whether or not it's the kind of thing they should investigate, I don't know yet." He strode off to talk to Weiss. Lattesta was looking up at the body, shaking his head, as if he was noting a level of awfulness he'd thought couldn't be reached.

I didn't know what to do with myself. I was in charge of the bar, and the crime scene was on bar property, so I was determined to stay.

Alcee Beck called, "All people on the scene who are not police officers, leave the area! All police officers who are non-essential to the crime scene, step into the front parking lot!" His gaze fell on me, and he jabbed a finger toward the front. So I went back to lean against my car. Though it was cold enough, it was lucky for all of us that the day was bright and the wind wasn't blowing. I pulled my coat collar up around my ears and reached into the car to get my black gloves. I tugged them on and waited.

Time passed. I watched various police officers come and go. When Holly showed up for her shift, I explained what had happened and sent her home, telling her I'd call when I'd gotten permission to reopen. I couldn't think of any other course of action. Antoine and D'Eriq had left long ago, after I'd entered their cell numbers on my phone.

Jason's truck screeched to a halt beside my car, and he leaped out to stand in front of me. We hadn't spoken in weeks, but this was no time to talk about our differences. "Is it true?" my brother asked.

"I'm sorry. It's true."

"The baby, too?"

"Yeah."

"Alcee come out to the job site," he said numbly. "He come asking how long it had been since I'd seen her. I haven't talked to her in four or five weeks, except to send her some money for the doctor visits and her vitamins. I saw her once at Dairy Queen."

"Who was she with?"

"Her sister." He took a long, shuddering breath. "You think . . . Was it bad?"

No point beating around the bush. "Yes," I said.

"Then I'm sorry she had to go that way," he said. He wasn't used to expressing complex emotions, and it sat awkwardly on him, this combination of grief and regret and loss. He looked five years older. "I was so hurt by her and mad at her, but I wouldn't want her to suffer and be afraid. God knows we probably wouldn't have been good as parents, but we didn't get a chance to try."

I agreed with every part of what he'd said.

"Did you have company last night?" I said finally.

"Yeah, I took Michele Schubert home from the Bayou," he said. The Bayou was a bar in Clarice, only a few miles away.

"She stay all night?"

"I made her scrambled eggs this morning."

"Good." For once my brother's promiscuity paid off—Michele was a single divorcée without children and forthright to boot. If anyone would be willing to tell the police exactly where she'd been and what she'd done, Michele was the woman. I said as much.

"The police have already talked to her," Jason told me.

"That was fast."

"Bud was in the Bayou last night."

So the sheriff would have seen Jason leave and would have noted whom he'd left with. Bud hadn't kept the job of sheriff this long without being shrewd. "Well, that's good," I said, and couldn't think of anything else to say.

"You think maybe she was killed because she was a panther?" Jason asked hesitantly.

"Maybe. She was partially changed when she was killed."

"Poor Crystal," he said. "She would have hated anyone to see her like that." And to my amazement, tears ran down his face.

I didn't have the slightest idea how to react. All I could do was fetch a Kleenex from the box in my car and shove it in his hand. I hadn't seen Jason cry in years. Had he even cried when Gran had died? Maybe he really had loved Crystal. Maybe it hadn't been solely wounded pride that had caused him to set up her exposure as an adulteress. He'd fixed it so both her uncle Calvin and I would catch her in the act. I'd been so disgusted and furious with being forced to be a witness—and with the consequences—that I'd avoided Jason for weeks. Crystal's death had shunted aside that anger, at least for the moment.

"She's beyond that now," I said.

Calvin's battered truck pulled up on the other side of my car. Quicker than my eye could track, he stood in front of me, while Tanya Grissom scrambled out the other side. A stranger looked out of Calvin's eyes. Normally a peculiar golden green color, those eyes were now almost gold, and the irises were so large that there was almost no visible white. His pupils had elongated. He was not even wearing a light jacket. It made me cold to look at him in more ways than one.

I held up my hands. "I'm so sorry, Calvin," I said. "You need to know Jason did *not* do this." I looked up, not too far, to meet his eerie eyes. Calvin was a little grayer now than he'd been when I'd first met him several years ago, and a little stockier. He still looked solid and dependable and tough.

"I need to smell her," he said, ignoring my words. "They have to let me back there to smell her. I'll know."

"Come on, then; we'll go tell them that," I said, because not only was that a good idea, but also I wanted to keep him away from Jason. At least Jason was smart enough to stay on the far side of my car. I took Calvin's arm and we began to walk around the building, only to be stopped by the crime scene tape.

Bud Dearborn moved over to the other side of the tape when he saw us. "Calvin, I know you're rattled, and I'm real sorry about your niece," he began, and with a flash of claw Calvin ripped down the tape and began walking over to the cross.

Before he'd gotten three steps, the two FBI agents moved to intercept him. Suddenly they were on the ground. There was a lot of shouting and tumult, and then Calvin was being held back by Bud, Andy, and Alcee, with Lattesta and Weiss trying to assist from their undignified positions.

"Calvin," Bud Dearborn wheezed. Bud was not a young man, and it was clear that holding Calvin back was taking every bit of strength he possessed. "You gotta stay away, Calvin. Any evidence we collect is gonna be tainted if you don't stay away from the body." I was astonished at Bud's restraint. I would have expected him to crack Calvin in the head with his baton or a flashlight. Instead, he seemed as sympathetic as a strained and taxed man could be. For the first time, I understood that I wasn't the only one who'd known about the secret of the Hotshot community. Bud's wrinkled hand patted Calvin's arm in a gesture of consolation. Bud took care to avoid touching Calvin's claws. Special Agent Lattesta noticed them, and he drew in a harsh breath, making an incoherent warning noise.

"Bud," Calvin said, and his voice came out in a growl, "if you can't let me over there now, I have to smell her when they take her down. I'm trying to catch the scent of the ones who did this."

"I'll see if you can do that," Bud said steadily. "For right now, buddy, we got to get you out of here because they gotta pick up all this evidence around here, evidence that'll stand up in court. You got to stay away from her. Okay?"

Bud had never cared for me, nor I for him, but at that moment I sure thought well of him.

After a long moment, Calvin nodded. Some of the tension went out of his shoulders. Everyone who was holding on to him eased up on their grip.

Bud said, "You stay out front; we'll call you. You got my word."

"All right," Calvin said. The law enforcement crowd let go.

Calvin let me put my arm around him. Together, we turned to make for the front parking lot. Tanya was waiting for him, tension in every line of her body. She'd had the same expectations I'd had: that Calvin was going to get a good beating.

"Jason didn't do this," I said again.

"I don't care about your brother," he said, turning those strange eyes on me. "He doesn't matter to me. I don't think he killed her."

It was clear that he thought my anxiety about Jason was blocking my concern about the real problem, the death of his niece. It was clear he didn't appreciate that. I had to respect his feelings, so I shut my mouth.

Tanya took his hands, claws and all. "Will they let you go over her?" she asked. Her eyes never left Calvin's face. I might as well not have been there.

"When they take the body down," he said.

It would be so great if Calvin could identify the culprit. Thank God the werecreatures had come out. But . . . that might have been why Crystal had been killed.

"You think you'll be able to get a scent?" Tanya said. Her voice was quiet, intent. She was more serious than I'd ever seen her in our spotty acquaintance. She put her arms around Calvin and rested her head on his shoulder. She looked up at him.

"I'll get a score of scents after all these folks have touched her. I can only try to match them all. I wish I'd been here first." He held Tanya as if he needed to lean on someone.

Jason was standing a yard away, waiting for Calvin to notice him. His back was stiff, his face frozen. There was an awful moment of silence when Calvin looked over Tanya's shoulder and noted Jason's presence.

I don't know how Tanya reacted, but every muscle in my

body twanged from the tension. Slowly Calvin held out a hand to Jason. Though it was a human hand again, it was obviously battered. The skin was freshly scarred and one of the fingers was slightly bent.

I had done that. I'd stood up for Jason at his wedding, and Calvin had stood up for Crystal. After Jason had made us witness Crystal's infidelity, we'd had to stand in for them when the penalty had been pronounced: the maiming of a hand or paw. I'd had to bring a brick down on my friend's hand. I hadn't felt the same about Jason since then.

Jason bent and licked the back of the hand, emphasizing how subservient he was. He did it awkwardly, because he was still new to the ritual. I held my breath. Jason's eyes were rolled up to keep Calvin's face in sight. When Calvin nodded, we all relaxed. Calvin accepted Jason's obeisance.

"You'll be in at the kill," Calvin said, as if Jason had asked him something.

"Thanks," Jason said, and then backed away. He stopped when he'd gone a couple of feet. "I want to bury her," he said.

"We'll all bury her," Calvin said. "When they let us have her back." There was not a particle of concession in his voice.

Jason hesitated a moment and then nodded.

Calvin and Tanya got back in Calvin's truck. They settled in. Clearly they planned to wait there until the body was brought down from the cross. Jason said, "I'm going home. I can't stay here." He seemed almost dazed.

"Okay," I said.

"Are you . . . Do you plan on staying here?"

"Yes, I'm in charge of the bar while Sam is gone."

"That's a lot of trust he has in you," Jason said.

I nodded. I should feel honored. I did feel honored.

"Is it true his stepdad shot his mom? That's what I heard at the Bayou last night."

"Yes," I said. "He didn't know that Sam's mom was, you know, a shapeshifter."

Jason shook his head. "This coming-out thing," he said. "I don't know that's it been such a good idea after all. Sam's mom got shot. Crystal is dead. Someone who knew what she was put her up there, Sookie. Maybe they'll come after me next. Or Calvin. Or Tray Dawson. Or Alcide. Maybe they'll try to kill us all."

I started to say that couldn't happen, that the people I knew wouldn't turn on their friends and neighbors because of an accident of birth. But in the end, I didn't say that, because I wondered if it was the truth.

"Maybe they will," I said, feeling an icy tingle run down my back. I took a deep breath. "But since they didn't go after the vampires—for the most part—I'm thinking they'll be able to accept weres of all sorts. At least, I hope so."

Mel, wearing the slacks and sports shirt he wore daily at the auto parts place, got out of his car and walked over. I noticed that he was carefully not looking at Calvin, though Jason was still standing right beside the panther's pickup. "It's true, then," Mel said.

Jason said, "She's dead, Mel."

Mel patted Jason's shoulder in the awkward way men have when they have to comfort other men. "Come on, Jason. You don't need to be around here. Let's go to your house. We'll have a drink, buddy."

Jason nodded, looking dazed. "Okay, let's go." After Jason left for home with Mel following right behind, I climbed back in my own vehicle and fished the newspapers for the past few days from the backseat. I often picked them up from the driveway when I came out to go to work, tossed them in the back, and tried to read at least the front page within a reasonable length of time. What with Sam leaving and my business with the bar, I hadn't caught a glimpse of the news since the weres went public.

I arranged the papers in order and began to read.

The public reaction had ranged from the panicked to the calm. Many people claimed they'd had a suspicion that the world contained more than humans and vampires. The vampires themselves were 100 percent behind their furry brethren, at least in public. In my experience, the two major supernatural groups had had a very bumpy relationship. The shifters and Weres mocked the vampires, and the vampires jeered right back. But it looked like the supernaturals had agreed to present a united front, at least for a while.

The reactions of governments varied wildly. I think the U.S. policy had been formed by shifters in place within the system, because it was overwhelmingly favorable. There was a huge tendency to accept the weres as if they were completely human, to keep their rights as Americans exactly on a par with their previous status when no one knew they were two-natured. The vampires couldn't be too pleased about that, because they hadn't yet obtained full rights and privileges under the law. Legal marriage and inheritance of property were still forbidden in a few states, and vampires were barred from owning certain businesses. The human casino lobby had been successful in banning the vamps from direct ownership of gambling establishments, which I still couldn't understand, and though vampires could be police officers and firefighters, vampire doctors were not accepted in any field that included treating patients with open wounds. Vampires weren't allowed in competition sports, either. That I could understand; they were too strong. But there were already lots of athletes whose ancestry included full- and part-weres, because sports were a natural bent for them. The military ranks, too, were filled with men and women whose grandparents had bayed under the full moon. There were even some full-blooded weres in the armed services, though it was a very tricky occupation for people who had to find somewhere private to be three nights a month.

The sports pages were full of pictures of some part- and whole-weres who'd become famous. A running back for the New England Patriots, a fielder for the Cardinals, a marathon runner . . . they'd all confessed to being wereanimals of one kind or another. An Olympic champion swimmer had just discovered that his dad was a wereseal, and the number-one ranked women's tennis player in Britain had gone on record as saying that her mother was a wereleopard. The sports world hadn't been in such a tumult since the last drug scandal. Did these athletes' heritage give them an unfair advantage over other players? Should their trophies be taken away from them? Should their records be allowed to stand? Another day, I might enjoy debating this with someone, but right now I just didn't care.

I began to see an overall picture. The outing of the two-natured was a much different revelation from the vampires' announcement. The vampires had been completely off the human grid, except in legend and lore. They'd lived apart. Since they could subsist on the Japanese synthetic blood, they had presented themselves as absolutely nonthreatening. But wereanimals had been living among us all the time, integrated into our society yet maintaining their secret lives and alliances. Sometimes even their children (those who weren't firstborn and therefore not weres) didn't know what their parents were, especially if they were not wolves.

"I feel betrayed," one woman was quoted as saying. "My granddad turns into a lynx every month. He runs around and kills things. My beautician, I've been going to her for fifteen years, and she's a coyote. I didn't know! I feel I've been deceived in an ugly way."

Some people thought it was fascinating. "Our principal is a werewolf," said a kid in Springfield, Missouri. "How cool is that?"

The very fact of the existence of wereanimals frightened some people. "I'm scared I'll shoot my neighbor by accident if I see him trotting down the road," said a farmer in Kansas. "What if he gets after my chickens?"

Various churches were thrashing out their policy on weres. "We don't know what to think," a Vatican official confessed. "They're alive, they're among us, they must have souls. Even some priests are wereanimals." The fundamentalists were equally stymied. "We were worried about Adam and Steve," a Baptist minister said. "Should we have been more worried about Rover and Fluffy?"

While my head had been in the sand, all hell had broken loose.

Suddenly it was easier to see how my werepanther sister-in-law had ended up on a cross at a bar owned by a shifter.

Chapter 6

The moment the nails came out of her hands and feet, Crystal's body reverted to looking completely human. I watched from behind the crime scene tape. This process drew the horrified attention of everyone on the site. Even Alcee Beck flinched back. I'd been waiting for hours by then; I'd read all the newspapers twice, found a paperback in the glove compartment and gotten about a third of the way through it, and had a limp conversation with Tanya about Sam's mother. After we'd rehashed that news, she mostly talked about Calvin. I gathered that she had moved in with him. She'd gotten a part-time job at Norcross in the main office, doing something clerical. She loved the regular hours. "And I don't have to stand up all day," she said.

"Sounds good," I said politely, though I'd hate that kind of job. Working with the same people every day? I'd get to know them all too well. I wouldn't be able to stay out of their thoughts, and I'd reach the point of wanting to get away from them because I knew too much about them. At the bar, there were always different people coming in to keep me distracted.

"How'd the Great Reveal go for you?" I asked.

"I told 'em at Norcross the next day," she said. "When they found out I was a werefox, they thought that was funny." She looked disgusted. "Why do the big animals get all the press? Calvin got huge respect out in the plant from his crew. I get jokes about bushy tails."

"Not fair," I agreed, trying not to smile.

"Calvin is completely wiped out about Crystal," Tanya said abruptly. "She was his favorite niece. He felt awful bad for her when it turned out she was such a poor shifter. And about the babies." Crystal, the product of a lot of inbreeding, had taken forever to change into her panther form and had had a hard time reversing the process when she wanted to become a human again. She'd miscarried several times, too. The only reason she'd been allowed to marry Jason was that it had become obvious she would probably never carry a pureblood baby to term.

"Could be this baby was lost before the murder, or she aborted during the murder," I said. "Maybe the—whoever did this—didn't know."

"She was showing, but not a whole lot," Tanya said, nodding. "She was real picky about her food, 'cause she was determined to keep her figure." She shook her head, her face bitter. "But really, Sookie, does it really make any difference if the killer knew or not? The end is the same. The baby is dead, and so is Crystal, and she died afraid and alone."

Tanya was absolutely right.

"Do you think Calvin can track whoever did this from the smell?" I asked.

Tanya looked uneasy. "There were lots of scents," she said. "I don't know how he can tell which one's *the* scent. And look, they're all touching her. Some of 'em are wearing rubber gloves, but those have an odor, you know. See, there's Mitch Norris helping take her down, and he's one of us. So how will Calvin know?"

"Besides, it might be one of them," I said, nodding toward the group gathered around the dead woman. Tanya looked at me sharply.

"You mean law enforcement might be in on it?" she said. "Do you know something?"

"No," I said, sorry I'd opened my big mouth. "It's just . . . we don't know anything for sure. I guess I was thinking about Dove Beck."

"He's the one she was in bed with that day?"

I nodded. "That big guy, there—the black guy in the suit? That's his cousin Alcee."

"Think he might have had something to do with it?"

"Not really," I said. "I was just . . . speculating."

"I'll bet Calvin's thought of that, too," she said. "Calvin's very sharp."

I nodded. There was nothing flashy about Calvin, and he hadn't managed to go to college (I hadn't either), but there was nothing wrong with his brain.

Bud beckoned to Calvin then, and he got out of his truck and went over to the body, which had been laid on a gurney spread with an open body bag. Calvin approached the body carefully, his hands behind his back so he wouldn't touch Crystal.

We all watched, some with loathing and distaste, some with indifference or interest, until he'd finished.

He straightened, turned, and walked back in the direction

of his truck. Tanya got out of my car to meet him. She put her arms around him and looked up at him. He shook his head. I'd lowered my window so I could hear. "I couldn't make out much on the rest of her," he said. "Too many other smells. She just smelled like a dead panther."

"Let's go home, Calvin," Tanya said.

"Okay." They each raised a hand to me to let me know they were leaving, and then I was by myself in the front parking lot, still waiting. Bud asked me to open the employee entrance to the bar. I handed him the keys. He returned after a few minutes to tell me that the door had been securely locked and that there was no sign anyone had been inside the bar since it had closed. He handed the keys to me.

"So we can open up?" I asked. A few police vehicles had left, the body was gone, and it seemed to me that the whole process was winding down. I was willing to wait there if I could get into the building soon.

But after Bud told me it might be two or three more hours, I decided I'd go home. I'd spoken to every employee I could reach, and any customers could clearly see from the tape put across the parking lot that the bar was closed. I was wasting my time. My FBI agents, who'd spent hours with their cell phones clamped to their ears, seemed now to be more concerned about this crime than about me, which was great. Maybe they'd forget all about me.

Since no one seemed to be watching me or to care what I was doing, I started my car up and left. I didn't have the heart to run any errands. I went straight back to the house.

Amelia had long ago left for work at the insurance agency, but Octavia was home. She had set up the ironing board in her room. She was pressing the hem on a pair of pants she'd just shortened, and she had a pile of her blouses ready to iron.

I guess there wasn't any magic spell to get the wrinkles out. I offered to drive her into town, but she said her trip with Amelia the day before had taken care of all her needs. She invited me to sit on the wooden chair by the bed while she worked. "Ironing goes faster when you have someone to talk to," she said, and she sounded so lonely I felt guilty.

I told her about the morning I'd had, about the circumstances of Crystal's death. Octavia had seen some bad stuff in her time, so she didn't freak out. She made the appropriate answers and expressed the shock almost anyone would feel, but she hadn't really known Crystal. I could tell there was something on her mind.

Octavia put down the iron and moved to face me directly. "Sookie," she said, "I need to get a job. I know I'm a burden to you and Amelia. I used to borrow my niece's car during the day when she was working the night shift, but since I've moved out here, I've been having to ask you-all for rides. I know that gets old. I cleaned my niece's house and cooked and helped to watch the kids to pay her for my room and board, but you and Amelia are such cleaners that my two cents wouldn't really be a help."

"I'm glad to have you, Octavia," I said, not entirely truthfully. "You've helped me in a lot of ways. Remember that you got Tanya off my back? And now she seems to be in love with Calvin. So she won't be pestering me anymore. I know you'd feel better if you could get a job, and maybe something will come up. In the meantime, you're fine here. We'll think of something."

"I called my brother in New Orleans," she said to my astonishment. I hadn't even known she had a living brother. "He says the insurance company has decided to give me a payment. It's not much, considering I lost almost everything, but it'll be enough to buy a good secondhand car. There won't be anything there for me to go back to, though. I'm not going to rebuild, and there aren't too many places I could afford on my own."

"I'm sorry," I said. "I wish there was something I could do about it, Octavia. Make things better for you."

"You've already made things better for me," she said. "I'm grateful."

"Oh, please," I said miserably. "Don't. Thank Amelia."

"All I know how to do is magic," Octavia said. "I was so glad to help you out with Tanya. Does she seem to remember?"

"No," I said. "I don't think she remembers anything about Calvin bringing her over here, or the spell casting. I'll never be her favorite person, but at least she's not trying to make my life miserable anymore."

Tanya had been sent to sabotage me by a woman named Sandra Pelt, who bore me a grudge. Since Calvin had clearly taken a shine to Tanya, Amelia and Octavia had worked a little magic on her to cut her free from Sandra's influence. Tanya still seemed abrasive, but that was just her nature, I figured.

"Do you think we should do a reconstruction to find out who Crystal's killer was?" Octavia offered.

I thought it over. I tried to imagine staging an ectoplasmic reconstruction in the parking lot of Merlotte's. We'd have to find at least one more witch, I thought, because that was a large area, and I wasn't sure Octavia and Amelia could handle it by themselves. They'd probably think they could, though.

"I'm afraid we'd be seen," I said finally. "And that would be bad for you and Amelia. Besides, we don't know where the actual death took place. And you have to have that, right? The death site?"

Octavia said, "Yes. If she didn't die there in the parking lot, it wouldn't do a bit of good." She sounded a bit relieved.

"I guess we won't know until the autopsy if she died there or before they put up the cross." I didn't think I could stand to witness another ectoplasmic reconstruction, anyway. I'd seen two. Watching the dead—in a watery but recognizable form—reenact the last minutes of their lives was an indescribably eerie and depressing experience.

Octavia went back to her ironing, and I wandered into the kitchen and heated up some soup. I had to eat something, and opening a can was about as much effort as I could expend.

The dragging hours were absolutely negative. I didn't hear from Sam. I didn't hear from the police about opening Merlotte's. The FBI agents didn't return to ask me more questions. Finally I decided to drive to Shreveport. Amelia had returned from work, and she and Octavia were cooking supper together when I left the house. It was a homey scene; I was simply too restless to join in.

For the second time in as many days, I found myself on the way to Fangtasia. I didn't let myself think. I listened to a black gospel station all the way over, and the preaching helped me feel better about the awful events of the day.

By the time I arrived, it was full night, though it was too early for the bar to be crowded. Eric was sitting at one of the tables in the main room, his back to me. He was drinking some TrueBlood and talking to Clancy, who ranked under Pam, I thought. Clancy was facing me, and he sneered when he saw me walking toward the table. Clancy was no Sookie Stackhouse fan. Since he was a vampire, I couldn't discover why, but I thought he simply didn't like me.

Eric turned to see me approaching, and his eyebrows rose. He said something to Clancy, who got up and stalked back to the office. Eric waited for me to sit down at his table. "Hello, Sookie," he said. "Are you here to tell me how angry you are at me about our pledging? Or are you ready to have that long talk we must have sooner or later?"

"No," I said. We sat for a while in silence. I felt exhausted but oddly peaceful. I should be giving Eric hell about his high-handed handling of Quinn's request and the knife presentation. I should be asking him all kinds of questions . . . but I couldn't summon up the necessary fire.

I just wanted to sit beside him.

There was music playing; someone had turned on the all-vampire radio station, KDED. The Animals were singing "The Night." After he finished his drink and there was only a red residue staining the sides of the bottle, Eric lay his cold white hand on top of mine. "What happened today?" he asked, his voice calm.

I began to tell him, starting with the FBI visit. He didn't interrupt to exclaim or to ask questions. Even when I ended my tale with the removal of Crystal's body, he didn't speak for a while. "Even for you, that's a busy day, Sookie," he said finally. "As for Crystal, I don't think I ever met her, but she sounds worthless."

Eric never waffled around to be polite. Though I actually enjoyed that, I was also glad it wasn't a widely held trait. "I don't know that anyone is worthless," I said. "Though I have to admit, if I had to pick one person to get in a lifeboat with me, she wouldn't have made even my long list."

Eric's mouth quirked up in a smile.

"But," I added, "she was pregnant, that's the thing, and the baby was my brother's."

"Pregnant women were worth twice as much if they were killed in my time," Eric said.

He'd never volunteered much information about his life before he'd been turned. "What do you mean, worth?" I asked.

"In war, or with foreigners, we could kill whom we pleased," he said. "But in disputes between our own people, we had to pay silver when we killed one of our own." He looked like he was dredging up the memory with an effort. "If the person killed was a woman with child, the price was double."

"How old were you when you got married? Did you have children?" I knew Eric had been married, but I didn't know anything else about his life.

"I was counted a man at twelve," he said. "I married at sixteen. My wife's name was Aude. Aude had . . . We had . . . six children."

I held my breath. I could tell he was looking down the immense swell of time that had passed between his present—a bar in Shreveport, Louisiana—and his past—a woman dead for a thousand years.

"Did they live?" I asked very quietly.

"Three lived," he said, and he smiled. "Two boys and a girl. Two died at birth. And with the sixth child, Aude died, too."

"Of what?"

He shrugged. "She and the baby caught a fever. I suppose it was from some sort of an infection. Then, if people got sick, they mostly died. Aude and the baby perished within hours of each other. I buried them in a beautiful tomb," he said proudly. "My wife had her best broach on her dress, and I laid the baby on her breast."

He had never sounded less like a modern man. "How old were you?"

He considered. "I was in my early twenties," he said. "Perhaps twenty-three. Aude was older. She had been my elder brother's wife, and when he was killed in battle, it fell to me to marry her so our families would still be bonded. But I'd always liked her, and she was willing. She wasn't a silly girl; she'd lost two babies of my brother's, and she was glad to have more that lived."

"What happened to your children?"

"When I became a vampire?"

I nodded. "They can't have been very old."

"No, they were small. It happened not long after Aude's death," he said. "I missed her, you see, and I needed someone to raise the children. No such thing as a househusband then." He laughed. "I had to go raiding. I had to be sure the slaves were doing what they ought in the fields. So I needed another wife. One night I went to visit the family of a young woman I hoped would marry me. She lived a mile or two away. I had some worldly goods, and my father was a chief, and I was thought a handsome man and was a noted fighter, so I was a good prospect. Her brothers and her father were glad to greet me, and she seemed . . . agreeable. I was trying to get to know her a bit. It was a good evening. I had high hopes. But I had a lot to drink there, and on my way home that night . . ." Eric paused, and I saw his chest move. In remembering his last moments as a human, he had actually taken a deep breath. "It was the full moon. I saw a man lying hurt by the side of the road. Ordinarily I would have looked around to find those who had attacked him, but I was drunk. I went over to help him; you can probably guess what happened after that."

"He wasn't really hurt."

"No. But I was, soon after. He was very hungry. His name

was Appius Livius Ocella." Eric actually smiled, though without much humor. "He taught me many things, and the first was not to call him Appius. He said I didn't know him well enough."

"The second thing?"

"How to get to know him."

"Oh." I figured I understood what that meant.

Eric shrugged. "It was not so bad . . . once we left the area I knew. In time, I stopped pining after my children and my home. I had never been away from my people. My father and mother were still alive. I knew my brothers and my sisters would make sure the children were brought up to be as they ought, and I had left enough to keep them from being a burden. I worried, of course, but there was no helping it. I had to stay away. In those days, in small villages, any stranger was instantly noticed, and if I ventured anywhere close to where I'd lived, I'd be recognized and hunted. They would know what I was, or at least know I was . . . wrong."

"Where did you and Appius go?"

"We went to the biggest cities we could find, which were few enough then. We traveled all the time, parallel to the roads so we could prey on travelers."

I shuddered. It was painful to imagine Eric, so flamboyant and quick-witted, skulking through the woods in search of easy blood. It was awful to think of the unfortunates he'd ambushed.

"There were not so many people," he said. "Villagers would miss their neighbors immediately. We had to keep moving. Young vampires are so hungry; at first, I killed even when I didn't mean to."

I took a deep breath. This was what vampires did; when they were young, they killed. There had been no substitute for fresh blood then. It was kill, or die. "Was he good to you? Appius Livius Ocella?" How much worse could you have it than to be the constant companion of the man who had murdered you?

"He taught me all he knew. He had been in the legions, and he was a fighter, as I was, so we had that in common. He liked men, of course, and that took some getting used to. I had never done that. But when you're a new vampire, anything sexual seems exciting, so even that I enjoyed . . . eventually."

"You had to comply," I said.

"Oh, he was much stronger . . . though I was a bigger man than him—taller, longer arms. He had been vampire for so many centuries, he'd lost count. And of course, he was my sire. I had to obey." Eric shrugged.

"Is that a mystical thing or a made-up rule?" I asked, curiosity finally getting the better of me.

"It's both," Eric said. "It's a compulsion. It's impossible to resist, even when you want to . . . even when you're desperate to get away." His white face was closed and brooding.

I couldn't imagine Eric doing something he didn't want to do, being in a subservient position. Of course, he had a boss now; he wasn't autonomous. But he didn't have to bow and scrape, and he made most of his own decisions.

"I can't imagine it," I said.

"I wouldn't want you to." His mouth pulled down at one corner, a wry expression. Just when I began to ponder the irony of that, since he'd perhaps married me vampire-style without asking me, Eric changed the subject, slamming shut the door on his past. "The world has changed a great deal since I was human. The past hundred years have been especially exciting. And now the Weres are out, and all the other two-natured. Who knows? Maybe the witches or the fae will step forward next." He smiled at me, though it was a little stiff.

His idea gave me a happy fantasy of seeing my great-grandfather Niall every day. I'd only learned of his existence a few months before, and we hadn't spent much time together, but learning I had a living ancestor had been very important to me. I had so few blood kin. "That would be wonderful," I said wistfully.

"My lover, it will never happen," Eric said. "The creatures that make up the fae are the most secret of all the supernatural beings. There are not many remaining in this country. In fact, there are not so many remaining in the world. The number of their females, and the fertility of those females, is dropping every year. Your great-grandfather is one of the few survivors with royal blood. He would never condescend to treat with humans."

"He talks to me," I said, because I wasn't sure what "treat" meant.

"You share his blood." Eric waved his free hand. "If you didn't, you would never have seen him."

Well, no, Niall wasn't going to stop in at Merlotte's for a brew and a chicken basket and shake hands all around. I looked at Eric unhappily. "I wish he'd help Jason out," I said, "and I never thought I'd say that. Niall doesn't seem to like Jason at all, but Jason's going to be in a lot of trouble about Crystal's death."

"Sookie, if you're asking for my thoughts, I have no idea why Crystal was killed." And he really didn't care much. At least with Eric, you could tell where you stood.

In the background the KDED DJ said, "Next, Thom

Yorke's 'And It Rained All Night.'" While Eric and I had been having our one-on-one, the bar sounds had seemed muted, faraway. Now they came back with a rush.

"The police and the werepanthers, they'll track whoever did it," he said. "I'm more concerned about these FBI agents. What is their goal? Do they want to take you away? Can they do that in this country?"

"They wanted to identify Barry. Then they wanted to find out what Barry and I could do, and how we could do it. Maybe they were supposed to ask if we'd work for them, and Crystal's death interrupted our conversation before they could say anything."

"And you don't want to work for them." Eric's bright blue eyes were intent on my face. "You don't want to leave."

I pulled my hand out from under his. I watched my hands clasp each other, twist. "I don't want people to die because I wouldn't help them," I said. I felt my eyes brim with tears. "But I'm selfish enough that I don't want to go wherever they send me, trying to find dying people. I couldn't stand the wear and tear of seeing disaster every day. I don't want to leave home. I've been trying to imagine what it would be like, what they might have me do. And it scares me to death."

"You want to own your own life," Eric said.

"As much as anyone can."

"Just when I think you're very simple, you say something complex," Eric said.

"Are you complaining?" I tried to smile, failed.

"No."

A heavy girl with a big jaw came up and thrust an autograph book in front of Eric. "Could you please sign this?" she said. Eric gave her a blinding smile and scribbled on the blank page. "Thank you," she said breathlessly, and went back to her table. Her friends, all women just old enough to be in the bar, were exclaiming at her courage, and she leaned forward, telling them all about her encounter with the vampire. As she finished, one of the human waitresses drifted up to their table and took another order for drinks. The staff here was well-trained.

"What was she thinking?" Eric asked me.

"Oh, she was very nervous and she thought you were lovely, but . . ." I struggled to put it into words. "Not handsome in a way that was very real to her, because she would never think she would actually get to have you. She's very . . . She doesn't think much of herself."

I had one of those flashes of fantasy. *Eric would walk over to her, bow to her, give her a reverent kiss on the cheek, ignore her prettier friends. This gesture would make every man in the bar wonder what the vampire saw in her that they couldn't see. Suddenly the plain girl would be overwhelmed with attention from the men who'd witnessed the interchange. Her friends would give her respect because Eric had. Her life would change.*

But none of that happened, of course. Eric forgot about the girl as soon as I'd finished speaking. I didn't think it would work out like my fantasy, even if he did approach her. I felt a flash of disappointment that fairy tales didn't come true. I wondered if my fairy great-grandfather had ever heard one of what we thought of as a fairy tale. Did fairy parents tell fairy children human tales? I was willing to bet they didn't.

I felt a moment of disconnect, as if I were standing back from my own life and viewing it from afar. The vampires owed me money and favors for my services to them. The Weres had declared me a friend of the pack for my help during the just-completed war. I was pledged to Eric, which seemed to mean I was engaged or even married. My brother was a werepanther. My great-grandfather was a fairy. It took me a moment to pull myself back into my own skin. My life was too weird. I had that out-of-control feeling again, as if I were spinning too fast to stop.

"Don't talk to the FBI people alone," Eric was saying. "Call me if it's at night. Call Bobby Burnham if they come in the day."

"But he hates me!" I said, dragged back into reality and thus not too cautious. "Why would I call him?"

"What?"

"Bobby hates me," I said. "He'd love it if the feds carted me off to some underground bunker in Nevada for the rest of my life."

Eric's face looked frozen. "He said this?"

"He didn't have to. I can tell when someone thinks I'm slime."

"I'll have a talk with Bobby."

"Eric, it's not against the law for someone to dislike me," I said, remembering how dangerous it could be to complain to a vampire.

He laughed. "Maybe I'll make it against the law," he said teasingly, his accent more apparent than usual. "If you can't reach Bobby—and I am absolutely sure he will help you— you should call Mr. Cataliades, though he's down in New Orleans."

"He's doing well?" I hadn't seen or heard from the mostly demon lawyer since the collapse of the vampire hotel in Rhodes.

Eric nodded. "Never better. He is now representing Felipe de Castro's interests in Louisiana. He would help if you asked him. He's quite fond of you."

I stored that piece of information away to ponder. "Did his niece survive?" I asked. "Diantha?"

"Yes," Eric said. "She was buried for twelve hours, and the rescuers knew she was there. But there were beams wedged over the place where she was trapped, and it took time to remove them. They finally dug her out."

I was glad to hear Diantha was alive. "And the lawyer, Johan Glassport?" I asked. "He had a few broken bones, Mr. Cataliades said."

"He will recover fully. He collected his fee and then he vanished into the depths of Mexico."

"Mexico's gain is Mexico's loss," I said. I shrugged. "I guess it takes a lawyer to get your money when the hirer is dead. I never got mine. Maybe Sophie-Anne thought Glassport did more for her, or he had the wits to ask even though she'd lost her legs."

"I didn't know you still hadn't been paid." Eric looked displeased all over again. "I'll talk to Victor. If Glassport collected for his services to Sophie, you certainly should. Sophie left a large estate, and no children. Victor's king owes you a debt. He'll listen."

"That would be great," I said. I may have sounded a little too relieved.

Eric eyed me sharply. "You know," he said, "if you need money, you have only to ask. I will not have you going without anything you need, and I know you enough to be sure you wouldn't ask for money for something frivolous."

He almost didn't sound like that was such an admirable attribute. "I appreciate the thought," I said, and I could hear my voice get all stiff. "I just want what's due me."

There was a long silence between us, though the bar was at its usual noise level around Eric's table.

"Tell me the truth," Eric said. "Is it possible you came here simply to spend time with me? You haven't yet told me how angry you are with me that I tricked you over the knife. Apparently you're not going to, at least not tonight. I haven't yet discussed with you all my memories of the time we spent together when you were hiding me at your house. Do you know why I ended up so close to your home, running down that road in the freezing cold?"

His question was so unexpected that I was struck silent. I wasn't sure I wanted to know the answer. But finally I said, "No, I don't."

"The curse contained within the witch, the curse that activated when Chow killed her . . . It was that I would be close to my heart's desire without ever realizing it. A terrible curse and one that Hallow must have constructed with great subtlety. We found it dog-eared when we found her spell book."

There was nothing for me to say. I'd think about that, though.

It was the first time I'd come to Fangtasia simply to talk, without having been called there for some vampire reason. Blood bond or something much more natural? "I think . . . I just wanted some company," I said. "No soul-shaking revelations."

He smiled. "This is good."

I didn't know if it was or not.

"You know we're not really married, right?" I said. I had to say something, as much as I wanted to forget the whole thing had ever happened. "I know vamps and humans can get married now, but that wasn't a ceremony I recognize, nor does the State of Louisiana."

"I know that if I hadn't done it, you'd be sitting in a little room in Nevada right now, listening to Felipe de Castro while he does business with humans."

I hate it when my suspicions are correct. "But I saved him," I said, trying not to whine. "I saved his life, and he promised I had his friendship. Which means his protection, I thought."

"He wants to protect you right by his side now that he knows what you can do. He wants the leverage having you would give him over me."

"Some gratitude. I should have let Sigebert kill him." I closed my eyes. "Dammit, I just can't come out ahead."

"He can't have you now," Eric said. "We are wed."

"But, Eric . . ." I thought of so many objections to this arrangement I couldn't even begin to voice them. I had promised myself I wouldn't start arguing about this tonight, but the issue was like the eight-hundred-pound gorilla. It simply couldn't be ignored. "What if I meet someone else? What if you . . . Hey, what are the ground rules of being officially married? Just tell me."

"You're too upset and tired tonight for a rational conversation," Eric said.

He shook his hair back over his shoulders, and a woman at the next table said, *"Ooooooooooh."*

"Understand that he can't touch you now, that no one can unless they petition me first. This is under penalty of final death. And this is where my ruthlessness will be of service to both of us."

I took a deep breath. "Okay. You're right. But this isn't the end of the subject. I want to know everything about our new situation, and I want to know I can get out of this if I can't stand it."

His eyes looked as blue as a clear autumn sky, and as guile-less. "You will know everything when you want to know," he said.

"Hey, does the new king know about my great-grandfather?"

Eric's face settled into lines of stone. "I can't predict Felipe's reaction if he finds out, my lover. Bill and I are the only ones who have that knowledge now. It has to stay that way."

He reached over to take my hand again. I could feel each muscle, each bone, through the cool flesh. It was like hold-ing hands with a statue, a very beautiful statue. Again, I felt oddly peaceful for a few minutes.

"I have to go, Eric," I said, sorry but not sorry to be leav-ing. He leaned over to me and kissed me lightly on the lips. When I pushed back my chair, he rose to walk me to the door. I felt the wannabes hammer me with looks of envy all the way out of Fangtasia. Pam was at her station, and she looked at us with a chilly smile.

Lest we part on too lovey-dovey a note, I said, "Eric, when I'm back to being myself, I'm going to nail your ass for put-ting me in this position of being pledged to you."

"Darling, you can nail my ass anytime," he said charm-ingly, and turned to go back to his table.

Pam rolled her eyes. "You two," she said.

"Hey, this isn't any of *my* doing," I said, which wasn't entirely true. But it was a good exit line, and I took advan-tage of it to leave the bar.

Chapter 7

The next morning, Andy Bellefleur called to give me the green light to reopen.

By the time the crime scene tape was down, Sam had returned to Bon Temps. I was so glad to see my boss that my eyes got weepy. Managing Merlotte's was a lot harder than I'd ever realized. There were decisions to make every day and a huge crowd of people who needed to be kept happy: the customers, the workers, the distributors, the deliverymen. Sam's tax guy had called with questions I couldn't answer. The utility bill was due in three days, and I didn't have check-writing privileges. There was a lot of money that needed to be deposited into the bank. It was almost payroll time.

Though I felt like blurting out all these problems the minute Sam walked in the back door of the bar, I drew in a calming breath and asked about his mother.

After giving me a half hug, Sam had thrown himself into his creaking chair behind his desk. He swiveled to face me directly. He propped his feet up on the edge of the desk with an air of relief. "She's talking, walking, and mending," he said. "For the first time, we don't have to make up a story to cover how fast she can heal. We took her home this morning, and she's already trying to do stuff around the house. My brother and sister are asking her a million questions now that they've gotten used to the idea. They even seem kind of envious I'm the one who inherited the trait."

I was tempted to ask about his stepfather's legal situation, but Sam seemed awful anxious to get back into his normal routine. I waited a moment to see if he would bring it up. He didn't. Instead, he asked about the utility bill, and with a sigh of relief I was able to refer him to the list of things that needed his attention. I'd left it on his desk in my neatest handwriting.

First on the list was the fact that I'd hired Tanya and Amelia to come in some evenings to make up for Arlene's defection.

Sam looked sad. "Arlene's worked for me since I bought the bar," he said. "It's going to be strange, her not being here. She's been a pain in the butt in the past few months, but I figured she'd swing around to being her old self sooner or later. You think she'll reconsider?"

"Maybe, now that you're back," I said, though I had severe doubts. "But she's gotten to be so intolerant. I don't think she can work for a shifter. I'm sorry, Sam."

He shook his head. His dark mood was no big surprise, considering his mom's situation and the not-completely-ecstatic reaction of the American populace to the weird side of the world.

It amazed me that, once upon a time, I hadn't known,

either. I hadn't realized some of the people I knew were shifters because I didn't comprehend there was such a thing. You can misinterpret every mental cue you get if you don't understand where it's coming from. I'd always wondered why some people were so hard to read, why their brains gave me a different image from others. It simply hadn't occurred to me it was because those brains belonged to people who literally turned into animals.

"You think business'll slack off because I'm a shapeshifter or because of the murder?" Sam asked. Then he shook himself and said, "Sorry, Sook. I wasn't thinking about Crystal being your in-law."

"I wasn't ever nuts about her, as you well know," I said, as matter-of-factly as I could. "But I think it's awful what was done to her, no matter what she was like."

Sam nodded. I'd never seen his face so gloomy and serious. Sam was a creature of sunshine.

"Oh," I said, getting up to leave, and then I stopped, shifting from foot to foot. I took a deep breath. "By the way, Eric and I are married now." If I'd hoped I'd get to make my exit on a light note, my judgment was way, way off. Sam leaped to his feet and grabbed me by the shoulders.

"What have you done?" he asked. He was deadly serious.

"I haven't done anything," I said, startled by his vehemence. "It was Eric's doing." I told Sam about the knife.

"Didn't you realize there was some significance to the knife?"

"I didn't know it was a knife," I said, beginning to feel pretty pissed but still maintaining my reasonable voice. "Bobby didn't tell me. I guess he didn't know himself, so I couldn't very well pick it up from his brain."

"Where was your sense? Sookie, that was an *idiotic* thing to do."

This was not exactly the reaction I had anticipated from a man I'd been worried about, a man on whose behalf I'd been working my butt off for days. I gathered my hurt and pride around me like a jacket. "Then let me just take my *idiotic* self home, so you won't have to put up with my idiocy any longer," I said, my voice even enough to support a level. "I guess I'll go home now that you're back and I don't have to be here *every single minute of my day* to make sure things are running okay."

"I'm sorry," he said, but it was too late. I was on my high horse, and I was riding it out of Merlotte's.

I was out the back door before our heaviest drinker could have counted to five, and then I was in my car and on the way home. I was mad, and I was sad, and I suspected that Sam was right. That's when you get the angriest, isn't it? When you know you've done something stupid? Eric's explanation hadn't exactly erased my concerns.

I was scheduled to work that evening, so I had until then to get my act together. There was no question of my not showing up. Whether or not Sam and I were on the outs, I had to work.

I wasn't ready to be at home, where I'd have to think about my own confused feelings.

Instead of going home, I turned and went to Tara's Togs. I hadn't seen a lot of my friend Tara since she'd eloped with JB du Rone. But my inner compass was pointing in her direction. To my relief, Tara was in the store alone. McKenna, her "helper," was not a full-time employee. Tara came out of the back when the bell on the door rang. She looked a little surprised to see me at first, but then she smiled. Our friendship has had its ups and downs, but it looked like we were okay now. Great.

"What's up?" Tara asked. She looked attractive and snuggly in a teal sweater. Tara is taller than I am, and real pretty, and a real good businesswoman.

"I've done a stupid thing, and I don't know how I feel about it," I said.

"Tell me," she commanded, and we went to sit at the table where the wedding catalogs were kept. She shoved the box of Kleenex over to me. Tara knows when I'm going to cry.

So I told her the long story, beginning with the incident in Rhodes where I'd exchanged blood with Eric for what turned out to be one too many times. I told her about the weird bond we had as a result.

"Let me get this straight," she said. "He offered to take your blood so an even worse vamp wouldn't bite you?"

I nodded, dabbing at my eyes.

"Wow, such self-sacrifice." Tara had had some bad experiences with vampires. I wasn't surprised at her sarcastic summation.

"Believe me, Eric doing it was by far the lesser of two evils," I assured her.

Suddenly, I realized *I'd be free now if Andre had taken my blood that night.* Andre had died at the bombing site. I considered that for a second and moved on. That hadn't happened and I wasn't free, but the chains I wore now were a lot prettier.

"So how are you feeling about Eric?" Tara asked.

"I don't know," I said. "There are things I almost love about him, and things about him that scare the hell out of me. And I really . . . you know . . . *want* him. But he pulls tricks for what *he* says is my own good. I believe he cares about me. But he cares about himself mostly." I took a deep breath. "I'm sorry. I'm babbling."

"This is why I married JB," she said. "So I wouldn't have to worry about shit like this." She nodded, confirming her own good decision.

"Well, you've taken him, so I can't do that," I said. I tried to smile. Marriage to someone as simple as JB sounded really relaxing. But was marriage supposed to be like settling back in a La-Z-Boy? *At least spending time with Eric is never boring,* I thought. Sweet as he was, JB had a finite capacity for entertaining conversation.

Plus, Tara was always going to have to be in charge. Tara was no fool, and she'd never be blinded by love. Other things, maybe, but not love. I knew Tara clearly understood the rules of her marriage to JB, and she didn't seem to mind. For her, being the navigator/captain was a comforting and empowering role. I definitely liked to be in charge of my own life—I didn't want anyone owning me—but my concept of marriage was more in the nature of a democratic partnership.

"So, let me summarize," Tara said in a good imitation of one of our high school teachers. "You and Eric have done the nasty in the past."

I nodded. Boy howdy, had we.

"Now the whole vampire organization owes you for some service you performed. I don't want to know what it was, and I don't want to know why you did it."

I nodded again.

"Also, Eric more or less owns a piece of you because of this blood-bond thing. Which he didn't necessarily plan out in advance, to give him credit."

"Yep."

"And now he's maneuvered you into the position of being his fiancée? His wife? But you didn't know what you were doing."

"Right."

"And Sam called you idiotic because you obeyed Eric."

I shrugged. "Yeah, he did."

Tara had to help a customer then, but only for a couple of minutes. (Riki Cunningham wanted to pay on a prom dress she'd put on layaway for her daughter.) When Tara resumed her seat, she was ready to give me feedback. "Sookie, at least Eric does care about you some, and he's never hurt you. You could've been smarter. I don't know if you weren't because of this bond thing you have with him or because you're so gone on him that you don't ask enough questions. Only you can figure that out. But it could be worse. No humans need to know about this knife thing. And Eric can't be around during the day, so you'll have Eric-free time to think. Also, he's got his own business to run, so he's not going to be following you around. And the new vampire execs have to leave you alone because they want to keep Eric happy. Not so bad, right?" She smiled at me, and after a second, I smiled back.

I began to perk up. "Thanks, Tara," I said. "You think Sam will stop being mad?"

"I wouldn't exactly expect him to apologize for saying you acted like an idiot," Tara warned me. "A, it's true, and B, he's a man. He's got that chromosome. But you two have always gotten along great, and he owes you for you taking care of the bar. So he'll come around."

I pitched my used Kleenex into the little trash can by the table. I smiled, though it probably wasn't my best effort.

"Meanwhile," Tara said, "I have some news for you, too." She took a deep breath.

"What is it?" I asked, delighted that we were back on best-friend footing.

"I'm going to have a baby," Tara said, and her face froze in a grimace.

Ah-oh. *Dangerous* footing. "You don't look super-happy," I said, cautiously.

"I hadn't planned on having children at all," she said. "Which was okay with JB."

"So . . . ?"

"Well, even multiple birth control methods don't always work," Tara said, looking down at her hands, which were folded on top of a bridal magazine. "And I just can't have it taken care of. It's ours. So."

"Might . . . might you come around to being glad about this?"

She tried to smile. "JB is really happy. It's hard for him to keep it a secret. But I wanted to wait for the first three months to pass. You're the first one I've told."

"I swear," I said, reaching over to pat her shoulder, "you'll be a good mother."

"You really think so?" She looked, and felt, terrified. Tara's folks had been the kind of parents who occasionally get shotgunned by their offspring. Tara's abhorrence of violence had prevented her from taking that path, but I don't think anyone would have been surprised if the older Thorntons had vanished one night. A few people would have applauded.

"Yeah, I really think so." I meant it. I could *hear*, directly from her head, Tara's determination to wipe out everything her own mother had done to her by being the best mother she could be to her own child. In Tara's case, that meant she would be sober, gentle-handed, clean of speech, and full of praise.

"I'll show up at every classroom open house and teacher conference," she said, now in a voice that was almost frightening in its intensity. "I'll bake brownies. My child will have new clothes. Her shoes will fit. She'll get her shots, and she'll get her braces. We'll start a college fund next week. I'll tell her I love her every damn day."

If that wasn't a great plan for being a good mother, I couldn't imagine what a better one could be.

We hugged each other when I got up to leave. *This is the way it's supposed to be,* I thought.

I went home, ate a belated lunch, and changed into my work clothes.

When the phone rang, I hoped it was Sam calling to smooth things over, but the voice on the other end was an older man's and unfamiliar.

"Hello? Is Octavia Fant there, please?"

"No, sir, she's out. May I take a message?"

"If you would."

"Sure." I'd answered the phone in the kitchen, so there was a pad and pencil handy.

"Please tell her Louis Chambers called. Here's my number." He gave it to me slowly and carefully, and I repeated it to make sure I'd put it down correctly. "Ask her to call me, please. I'll be glad to take a collect call."

"I'll make sure she gets your message."

"Thank you."

Hmmm. I couldn't read thoughts over the phone, which normally I considered a great relief. But I would have enjoyed learning a little more about Mr. Chambers.

When Amelia came home a little before five, Octavia was in the car. I gathered Octavia had been walking around downtown Bon Temps filling out job applications, while

Amelia had put in an afternoon at the insurance agency. It was Amelia's evening to cook, and though I had to leave for Merlotte's in a few minutes, I enjoyed watching her leap into action, creating spaghetti sauce. I handed Octavia her message while Amelia was chopping onions and a bell pepper.

Octavia made a choked sound and grew so still that Amelia stopped chopping and joined me in waiting for the older woman to look up from the piece of paper and give us a little backstory. That didn't happen.

After a moment, I realized Octavia was crying, and I hurried to my bedroom and got a tissue. I tried to slip it to Octavia tactfully, like I hadn't noticed anything amiss but just happened to have an extra Kleenex in my hand.

Amelia carefully looked down at the cutting board and resumed chopping while I glanced at the clock and began fishing around in my purse for my car keys, taking lots of unnecessary time to do it.

"Did he sound well?" Octavia asked, her voice choked.

"Yes," I said. There was only so much I could get from a voice on the other end of a phone line. "He sounded anxious to talk to you."

"Oh, I have to call him back," she said, and her voice was wild.

"Sure," I said. "Just punch in the number. Don't worry about calling collect or anything; the phone bill'll tell us how much it was." I glanced over at Amelia, cocking an eyebrow. She shook her head. She didn't know what the hell was going on, either.

Octavia placed the call with shaking fingers. She pressed the phone to her ear after the first ring. I could tell when Louis Chambers answered. Her eyes shut tight, and her hand clenched the phone so hard the muscles stood out.

"Oh, Louis," she said, her voice full of raw relief and amazement. "Oh, thank God. Are you all right?"

Amelia and I shuffled out of the kitchen at that point. Amelia walked to my car with me. "You ever heard of this Louis guy?" I asked.

"She never talked about her private life when she was working with me. But other witches told me Octavia had a steady boyfriend. She hasn't mentioned him since she's been here. It looks like she hasn't heard from him since Katrina."

"She might not have thought he survived," I said, and we widened our eyes at each other.

"That's big stuff," Amelia said. "Well. We may be losing Octavia." She tried to stifle her relief, but of course, I could read it. As fond as Amelia was of her magical mentor, I'd realized that for Amelia, living with Octavia was like living with one of your junior high teachers.

"I got to go," I said. "Keep me posted. Text me if there's any big news." Texting was one of my new Amelia-taught skills.

Despite the chilly air, Amelia sat on one of the lawn chairs that we'd recently hauled out of the storage shed to encourage ourselves to anticipate spring. "The minute I know something," she agreed. "I'll wait here a few minutes, then go check on her."

I got in my car and hoped the heater would warm up soon. In the gathering dusk, I drove to Merlotte's. I saw a coyote on the way. Usually they were too clever to be seen, but this one was trotting along the side of the road as if he had an appointment in town. Maybe it was really a coyote, or maybe it was a person in another form. When I considered the possums and coons and the occasional armadillo I saw squashed by the road every morning, I wondered how many

werecreatures had gotten killed in their animal forms in such
careless ways. Maybe some of the bodies the police labeled
murder victims were actually people killed by accident in
their alternate form. I remembered all animal traces had vanished from Crystal's body when she'd been taken down from
the cross, after the nails had been removed. I was willing to
bet those nails had been silver. There was so much I didn't
know.

When I came in Merlotte's back door, full of plans to
reconcile with Sam, I found my boss having an argument
with Bobby Burnham. It was almost dark now, and Bobby
should be off the clock. Instead, he was standing in the hall
outside of Sam's office. He was red in the face and fit to be
tied.

"What's up?" I said. "Bobby, did you need to talk to me?"

"Yeah. This guy wouldn't tell me when you were going to
get here," Bobby said.

"This guy is my boss, and he isn't obliged to tell you anything," I said. "Here I am. What do you need to say to me?"

"Eric sent you this card, and he ordered me to tell you I'm
at your disposal whenever you need me. I'm supposed to wash
your car if you want me to." Bobby's face went even redder
as he said this.

If Eric had thought Bobby would be made humble and
compliant after a public humiliation, he was nuts. Now
Bobby would hate me for a hundred years, if he lived that
long. I took the card Bobby handed me and said, "Thanks,
Bobby. Go back to Shreveport."

Before the last syllable left my mouth, Bobby was out the
back door. I examined the plain white envelope and then
stuck it in my purse. I looked up to meet Sam's eyes.

"Like you needed another enemy," he said, and stomped into his office.

Like I needed another friend acting like an asshole, I thought. So much for us having a good laugh over our disagreement. I followed Sam in to drop my purse in the drawer he kept empty for the barmaids. We didn't say a word to each other. I went to the storeroom to get an apron. Antoine was changing his stained apron for a clean one.

"D'Eriq bumped into me with a jar full of jalapeños, and the juice slopped out," he said. "I can't stand the smell of 'em."

"Whoo," I said, catching a whiff. "I don't blame you."

"Sam's mama doing okay?"

"Yeah, she's out of the hospital," I said.

"Good news."

As I tied the strings around my waist, I thought Antoine was about to say something else, but if he was, he changed his mind. He crossed the hall to knock on the kitchen door, and D'Eriq opened it from the inside and let him in. People had wandered into the kitchen by mistake too often, and the door was kept locked all the time. There was another door from the kitchen that led directly out back, and the Dumpster was right outside.

I walked past Sam's office without looking in. He didn't want to talk to me; okay, I wouldn't talk to him. I realized I was being childish.

The FBI agents were still in Bon Temps, which shouldn't have surprised me. Tonight, they came into the bar. Weiss and Lattesta were sitting opposite each another in a booth, a pitcher of beer and a basket of French-fried pickles between them, and they were talking intently. And at a table close to them, looking regal and beautiful and remote, was my great-grandfather Niall Brigant.

This day was going to win a prize for most peculiar. I blew out a puff of air and went to wait on my great-grandfather first. He stood as I approached. His pale straight hair was tied back at the nape of his neck. He was wearing a black suit and a white shirt, as he always did. Tonight, instead of the solid black tie he usually wore, he had on a tie I'd given him for Christmas. It was red, gold, and black striped, and he looked spectacular. Everything about him gleamed and shone. The shirt wasn't simply white—it was snowy and starched; and his coat wasn't just black—it was spotlessly inky. His shoes showed not a speck of dust, and the myriad of fine, fine wrinkles in his handsome face only set off its perfection and his brilliant green eyes. His age enhanced rather than diminished his looks. It almost hurt to look at him. Niall put his arms around me and kissed my cheek.

"Blood of my blood," he said, and I smiled into his chest. He was so dramatic. And he had such a hard time looking human. I'd had one glimpse of him in his true form, and it had been nearly blinding. Since no one else in the bar was gasping at the sight of him, I knew they weren't seeing him the same way I did.

"Niall," I said. "I'm so happy to see you." I always felt pleased and flattered when he visited. Being Niall's great-granddaughter was like being kin to a rock star; he lived a life I couldn't imagine, went places I would never go, and had power I couldn't fathom. But every now and then he spent time with me, and that time was always like Christmas.

He said very quietly, "These people opposite me, they do nothing but talk of you."

"Do you know what the FBI is?" Niall's fund of knowledge was incredible, since he was so old he'd stopped counting at a thousand and sometimes missed accurate dates by more than a century, but I didn't know how specific his information about the modern day might be.

"Yes," he said. "FBI. A government agency that collects data about law breakers and terrorists inside the United States."

I nodded.

"But you're such a good person. You're not a killer or terrorist," Niall said, though he didn't sound as if he believed my innocence would protect me.

"Thank you," I said. "But I don't think they want to arrest me. I suspect they want to find out how I get results with my little mental condition, and if they decide I'm not nuts, they probably want me to work for them. That's why they came to Bon Temps . . . but they got sidetracked." And that brought me to the painful subject. "Do you know what happened to Crystal?"

But some other customers called me then, and it was a while before I got back to Niall, who was waiting patiently. He somehow made the scarred chair look like a throne. He picked the conversation up right where we'd left off.

"Yes, I know what happened to her." His face didn't seem to change, but I felt the chill rolling off of him. If I'd had anything to do with Crystal's death, I would have felt very afraid.

"How come you care?" I asked. He'd never paid any attention to Jason; in fact, Niall seemed to dislike my brother.

Niall said, "I'm always interested in finding out why someone connected to me has died." Niall had sounded totally impersonal when he spoke of Crystal's death, but if he was interested, maybe he would help. You'd think he'd want to clear Jason, since Jason was his great-grandson just as surely as I was his great-granddaughter, but Niall had never shown any sign of wanting to meet Jason, much less get to know him.

Antoine rang the bell in the kitchen to tell me one of my orders was up, and I scurried off to serve Sid Matt Lancaster and Bud Dearborn their cheesy chili bacon fries. The recently widowed Sid Matt was so old I guess he figured his arteries couldn't harden much more than they already had, and Bud had never been one for health food.

When I could return to Niall, I said, "Do you have any idea who did it? The werepanthers are searching, too." I put down an extra napkin on the table in front of him so I'd look busy.

Niall didn't disdain the panthers. In fact, though fairies seemed to consider themselves apart and superior to all other species of supernaturals, Niall (at least) had respect for all shapechangers, unlike the vampires, who regarded them as second-rate citizens. "I'll look a little. I've been preoccupied, and that is why I haven't visited. There is trouble." I saw that Niall's expression was even more serious than usual.

Oh, shit. More trouble.

"But you need not concern yourself," he added regally. "I will take care of it."

Did I mention Niall is a little proud? But I couldn't help but feel concerned. In a minute I'd have to go get someone else another drink, and I wanted to be sure I understood him. Niall didn't come around often, and when he did, he seldom dallied. I might not get another chance to talk to him. "What's up, Niall?" I asked directly.

"I want you to take special care of yourself. If you see any fairies other than myself or Claude and Claudine, call me at once."

"Why would I worry about other fairies?" The other shoe dropped. "Why would other fairies want to hurt me?"

"Because you are my great-granddaughter." He stood, and I knew I'd get no more explanation than that.

Niall hugged me again, kissed me again (fairies are very touchy-feely), and left the bar, his cane in his hand. I'd never seen him use it as an aid to walking, but he always had it with him. As I stared after him, I wondered if it had a knife concealed inside. Or maybe it might be an extra-long magic wand. Or both. I wished he could've stuck around for a while, or at least issued a more specific danger bulletin.

"Ms. Stackhouse," said a polite male voice, "could you bring us another pitcher of beer and another basket of pickles?"

I turned to Special Agent Lattesta. "Sure, be glad to," I said, smiling automatically.

"That was a very handsome man," Sara Weiss said. Sara was feeling the effects of the two glasses of beer she'd already had. "He sure looked different. Is he from Europe?"

"He does look foreign," I agreed, and took the empty pitcher and fetched them a full one, smiling all the while. Then Catfish, my brother's boss, knocked over a rum and Coke with his elbow, and I had to call D'Eriq to come with a washcloth for the table and a mop for the floor.

After that, two idiots who'd been in my high school class got into a fight about whose hunting dog was better. Sam had to break that up. They were actually quicker to come to their senses now that they knew what Sam was, which was an unexpected bonus.

A lot of the discussion in the bar that evening dealt

with Crystal's death, naturally. The fact that she'd been a
werepanther had seeped into the town's consciousness. About
half of the bar patrons believed she'd been killed by someone who hated the newly revealed underworld. The other
half wasn't so sure that she'd been killed because she was a
werepanther. That half thought her promiscuity was enough
motivation. Most of them assumed Jason was guilty. Some
of them felt sympathy for him. Some of them had known
Crystal or her reputation, and they felt Jason's actions were
justifiable. Almost all of these people thought of Crystal only
in terms of Jason's guilt or innocence. I found it real sad that
most people would only remember her for the manner of her
death.

I should go see Jason or call him, but I couldn't find it in
my heart. Jason's actions over the past few months had killed
something in me. Though Jason was my brother, and I loved
him, and he was showing signs of finally growing up, I no
longer felt that I had to support him through all the trials
his life had brought him. That made me a bad Christian, I
realized. Though I knew I wasn't a deep theological thinker, I
sometimes wondered if crisis moments in my life hadn't come
down to two choices: be a bad Christian or die.

I'd chosen life every time.

Was I looking at this right? Was there another point of
view that would enlighten me? I couldn't think of anyone to
ask. I tried to imagine the Methodist minister's face if I asked
him, "Would it be better to stab someone to keep yourself
safe, or let them go on and kill you? Would it be better to
break a vow I made in front of God, or refuse to break my
friend's hand to bits?" These were choices I had faced. Maybe
I owed God a big debt. Or maybe I was protecting myself

like he wanted me to. I just didn't know, and I couldn't think deep enough to figure out the Ultimate Right Answer.

Would the people I was serving laugh, if they knew what I was thinking? Would my anxiety over the state of my soul amuse them? Lots of them would probably tell me that all situations are covered in the Bible, and that if I read the Book more, I'd find my answers there.

That hadn't worked for me so far, but I wasn't giving up. I abandoned my circular thoughts and listened in on the people around me to give my brain a rest.

Sara Weiss thought that I seemed like a simple young woman, and she decided I was incredibly lucky to have been given a gift, as she considered it. She believed everything Lattesta had told her about what had happened at the Pyramid, because underneath her practical approach to life there was a streak of mysticism. Lattesta, too, thought it was almost possible I was psychic; he'd listened to accounts of the Rhodes first responders with great interest, and now that he'd met me, he'd come to think they were speaking the truth. He wanted to know what I could do for my country and his career. He wondered if he'd get a promotion if he could get me to trust him enough to be my handler throughout my time of helping the FBI. If he could acquire my male accomplice, as well, his upward trajectory would be assured. He would be stationed at FBI headquarters in Washington. He would be launched up the ladder.

I considered asking Amelia to lay a spell on the FBI agents, but that seemed like cheating somehow. They weren't supes. They were just doing what they'd been told to do. They didn't bear me any ill will; in fact, Lattesta believed he was doing me a favor, because he could get me out of this parish backwater and into the national limelight, or at least high in the esteem of the FBI.

As if that mattered to me.

As I went about my duties, smiling and exchanging chit-chat with the regular customers, I tried to imagine leaving Bon Temps with Lattesta. They'd devise some test to measure my accuracy. They'd finally believe I wasn't psychic but telepathic. When they found out what the limits of my talent were, they'd take me places where awful things had happened so I could find survivors. They'd put me in rooms with the intelligence agents of other countries or with Americans they suspected of awful things. I'd have to tell the FBI whether or not those people were guilty of whatever crime the FBI imagined they might have committed. I'd have to be close to mass murderers, maybe. I imagined what I might see in the mind of such a person, and I felt sick.

But wouldn't the knowledge I gained be a great help to the living? Maybe I'd learn about plots far enough in advance to prevent deaths.

I shook my head. My mind was wandering too far afield. All that *might* happen. A serial killer *might* be thinking of where his victims were buried just at the moment I was listening to his thoughts. But in my extensive experience, people seldom thought, "Yes, I buried that body at 1218 Clover Drive under the rosebush," or, "That money I stole sure is safe in my bank account numbered 12345 in the Switzerland National Bank." Much less, "I'm plotting to blow up the XYZ building on May 4, and my six confederates are . . ."

Yes, there would be some good I could do. But whatever I could achieve would never reach the expectations of the government. And I'd never be free again. I didn't think they'd hold me in a cell or anything—I'm not that paranoid. But I didn't think I'd ever get to live my own life as I wanted.

So once again, I decided that maybe I was being a bad Christian, or at least a bad American. But I knew that unless I was forced to do so, I wasn't going to leave Bon Temps with Agent Weiss or Special Agent Lattesta. Being married to a vampire was way better.

Chapter 8

I was mad at almost everybody when I drove home that night. Every now and then, I had spells like that; maybe everyone does. It's hormonal or cyclical in some other way. Or maybe it's just the chance alignment of the stars.

I was angry with Jason because I'd been angry with him for months. I was angry with Sam in a kind of hurt way. I was pissed at the FBI agents because they were here to put pressure on me—though in truth they hadn't done that yet. I was outraged at Eric's stunt with the knife and his high-handed banishment of Quinn, though I had to admit Eric had spoken the truth when he said I'd given Quinn the heave-ho first. That didn't mean I never wanted to see him again. (Or did it?) It *sure* didn't mean that Eric could dictate to me who I saw and who I didn't.

And maybe I was angry with myself, because when I'd had the chance to confront Eric about all kinds of stuff, I'd gone all goopy and listened to his reminiscences. Like the flashbacks on *Lost*, Eric's Viking memories had broken into the flow of the current story.

To make me even angrier, there was a car I didn't recognize parked at the front door, where only visitors parked. I went to the back door and up the porch steps, frowning and feeling totally contrary. I didn't want company. All I wanted to do was put on my pajamas, wash my face, and get into bed with a book.

Octavia was sitting at the kitchen table with a man I'd never met. He was one of the blackest men I'd ever seen, and his face was tattooed with circles around the eyes. Despite his fearsome decorations, he looked calm and agreeable. He rose to his feet when I came in.

"Sookie," Octavia said in a trembling voice, "this is my friend Louis."

"Nice to meet you," I said, and extended my hand for him to shake. He gave mine a carefully gentle grip, and I sat down so he would. Then I noticed the suitcases sitting in the hall. "Octavia?" I said, pointing at them.

"Well, Sookie, even us old ladies have some romance in our lives," Octavia said, smiling. "Louis and I were close friends before Katrina. He lived about ten minutes' drive away from me in New Orleans. After it happened, I looked for him. I gave up, finally."

"I spent a lot of time trying to find Octavia," Louis said, his eyes on her face. "I finally tracked down her niece two days ago, and her niece had the phone number here. I couldn't believe I'd finally found her."

"Did your house survive the . . . ?" Incident, catastrophe, disaster, apocalypse—pick your word; they all would serve.

"Yes, praise the gods, it did. And I have electricity. There's a lot to do, but I have light and heat. I can cook again. My refrigerator's humming and my street's almost clean. I put my own roof back on. Now Octavia can come home with me to a place fit for her."

"Sookie," she said very gently, "you've been so kind, letting me stay with you. But I want to be with Louis, and I need to be back in New Orleans. There'll be something I can do to help rebuild the city. It's home to me."

Octavia obviously felt she was delivering a heavy blow. I tried to look chagrined. "You have to do what's best for you, Octavia. I've loved having you in my house." I was so grateful Octavia wasn't telepathic. "Is Amelia here?"

"Yes, she's upstairs getting something for me. Bless her heart, she got me a good-bye present somehow."

"Awww," I said, trying not to overdo it. I got a sharp look from Louis, but Octavia beamed at me. I'd never seen Octavia beam before, and I liked the look on her.

"I'm just glad I was able to be a help to you," she said, nodding wisely.

It was a little trouble to maintain my slightly-sad-but-brave smile, but I managed. Thank goodness Amelia clattered down the stairs at that moment with a wrapped package in her hands, a thin, flimsy red scarf tied around it and secured with a big bow. Without looking at me, Amelia said, "Here's a little something from Sookie and me. I hope you enjoy it."

"Oh, you're so sweet. I'm sorry I ever doubted your skill, Amelia. You're one heck of a witch."

"Octavia, it means so much to me to hear you say that!" Amelia was genuinely touched and tearful.

Thank goodness Louis and Octavia got up then. Though I liked and respected the older witch, she had provided a series of speed bumps in the smooth running of the household Amelia and I had formed.

I actually found myself breathing a profound sigh of relief when the front door shut on her and her partner. We'd all said good-bye to one another over and over, and Octavia had thanked both of us for various things repeatedly, and she'd also found ways to remind us of all sorts of mysterious things she'd done for us that we were having a hard time recalling.

"Heavens be praised," said Amelia, collapsing on the stairs. Amelia was not a religious woman, or at least she wasn't a conventional Christian religious woman, so this was a quite a demonstration from her.

I sat on the edge of the couch. "I hope they're very happy," I said.

"You don't think we should have checked up on him somehow?"

"A witch as strong as Octavia can't take care of herself?"

"Good point. But did you see those tattoos?"

"They were something, weren't they? I guess he's some kind of sorcerer."

Amelia nodded. "Yeah, I'm sure he practices some form of African magic," she said. "I don't think we need to worry about the high crime rate in New Orleans affecting Octavia and Louis. I don't think anyone's going to be mugging them."

"What was the present we gave her?"

"I called my dad, and he faxed me a gift certificate to his home supplies store."

"Hey, good idea. What do I owe you?"

"Not a dime. He insisted it be on him."

At least this happy incident took the edge off my generalized anger. I felt more companionable with Amelia, too, now that I no longer harbored a vague resentment for her bringing Octavia into my house. We sat in the kitchen and chatted for about an hour before I turned in, though I was too exhausted to try to explain the saga of what had been happening lately. We went to bed better friends than we'd been in weeks.

As I was getting ready for bed, I was thinking about our practical gift to Octavia, and that reminded me of the card Bobby Burnham had handed me. I got it out of my purse and slit the envelope with my nail file. I pulled out the card inside. Enclosed in it was a picture I'd never seen, clearly taken during Eric's photo shoot for the calendar you could buy in the gift shop at Fangtasia. In the calendar shot, Eric (Mr. January) stood by a huge bed made up all in white. The background was gray, with glittering snowflakes hanging down all around. Eric had one foot on the floor, the other knee bent and resting on the bed. He was holding a white fur robe in a strategic position. In the picture Eric had given me today, he was in somewhat the same pose, but he was holding a hand out to the camera as if he was inviting the viewer to come join him on the bed. And the white fur wasn't covering quite everything. "I wait for the night you join me," he'd written on the otherwise blank card in his crabbed handwriting.

Faintly cheesy? Yes. Gulp inducing? Oh, you betcha. I could practically feel my blood heat up. I was sorry I'd opened it right before I climbed in the bed. It definitely took me a long time to drift off to sleep.

It felt funny not to hear Octavia buzzing around the house when I woke up the next morning. She'd vanished from my life as quickly as she'd entered it. I hoped that in some of their time together, Octavia and Amelia had discussed Amelia's status with what remained of her New Orleans coven. It was hard to believe Amelia could turn a young man into a cat (during the course of some very adventurous sex), I thought, as I watched my roommate hurry out the back door to get to the insurance office. Amelia, dressed in navy pants and a tan and navy sweater, looked like she was ready to sell Girl Scout cookies. When the door slammed behind her, I drew a long breath. I was alone in the house for the first morning in ages.

The solitude didn't last long. I was drinking a second cup of coffee and eating a toasted biscuit when Andy Bellefleur and Special Agent Lattesta came to the front door. I hastily pulled on some jeans and a T-shirt to answer the door.

"Andy, Special Agent Lattesta," I said. "Come on in." I led the way back to the kitchen. I wasn't going to let them keep me away from my coffeepot. "Do you want a cup?" I asked them, but they both shook their heads.

"Sookie," Andy said, his face serious, "we're here about Crystal."

"Sure." I bit off some biscuit, chewed, and swallowed. I wondered if Lattesta was on a diet or something. He followed my every move. I dipped into his brain. He wasn't happy that I wasn't wearing a bra, because my boobs distracted him. He was thinking I was a bit too curvy for his taste. He was thinking he'd better not think about me that way anymore. He was missing his wife. "I figured that would take priority over the other thing," I said, forcing my attention back to Andy.

I couldn't tell how much Andy knew—how much Lattesta had shared—about what had happened in Rhodes, but Andy nodded. "We think," he said, after glancing from me to Lattesta, "that Crystal died three nights ago, sometime between one a.m. and three or four a.m."

"Sure," I said again.

"You knew that?" Lattesta went practically on point, like a bird dog.

"It stands to reason. There's always someone around the bar until one or two, and then normally Terry comes in to clean the floors sometime between six and eight a.m. Terry wasn't coming so early that day because he'd been tending bar and needed to sleep late, but most people wouldn't think of that, right?"

"Right," Andy said after an appreciable pause.

"So," I said, my point made, and poured myself some more coffee.

"How well do you know Tray Dawson?" Andy asked.

That was a loaded question. The accurate answer was, "Not as well as you think." I'd once been caught in an alley with Tray Dawson and he'd been naked, but it wasn't what people thought. (I'd been aware they'd thought quite a bit.) "He's been dating Amelia," I said, which was pretty safe to say. "She's my roommate," I reminded Lattesta, who was looking a little blank. "You met her two days ago. She's at work right now. And of course, Tray's a werewolf."

Lattesta blinked. It would take a while for him to get used to people saying that with straight faces. Andy's own expression didn't change.

"Right," Andy said. "Was Amelia out with Tray the night Crystal died?"

"I don't remember. Ask her."

"We will. Has Tray ever said anything to you about your sister-in-law?"

"I don't recall anything. Of course, they knew each other, at least a little bit, since they were both wereanimals."

"How long have you known about . . . werewolves? And the other wereanimals?" Andy asked, as though he just couldn't help himself.

"Oh, for a while," I said. "Sam first, and then others."

"And you didn't tell anyone?" Andy asked incredulously.

"Of course not," I said. "People think I'm weird enough as it is. Besides, it wasn't my secret to tell." It was my turn to give him a look. "Andy, you knew, too." After that night in the alley when we'd been attacked by a were-hater, Andy had at least heard Tray in his animal form and then seen him as a naked human. Any basic connect-the-dots would draw a picture of a werewolf.

Andy looked down at the notepad he'd taken out of his pocket. He didn't write anything down. He took a deep breath. "So that time I saw Tray in the alley, he had just changed back? I'm kind of glad. I never figured you for the kind of woman who'd have sex in public places with someone she scarcely knew." (That surprised me; I'd always thought Andy believed just about anything bad about me.) "What about that bloodhound that was with you?"

"That was Sam," I said, rising to rinse out my coffee cup.

"But at the bar he changed into a collie."

"Collies are cute," I said. "He figured more people would relate. It's his usual form."

Lattesta's eyes were bugging out. He was one tightly wound guy. "Let's get back on topic," he said.

"Your brother's alibi seems to be true," Andy said. "We've talked to Jason two or three times, and we've talked to Michele twice, and she's adamant that she was with him the whole time. She told us everything that happened that night in detail." Andy half smiled. "Too much detail."

That was Michele. She was forthright and downright. Her mom was the same way. I'd gone to vacation Bible school one summer when Mrs. Schubert was teaching my age group. "Tell the truth and shame the devil," she'd advised us.

Michele had taken that adage to heart, though maybe not in the way her mother had intended it.

"I'm glad you believe her," I said.

"We also talked to Calvin." Andy leaned on his elbows. "He gave us the background on Dove and Crystal. According to him, Jason knew all about their affair."

"He did." I shut my mouth tight. I wasn't going to talk about that incident if I could help it.

"And we talked to Dove."

"Of course."

"Dove Beck," Lattesta said, reading from his own notes. "He's thirty, married, two kids."

Since I knew all that, I had nothing to say.

"His cousin Alcee insisted on being there when we talked to him," Lattesta said. "Dove says he was home all that night, and his wife corroborates that."

"I don't think Dove did it," I said, and they both looked surprised.

"But you gave us the lead that she and Dove had had an affair," Andy said.

I flushed with mortification. "I'm sorry I did. I hated it when everyone looked at Jason like they were sure he'd done it, when I knew he hadn't. I don't think Dove murdered Crystal. I don't think he cared enough about her to do that to her."

"But maybe she ruined his marriage."

"Still, he wouldn't do that. Dove would be mad at himself, not at her. And she was pregnant. Dove wouldn't kill a pregnant woman."

"How can you be so sure?"

Because I can read his mind and see his innocence, I thought.

But the vampires and weres had come out, not me. I was hardly a supernatural creature. I was just a variation on human. "I don't think that's in Dove," I said. "I don't see it."

"And we're supposed to accept that as proof?" Lattesta said.

"I don't care what you do with it," I said, stopping short of offering a suggestion as to exactly what he might try. "You asked me; I answered you."

"So you do think this was a hate crime?"

It was my turn to look down at the table. I didn't have a notepad to scribble on, but I wanted to consider what I was about to say. "Yes," I told them finally. "I think it was a hate crime. But I don't know if it was personal hate, because Crystal was a slut . . . or racial hate, because she was a werepanther." I shrugged. "If I hear anything, I'll tell you. I want this solved."

"Hear anything? In the bar?" Lattesta's expression was avid. Finally, a human man saw me as intensely valuable. Just my luck he was happily married and thought I was a freak.

"Yes," I said. "I might hear something in the bar."

They left after that, and I was glad to see them go. It was my day off. I felt I should do something special today to celebrate, since I was coming off such a difficult time, but I couldn't think of anything to do. I looked at the Weather Channel and saw the high for today was supposed to be in the sixties. I decided winter was officially over, even though it was still January. It would get cold again, but I was going to enjoy the day.

I got my old chaise longue out of the storage shed and set it up in the backyard. I slicked my hair up in a ponytail and doubled it over so it wouldn't hang down. I put on my smallest bikini, which was bright orange and turquoise. I covered myself in tanning lotion. I took a radio and the book I was reading and a towel, and went out to the yard. Yep, it was cool. Yep, I got goose bumps when a breeze came up. But this was always a happy day on my calendar, the first day I got to sunbathe. I was going to enjoy it. I needed it.

Every year I thought of all the reasons I shouldn't lie out in the sun. Every year I added up my virtues: I didn't drink, I didn't smoke, and I very seldom had sex, though I was willing to change that. But I loved my sun, and it was bright in the sky today. Sooner or later I'd pay for it, but it remained my weakness. I wondered if maybe my fairy blood would give me a pass on the possibility of skin cancer. Nope: my aunt Linda had died of cancer, and she'd had more fairy blood than I had. Well . . . dammit.

I lay on my back, my eyes closed, dark glasses keeping the glare to a minimum. I sighed blissfully, ignoring the fact that I was a little on the cold side. I carefully didn't think about many things: Crystal, mysterious ill-wishing fairies, the FBI. After fifteen minutes, I switched to my stomach, listening to the country-and-western station from Shreveport, singing along from time to time since no one was around to hear me. I have an awful voice.

"Whatchadoing?" asked a voice right by my ear.

I'd never levitated before, but I think I did then, rising about six inches off the low folding chaise. I squawked, too.

"Jesus Christ, Shepherd of Judea," I wheezed when I finally realized that the voice belonged to Diantha, half-demon niece of the mostly demon lawyer Mr. Cataliades. "Diantha, you scared me so bad I almost jumped out of my skin."

Diantha was laughing silently, her lean, flat body bobbing up and down. She was sitting cross-legged on the ground, and she was wearing red Lycra running shorts and a black-and-green patterned T-shirt. Red Converses with yellow socks completed her ensemble. She had a new scar, a long red puckered one that ran down her left calf.

"Explosion," she said when she saw I was looking at it. Diantha had changed her hair color, too; it was a gleaming platinum. But the scar was bad enough to recapture my attention.

"You okay?" I asked. It was easy to adopt a terse style when you were talking to Diantha, whose conversation was like reading a telegram.

"Better," she said, looking down at the scar herself. Then her strange green eyes met mine. "My uncle sent me." This was the prelude to the message she had come to deliver, I understood, because she said it so slowly and distinctly.

"What does your uncle want to tell me?" I was still on my stomach, propped on my elbows. My breathing was back to normal.

"He says the fairies are moving around in this world. He says to be careful. He says they'll take you if they can, and they'll hurt you." Diantha blinked at me.

"Why?" I asked, all my pleasure in the sun evaporating as if it had never been. I felt cold. I cast a nervous glance around the yard.

"Your great-grandfather has many enemies," Diantha said slowly and carefully.

"Diantha, do you know why he has so many enemies?" That was a question I couldn't ask my great-grandfather himself, or at least I hadn't worked up the courage to do so.

Diantha looked at me quizzically. "They're on one side; he's on the other," she said as if I were slow. "Theygotyergrandfather."

"They . . . These other fairies killed my grandfather Fintan?"

She nodded vigorously. "Hedidn'ttellya," she said.

"Niall? He just said his son had died."

Diantha broke into a hoot of shrill laughter. "Youcouldsaythat," she said, and doubled over, still laughing. "Choppedintapieces!" She slapped me on the arm in her excess of amusement. I winced.

"Sorry," she said. "Sorrysorrysorry."

"Okay," I said. "Just give me a minute." I rubbed the arm vigorously to restore the feeling. How did you protect yourself if marauding fairies were after you?

"Who exactly am I supposed to be scared of?" I asked.

"Breandan," she said. "Itmeanssomething; Iforgot."

"Oh. What does 'Niall' mean?" Easily sidetracked, that was me.

"Cloud," Diantha said. "All Niall's people got sky names."

"Okay. So Breandan is after me. Who is he?"

Diantha blinked. This was a very long conversation for her. "Your great-grandfather's enemy," she explained carefully, as if I were very dense. "The only other fairy prince."

"Why did Mr. Cataliades send you?"

"Didyerbest," she said in one breath. Her unblinking bright eyes latched onto mine, and she nodded and very gently patted my hand.

I *had* done my best to get everyone out of the Pyramid alive. But it hadn't worked. It was kind of gratifying to know that the lawyer appreciated my efforts. I'd spent a week being angry at myself because I hadn't uncovered the whole bombing plot more quickly. If I'd paid more attention, hadn't let

myself get so distracted by the other stuff going on around
me . . .

"Also, yercheck'llcome."

"Oh, good!" I could feel myself brighten, despite the worry
caused by the rest of Diantha's message. "Did you bring a let-
ter for me, or anything like that?" I asked, hoping for a little
more enlightenment.

Diantha shook her head, and the gelled spikes of her
bright platinum hair trembled all over her head, making her
look like an agitated porcupine. "Uncle has to stay neutral,"
she said clearly. "Nopapernophonecallsnoemails. That's why
he sent me."

Cataliades had really stuck his neck out for me. No, he'd
stuck *Diantha's* neck out. "What if they capture you, Diantha?" I said.

She shrugged a bony shoulder. "Godownfightin'," she said.
Her face grew sad. Though I can't read demon minds in the
same way I can read human ones, any fool could tell Diantha
was thinking about her sister, Gladiola, who had died from
the sweep of a vampire's sword. But after a second, Diantha
looked simply lethal. "Burn'em," Diantha said. I sat up and
raised my eyebrows to show I didn't understand.

Diantha turned her hand up and looked at the palm. A
tiny flicker of flame hovered right above it.

"I didn't know you could do that," I said. I was not a little
impressed. I reminded myself to always stay on Diantha's
good side.

"Little," she said, shrugging. I deduced from that that
Diantha could make only a small flame, not a large one.
Gladiola must have been taken completely by surprise by the
vampire who'd killed her, because vampires were flammable,
much more so than humans.

"Do fairies burn like vamps?"

She shook her head. "Buteverything'llburn," she said, her voice certain and serious. "Sooner, later."

I suppressed a shiver. "Do you want a drink or something to eat?" I asked.

"Naw." She got up from the ground, dusted off her brilliant outfit. "Igottago." She patted me on the head and turned, and then she was gone, running faster than any deer.

I lay back down on the chaise to think about all this. Now Niall had warned me, Mr. Cataliades had warned me, and I felt well and truly scared.

But the warnings, though timely, didn't give me any practical information about how to guard against this threat. It might materialize at any time or in any place, as far as I could tell. I could assume the enemy fairies wouldn't storm Merlotte's and haul me out of there, since the fae were so secretive; but other than that, I didn't have a clue about what form the attack would take or how to defend myself. Would locked doors keep fairies out? Did they have to be granted entry, like vampires? No, I couldn't recall having to tell Niall he could come in, and he'd been to the house.

I knew fairies weren't limited to the night, as the vamps were. I knew they were very strong, as strong as vampires. I knew the fae who were actual fairies (as opposed to the fae who were brownies or goblins or elves) were beautiful and ruthless; that even vampires respected the ferocity of the fairies. The oldest fairies didn't always live in this world, as Claudine and Claude did; there was somewhere else they could go, a shrinking and secret world they found vastly preferable to this one: a world without iron. If they could limit their exposure to iron, fairies lived so long that they couldn't keep track of the years. Niall, for example, tossed around hundreds of years in his conversational chronology in a very inconsistent way. He might describe some event as being five hundred years ago, when another event that predated it was earmarked two hundred years ago. He simply couldn't keep track of the passage of time, maybe partly because he didn't spend most of that time in our world.

I wracked my brain for any other information. I did know one other thing, and I couldn't believe I'd forgotten it even momentarily. If iron is bad for fairies, lemon juice is even worse. Claude and Claudine's sister had been murdered with lemon juice.

Now that I thought of them, I thought it might be helpful for me to talk to Claude and Claudine. Not only were they my cousins, but Claudine was my fairy godmother, and she was supposed to help me. She'd be at work at the department store where she handled complaints and wrapped packages and took layaway payments. Claude would be at the male strip club he now owned and managed. He'd be easier to reach. I went inside to look up the number. Claude actually answered the phone himself.

"Yes," he said, managing to convey indifference, contempt, and boredom in the one word.

"Hi, sweetie!" I said brightly. "I need to talk to you face-to-face. Can I run over there, or are you busy?"

"No, don't come here!" Claude sounded almost alarmed at the idea. "I'll meet you at the mall."

The twins lived in Monroe, which boasted a nice mall.

"Okay," I said. "Where and when?"

There was a moment of silence. "Claudine can get off late for lunch. We'll meet you in an hour and a half in the food court, around Chick-fil-A."

"See you there," I said, and Claude hung up. Mr. Charm. I hustled into my favorite jeans and a green and white T-shirt. I brushed my hair vigorously. It had gotten so long I found it a lot of trouble to deal with, but I couldn't bring myself to cut it.

Since I'd exchanged blood with Eric several times, not only had I not caught so much as a cold, but I didn't even have split ends. Plus, my hair was shinier and actually looked thicker.

I wasn't surprised that people bought vampire blood on the black market. It did surprise me that people were foolish enough to trust the sellers when they said that the red stuff was actually genuine vampire blood. Often the vials contained TrueBlood, or pig's blood, or even the Drainer's own blood. If the purchaser did get genuine vampire blood, it was aged and might easily drive the consumer mad. I would never have gone to a Drainer to buy vampire blood. But now that I'd had it several times (and very fresh), I didn't even need to use makeup base. My skin was flawless. Thanks, Eric!

I don't know why I bothered with being proud of myself, because no one was going to look at me twice when I was with Claude. He's six feet tall, with rippling black hair and brown eyes, the physique of a stripper (six-pack abs and all), and the jaw and cheekbones of a Renaissance statue. Unfortunately, he has the personality of a statue, too.

Today Claude was wearing khakis and a tight tank top under an open green silk shirt. He was playing with a pair of dark glasses. Though Claude's facial expressions when he wasn't "on" ranged from blank to sullen, today he actually seemed nervous. He scanned the food court area as if he suspected that someone had followed me, and he didn't relax when I dropped into a chair at his table. He had a Chick-fil-A cup in front of him, but he hadn't gotten anything to eat, so I didn't, either.

"Cousin," he said, "are you well?" He didn't even try to sound sincere, but at least he said the right words. Claude had gotten marginally more polite when I'd discovered my great-grandfather was his grandfather, but he'd never forget I was (mostly) human. Claude had as much contempt for humans as most fairies did, but he was definitely fond of bedding humans—as long as they had beard stubble.

"Yes, thank you, Claude. It's been a while."

"Since we met? Yes." And that was just fine with him. "How can I help you? Oh, here comes Claudine." He looked relieved.

Claudine was wearing a brown suit with big gold buttons and a brown, cream, and tan striped blouse. She dressed very conservatively for work, and though the outfit was becoming, something about the cut made her look somewhat less slim, I noticed. She was Claude's twin; there had been another sister, their triplet, Claudette, but Claudette had been murdered. I guess if there are two remaining out of three, you call the living two "twins"? Claudine was as tall as Claude, and as she bent to kiss him on the cheek, their hair (exactly the same shade) mingled in a cascade of dark ripples. She kissed me, too. I wondered if all the fae are as into physical contact as the fairies are. My cousin had a trayful of food: French fries, chicken nuggets, some kind of dessert, a big sugary drink.

"What kind of trouble is Niall in?" I asked, going directly to the point. "What kind of enemies does he have? Are they all actual fairies? Or are they some other kind of fae?"

There was a moment of silence while Claudine and Claude

noted my brisk mood. They weren't at all surprised at my questions, which I thought was significant.

"Our enemies are fairies," Claudine said. "The other fae don't mix in our politics, as a rule, though we're all variations on the same theme—like pygmies, Caucasians, and Asians are variations on human beings." She looked sad. "All of us are less than we used to be." She tore open a ketchup package and squirted it all over her fries. She stuck three fries in her mouth at one time. Wow, hungry.

"It would take hours to explain our whole lineage," Claude said, but he wasn't dismissing me. He was simply stating a fact. "We come from the line of fairies that claims kinship to the sky. Our grandfather, your great-grandfather, is one of the few surviving members of our royal family."

"He's a prince," I said, because that was one of the few facts I knew. *Prince Charming. Prince Valiant. Prince of the City.* The title carried a lot of weight.

"Yes. There is another prince, Breandan." Claude pronounced it "Bren-DAWN." Diantha had mentioned Breandan. "He is the son of Niall's older brother, Rogan. Rogan claimed kinship to the sea, and from there his influence spread to all bodies of water. Rogan recently has gone to the Summerlands."

"Dead," Claudine translated before she took a bite of her chicken.

Claude shrugged. "Yes, Rogan's dead. He was the only one who could rein in Breandan. And you should know, Breandan's the one who—" But Claude stopped in midsentence, because his sister had her hand clamped down on his arm. A woman who was feeding a little boy French fries looked over at us curiously, her attention attracted by Claudine's sudden gesture. Claudine gave Claude a look that could blister paint. He nodded, removed his arm from her grip, and began to speak again. "Breandan disagrees very strongly with Niall about policy. He . . ."

The twins looked at each other. Finally Claudine nodded.

"Breandan believes all the humans with fairy blood should be eradicated. He believes every time one of us mates with a human, we lose some of our magic."

I cleared my throat, trying to get rid of the lump of fear that had risen to block it. "So Breandan's an enemy. Any more royalty on Niall's side?" I asked in a choked voice.

"A less-than-prince. His title doesn't translate," Claude said. "Our father, Dillon, son of Niall and his first wife, Branna. Our mother is Binne. If Niall goes to the Summerlands, Dillon will replace him as prince. But of course he must wait."

The names were unfamiliar. The first one sounded almost like Dylan, the last sounded like BEE-nah. "Spell those, please," I said, and Claudine said, "B-I-N-N-E. D-I-L-L-O-N. Niall didn't live happily with Branna, and it took him a long time to love our father, Dillon. Niall preferred his half-human sons." She smiled at me to reassure me that humans were okay with her, I guess.

Niall had told me once I was his only living relative. But that wasn't true. Niall was definitely swayed by emotion, not facts. I needed to remember that. Claude and Claudine didn't seem to blame Niall's partiality on me, to my huge relief.

"So who's on Breandan's side?" I asked.

"Dermot," said Claudine. She looked at me expectantly.

I knew that name. I struggled to remember where I'd heard it.

"He's my grandfather Fintan's brother," I said slowly.

"Niall's other son by Einin. But he's half human." Einin had been a human woman seduced by Niall centuries ago. (She'd thought he was an angel, which gives you some idea how good fairies can look when they don't need to look human.) My half-human great-uncle was trying to kill his dad?

"Did Niall tell you that Fintan and Dermot were twins?" Claude asked.

"Yes," I said.

"Dermot was the younger by a few minutes. The twins were not identical, you understand," he said. He was enjoying his role as informant. "They were . . ." He paused, looked baffled. "I don't know the right term," he said.

"Fraternal. Okay, interesting, but so?"

"Actually," Claudine said, looking down intently at her chicken, "your brother, Jason, is the spitting image of Dermot."

"Are you suggesting that . . . What are you suggesting?" I was ready to be indignant, once I knew why.

"We're only telling you that this is why Niall has been naturally inclined to favor you over your brother," Claude said. "Niall loved Fintan, but Dermot defied Niall at every turn. He openly rebelled against our grandfather and pledged his loyalty to Breandan, though Breandan despises him. In addition to Dermot's resemblance to Jason, which is only a quirk of genes, Dermot is an asshole like Jason. You can see why Niall doesn't claim kinship with your brother."

I felt a moment's pity for Jason until my common sense woke me up. "So Niall has enemies besides Breandan and Dermot?"

"They have their own followers and associates, including a few assassins."

"But your dad and your mom are on Niall's side?"

"Yes. Others are, too, of course. All of us sky people."

"So I have to watch out for any approaching fairies, and they might attack me at any time because I'm Niall's blood."

"Yes. The fae world is too dangerous. Especially now. That's one reason we live in the human world." Claude glanced at Claudine, who was wolfing chicken nuggets like she'd been starving.

Claudine swallowed, patted her mouth with the paper napkin, and said, "Here's the most important point." She popped in another nugget and glanced at Claude, signaling him to take over.

"If you see someone who looks like your brother, but isn't . . ." Claude said.

Claudine swallowed. "Run like hell," she advised.

Chapter 9

I drove home more confused than ever. Though I loved my great-grandfather as much as I could on our short acquaintance . . . and I was absolutely ready to love him even more, and I was willing to back him up to the limit because we were kin . . . I still didn't know how to fight this war, or how to dodge it, either. Fairies did not want to be known to the human world, and they never would. They weren't like the wereanimals or the vampires, who wanted to share in the planet with us. There was much less reason for the fairies to keep in line with human policies and rules. They could do anything they wished and vanish back into their secret place.

For about the millionth time, I wished I had a normal great-grandfather instead of this improbable, glorious, and inconvenient fairy prince version.

Then I was ashamed of myself. I should be happy for

what I'd been given. I hoped God hadn't noticed my lapse of appreciation.

I'd already had a busy day, and it was only two o'clock. This wasn't shaping up to be my normal day off. Usually I did laundry, cleaned house, went to the store, read, paid bills. . . . But today was so pretty I wanted to stay outside. I wanted to work on something that would allow me to think at the same time. There sure was plenty to mull over.

I looked at the flower beds around the house and decided to weed. This was my least favorite chore, maybe because it was the one I'd often been assigned as a child. Gran had believed we should be brought up to work. It was in her honor that I tried to keep the flower beds looking nice, and now I sighed and made up my mind to get the job done. I'd start with the bed by the driveway, on the south side of the house.

I went over to our metal toolshed, the latest in a series of toolsheds that had served the Stackhouse family over the generations we'd lived on this spot. I opened the door with the familiar mingled feelings of pleasure and horror, because someday I was going to have to put in some serious work cleaning out the interior. I still had my grandmother's old trowel; there was no telling who'd used it before her. It was ancient but so well taken care of that it was better than any modern substitute. I stepped into the shadowy shed and found my gardening gloves and the trowel.

I knew from watching *Antiques Roadshow* that there were people who collected old farm implements. This toolshed would be an Aladdin's cave to such a collector. My family didn't believe in letting things go if they still worked. Though chock-full, the shed was orderly, because that had been my grandfather's way. When we'd come to live with him and Gran, he'd drawn an outline for every commonly used tool.

That was where he'd wanted that tool to be replaced every time it was used, and that was where it was still kept now. I could reach unerringly for the trowel, which was maybe the oldest tool in the shed. It was heavy, sharper, and narrower than its modern counterparts, but its shape was familiar to my hand.

If it had been really, truly spring, I'd have changed back into my bikini to combine business with pleasure. But though the sun was still shining, I wasn't in a carefree mood any longer. I pulled my gardening gloves on, because I didn't want to ruin my fingernails. Some of these weeds seemed to fight back. One grew on a thick, fleshy stalk, and it had sharp points on its leaves. If you let it grow long enough, it blossomed. It was really ugly and prickly, and it had to be removed by its roots. There were quite a few of them springing up among the emerging cannas.

Gran would have had a fit.

I crouched and set to work. With my right hand, I sank the trowel in the soft dirt of the flower bed, loosening the roots of the nasty weed, and pulled it up with my left hand. I shook the stalk to get the dirt off the roots and then tossed it aside. Before I'd started I'd put a radio out on the back porch. In no time at all, I was singing along with LeAnn Rimes. I began to feel less troubled. In a few minutes, I had a respectable pile of uprooted weeds and a glow of virtue.

If he hadn't spoken, it would have ended differently. But since he was full of himself, he had to open his mouth. His pride saved my life.

Also, he picked some unwise words. Saying, "I'll enjoy killing you for my lord," is just not the way to make my acquaintance.

I have good reflexes, and I erupted from my squatting

position with the trowel in my hand and I drove it upward into his stomach. It slid right in, as if it were designed to be a fairy-killing weapon.

And that was exactly what it turned out to be, because the trowel was iron and he was a fairy.

I leaped back and dropped into a half crouch, still gripping the bloody trowel, and waited to see what he'd do. He was looking down at the blood seeping through his fingers with an expression of absolute amazement, as if he couldn't believe I'd ruined his ensemble. Then he looked at me, his eyes pale blue and huge, and there was a big question on his face, as if he were asking me if I'd really done that to him, if it wasn't some kind of mistake.

I began backing up to the porch steps, never taking my eyes from him, but he wasn't a threat any longer. As I reached behind me to open the screen door, my would-be murderer crumpled to the ground, still looking surprised.

I retreated into the house and locked the door. Then I walked on trembling legs over to the window above the kitchen sink and peered out, leaning as far over the sink as I could. From this angle I could see only a bit of the crumpled body. "Okay," I said out loud. *"Okay."* He was dead, looked like. It had been so *quick.*

I started to pick up the wall phone, noticed how my hands were shaking, and spotted my cell phone on the counter where I'd been charging it. Since this was a crisis that definitely called for the head honcho, I speed-dialed my great-grandfather's big, secret emergency number. I thought the situation qualified. A male voice, not Niall's, answered. "Yes?" the voice said with a cautious tone.

"Ah, is Niall there?"

"I can reach him. Can I help you?"

Steady, I told myself. *Steady.* "Would you please tell him I've killed a fairy and he's laid out in my yard and I don't know what to do with the body?"

There was a moment of silence.

"Yes, I'll tell him that."

"Pretty soon, you think? Because I'm alone and I'm kind of freaked-out."

"Yes. Quite soon."

"And someone will come?" Geez Louise, I sounded whiny. I made my spine stiffen. "I mean, I can load him in my car trunk, I guess, or I could call the sheriff." I wanted to impress this unknown with the fact that I wasn't completely needy and helpless. "But there's the whole thing with you guys being secret, and he didn't seem to have a weapon, and obviously I can't prove this guy said he'd enjoy killing me."

"You . . . have killed a fairy."

"I *said* that. Way back." Mr. Slow-on-the-Uptake. I peered out the window again. "Yeah, he's still not moving. Dead and gone."

This time the silence lasted so long that I thought I must have blanked out and missed something. I said, "I'm sorry?"

"Are you really? We'll be there very soon." And he hung up.

I couldn't not look, and I couldn't bear to look. I'd seen the dead before, both human and nonhuman. And since the night I'd met Bill Compton in Merlotte's, I'd seen more than my share of bodies. Not that that was Bill's fault, of course.

I had goose pimples all over.

In about five minutes, Niall and another fairy walked out of the woods. There must be some kind of portal out there. Maybe Scotty had beamed them up. Or down. And maybe I wasn't thinking too clearly.

The two fairies stopped when they saw the body and then exchanged a few words. They seemed astonished. But they weren't scared, and they weren't acting like they expected the guy to get up and fight, so I crept across the back porch and out the screen door.

They knew I was there, but they continued their eyeballing of the body.

My great-grandfather raised his arm and I crept under it. He held me to him, and I glanced up to see that he was smiling.

Okay, *that* was unexpected.

"You're a credit to our family. You've killed my enemy," he said. "I was so right about humans." He looked proud as punch.

"This is a good thing?"

The other fairy laughed and looked at me for the first time. He had hair the color of butterscotch, and his eyes matched his hair, which to me was so weird that it was really off-putting—though like all the fairies I'd met, he was gorgeous. I had to suppress a sigh. Between the vampires and the fairies, I was doomed to be a plain Jane.

"I'm Dillon," he said.

"Oh, Claudine's dad. Nice to meet you. I guess your name means something, too?" I said.

"Lightning," he said, and gave me a particularly winsome smile.

"Who is this?" I said, jerking my head at the body.

"He was Murry," Niall said. "He was a close friend of my nephew Breandan."

Murry looked very young; to the human eye, he'd been perhaps eighteen. "He said he was looking forward to killing me," I told them.

"But instead, you killed him. How did you do it?" Dillon asked, as if he was asking how I rolled out a flaky piecrust.

"With my grandmother's trowel," I said. "Actually, it's been in my family for a long time. Not like we make a fetish of gardening tools or anything; it just works and it's there and there's no need to buy another one." Babbling.

They both looked at me. I couldn't tell if they thought I was nuts or what.

"Could you show us this gardening tool?" Niall said.

"Sure. Do you-all want some tea or something? I think we've got some Pepsi and some lemonade." No, no, not lemonade! They'd die! "Sorry, cancel the lemonade. Tea?"

"No," said Niall quite gently. "I think not now."

I'd dropped the bloody trowel in among the cannas. When I picked it up and approached them, Dillon flinched. "Iron!" he said.

"You don't have the gloves on," Niall said to his son chidingly, and took the trowel from me. His hands were covered with the clear flexible coating developed in fairy-owned chemical factories. Coated with this substance, fairies were able to go out in the human world with some degree of assurance that they wouldn't get poisoned in the process.

Dillon looked chastened. "No. Sorry, Father."

Niall shook his head as if he were disappointed in Dillon, but his attention was really on the trowel. He might have been prepared to handle something poisonous to him, but I noticed he still handled it very carefully.

"It went into him really easily," I said, and had to repress a sudden wave of nausea. "I don't know why. It's sharp, but it's not that sharp."

"Iron can part our flesh like a hot knife in butter," Niall said.

"Ugh." Well, at least I knew I hadn't suddenly gotten superstrong.

"He surprised you?" Dillon asked. Though he didn't have the fine, fine wrinkles that made my great-grandfather even more beautiful, Dillon looked only a little younger than Niall, which made their relationship all the more disorienting. But when I looked down at the corpse once more, I was completely back in the present.

"He sure did surprise me. I was just working away weeding the flower bed, and the next thing you know, he was standing right there telling me how much he was looking forward to killing me. I'd never done a thing to him. And he scared me, so I kind of came up in a rush with the trowel, and I got him in the stomach." Again, I wrestled with my own stomach's tendency to heave.

"Did he speak any more?" My great-grandfather was trying to ask me casually, but he seemed pretty interested in my answer.

"No, sir," I said. "He kind of looked surprised, and then he . . . he died." I walked over to the steps and sat down rather suddenly and heavily.

"It's not exactly like I feel guilty," I said in a rush of words. "It's just that he was trying to kill me and he was happy about it and I never did a thing to him. I didn't know anything about him, and now he's dead."

Dillon knelt in front of me. He looked into my face. He didn't exactly look kind, but he looked less detached. "He was your enemy, and now he is dead," he said. "This is cause for rejoicing."

"Not exactly," I said. I didn't know how to explain.

"You're a *Christian*," he said, as if he'd discovered I was a hermaphrodite or a fruitarian.

"I'm a real bad one," I said hurriedly. His lips compressed, and I could see he was trying hard not to laugh. I'd never felt less like mirth, with the man I'd killed lying a few feet away. I wondered how many years Murry had walked this earth, and now he was crumpled in a lifeless heap, his blood staining my gravel. Wait a minute! He wasn't anymore. He was turning to . . . dust. It wasn't anything like the gradual flaking away of a vampire; it was more like someone was erasing Murry.

"Are you cold?" Niall asked. He didn't seem to think the disappearance of bits of the body was anything unusual.

"No, sir. I'm just all upset. I mean, I was sunbathing and then I went to see Claude and Claudine, and now here I am." I couldn't take my eyes off the body's incremental disappearance.

"You've been lying in the sun and gardening. *We* like the sun and sky," he said, as if that was proof positive I had a special relationship with the fairy branch of my family. He smiled at me. He was so beautiful. I felt like an adolescent when I was around him, an adolescent with acne and baby fat. Now I felt like a *murderous* adolescent.

"Are you going to gather up his . . . ashes?" I asked. I rose, trying to look brisk and purposeful. Action would make me feel less miserable.

Two pairs of alien eyes stared at me blankly.

"Why?" Dillon asked.

"To bury them."

They looked horrified.

"No, not in the *ground*," Niall said, trying to sound less revolted than he was. "That isn't our way."

"Then what are you going to do with them?" There was quite a heap of glittering powder on my driveway and in my flower bed, and there was still his torso remaining. "I don't mean to be pushy, but Amelia might come home anytime. I don't get a lot of other visitors, but there's the odd UPS delivery person and the meter reader."

Dillon looked at my great-grandfather as if I'd suddenly begun speaking Japanese. Niall said, "Sookie shares her house with another woman, and this woman may return at any moment."

"Is anyone else going to come after me?" I asked, diverted from my question.

"Possibly," Niall said. "Fintan did a better job of protecting you than I am doing, Sookie. He even protected you from me, and I only want to love you. But he wouldn't tell me where you were." Niall looked sad, and harried, and tired for the first time since I'd met him. "I've tried to keep you out of it. I imagined I only wanted to meet you before they succeeded in killing me, and I arranged it through the vampire to make my movements less noticeable, but in arranging that meeting I've drawn you into danger. You can trust my son Dillon." He put his hand on the younger fairy's shoulder. "If he brings you a message, it's really from me." Dillon smiled charmingly, displaying supernaturally white and sharp teeth. Okay, he was scary, even if he was Claude and Claudine's dad.

"I'll talk to you soon," Niall said, bending over to give me a kiss. The fine, gleaming pale hair fell against my cheek. He smelled so good; fairies do. "I'm sorry, Sookie," he said. "I thought I could force them all to accept . . . Well, I couldn't." His green eyes glowed with intensity and regret. "Do you have—yes, a garden hose! We could gather up most of the dust, but I think it more practical if you simply . . . distribute it."

He put his arms around me and hugged me, and Dillon

gave me a mocking salute. The two took a few steps to the trees, and then they simply vanished into the undergrowth as deer do when you encounter them in the woods.

So that was that. I was left in my sunny yard, all by myself, with a sizeable pile of glittering powdery dust in a body-shaped heap on the gravel.

I added to my mental list of the odd things I'd done that day. I'd entertained the police, sunbathed, visited at a mall with some fairies, weeded, and killed someone. Now it was powdered-corpse removal time. And the day wasn't over yet.

I turned on the faucet, unwound the hose enough so the flow would reach the right area, and compressed the spray head to aim the water at the fairy dust.

I had a weird, out-of-body feeling. "You'd think I'd be getting used to it," I said out loud, startling myself even more. I didn't want to add up the people I'd killed, though technically most of them weren't people. Before the past two years (maybe even less if I counted down the months), I'd never laid a finger on another person in anger, aside from hitting Jason in the stomach with my plastic baseball bat when he tore my Barbie's hair out.

I pulled myself up sharply. The deed was done now. No going back.

I released the spray head and turned the hose off at the faucet.

In the fading sunlight, it was a little hard to tell, but I thought I'd dispersed the dust pretty thoroughly.

"But not from my memory," I said seriously. Then I had to laugh, and it sounded a little crazy. I was standing out in my backyard hosing down fairy dust and making melodramatic statements all to myself. Next I'd be doing the *Hamlet* soliloquy that I'd had to memorize in high school.

This afternoon had brought me down hard, to a real bad place.

I bit down on my bottom lip. Now that I was definitely over the intoxication of having a living relative, I had to face the fact that Niall's behavior was charming (mostly) but unpredictable. By his own admission, he'd inadvertently put me at great risk. Maybe I should have wondered before this what my grandfather Fintan had been like. Niall had told me he'd watched over me without ever making himself known, an image that seemed creepy but touching. Niall was creepy and touching, too. Great-uncle Dillon just seemed creepy.

The temperature was dropping with the creeping darkness, and I was shivering by the time I went in the house. The hose might freeze tonight, but I couldn't bring myself to care. There were clothes in the dryer, and I had to eat since I'd missed eating lunch at the mall. It was getting closer to suppertime. I had to concentrate on small things.

Amelia phoned while I was folding the laundry. She told me she was about to leave work and was going to meet Tray for dinner and a movie. She asked me if I wanted to come along, but I said I was busy. Amelia and Tray didn't need a third wheel, and I didn't need to feel like one.

It would have been nice to have some company. But what would I have done for social chitchat? *Wow, that trowel slid into his stomach like it was Jell-O.*

I shuddered and tried to think of what to do next. An uncritical companion, that was who I needed. I missed the cat we'd called Bob (though he hadn't been born a cat and wasn't one now). Maybe I could get another cat, a real one. It wasn't the first time I'd considered going to the animal shelter. I'd better wait until this fairy crisis was over before I did that. There wasn't any point in picking out a pet if I was liable to be abducted or killed at any moment, right? Wouldn't be fair to the animal. I caught myself giggling, and I knew that couldn't be good.

Time to stop brooding; time to get something done. First, I'd clean off the trowel and put it away. I carried it to the kitchen sink, and I scrubbed it and rinsed it. The dull iron seemed to have a new gloss on it, like a bush that had gotten watered after a drought. I held it to the light and stared at the old tool. I shook myself.

Okay, that had really been an unpleasant simile. I banished the idea and scrubbed. When I thought the trowel looked spotless, I washed it and dried it all over again. Then I walked quickly out the back door and through the dark to hang the damn thing back in the toolshed on its designated hook.

I wondered if I might not get a cheap new trowel at Wal-Mart after all. I wasn't sure I could use the iron one the next time I wanted to move some jonquil bulbs. It would feel like using a gun to pry out nails. I hesitated, the trowel poised to hang from its designated hook. Then I made up my mind and carried it back to the house. I paused on the back steps, admiring the last streak of light for a few moments until my stomach growled.

What a long day it had been. I was ready to settle in front of the television with a plate of something bad for me, watching some show that wouldn't improve my mind at all.

I heard the crunching of a car coming up the driveway as I was opening the screen door. I waited outside to see who my caller might be. Whoever it was, they knew me a little, because the car proceeded around to the back.

In a day full of shocks, here was another: my caller was Quinn, who was not supposed to stick his big toe into Area Five. He was driving a Ford Taurus, a rental car.

"Oh, *great*," I said. I'd wanted company earlier, but not this company. As much as I'd liked and admired Quinn, this conversation promised to be just as upsetting as the day had been.

He got out of his car and strode over to me, his walk graceful, as always. Quinn is a very large shaved-bald man with pansy purple eyes. He is one of the few remaining were-tigers in the world and probably the only male weretiger on the North American continent. We'd broken up the last time I'd seen him. I wasn't proud of how I'd told him or why I'd done it, but I thought I'd been pretty clear about us not being a couple.

Yet here he was, and his big warm hands were resting on my shoulders. Any pleasure I might have felt at seeing him again was drowned by the wave of anxiety that swept over me. I felt trouble in the air.

"You shouldn't be here," I said. "Eric turned down your request; he told me so."

"Did he ask you first? Did you know I wanted to see you?" The darkness was now intense enough to trigger the outside security light. Quinn's face had harsh lines in the yellow glare. His gaze locked with mine.

"No, but that's not the point," I said. I felt rage on the wind. It wasn't my rage.

"I think it is."

It was sunset. There simply wasn't time to get into an extended argument. "Didn't we say it all last time?" I didn't want to go through another scene, no matter how fond I was of this man.

"You said what you thought was all, babe. I disagree."

Oh, great. Just what I needed! But since I really do know that not everything is about me, I counted to ten and said, "I know I didn't give you any slack when I told you we shouldn't see each other anymore, Quinn, but I did mean what I said. What's changed in your personal situation? Is your mom able to take care of herself now? Or has Frannie grown up enough to be able to manage your mom if she escapes?" Quinn's mom had been through an awful time, and she'd come out of it more or less nuts. Actually, more. His sister, Frannie, was still a teenager.

He bowed his head for a moment, as if he were gathering himself. Then he looked directly into my eyes again. "Why are you harder on me than on anyone else?" he asked.

"I am not," I said instantly. But then I thought, *Am I?*

"Have you asked Eric to give up Fangtasia? Have you asked Bill to give up his computer enterprise? Have you asked Sam to turn his back on his family?"

"What . . . ?" I began, trying to work out the connection.

"You're asking me to give up other people I love—my mother and my sister—if I want to have you," he said.

"I'm not asking you to do *anything*," I said, feeling the tension inside me ratchet up to an almost intolerable level. "I told you that I wanted to be first with the guy in my life. And I figured—I still figure—that your family has got to come first with you because your mom and your sister are not exactly stand-on-their-own-two-feet kind of women. I haven't asked Eric to give up Fangtasia! Why would I do that? And where does Sam come into it?" I couldn't even think of a reason to mention Bill. I was so over him.

"Bill loves his status in the human and vampire worlds, and Eric loves his little piece of Louisiana more than he'll ever love you," Quinn said, and he sounded almost sorry for me. That was ridiculous.

"Where did all the hating come from?" I asked, holding

my hands spread in front of me. "I didn't quit dating you because of any feelings I had for someone else. I quit dating you because I thought your plate was full already."

"He's trying to wall you off from everyone else who cares for you," Quinn said, focusing on me with unnerving intensity. "And look at all the dependents *he* has."

"You're talking about Eric?" All Eric's "dependents" were vampires who could damn well take care of themselves.

"He'll *never* dump his little area for you. He'd never let his little pack of sworn vamps serve someone else. He'll never—"

I couldn't stand this anymore. I gave a scream of sheer frustration. I actually stomped my foot like a three-year-old. "I haven't asked him to!" I yelled. "What are you talking about? Did you show up to tell me no else will ever love me? What's wrong with you?"

"Yes, Quinn," said a familiar, cold voice. "What's wrong with you?"

I swear I jumped at least six inches. I'd let my quarrel with Quinn absorb my attention, and I hadn't felt Bill's arrival.

"You're frightening Sookie," Bill said from a yard behind me, and my spine shivered at the menace in his voice. "That won't happen, tiger."

Quinn snarled. His teeth began growing longer, sharper, before my eyes. Bill stood at my side in the next second. His eyes were glowing an eerie silvery brown.

Not only was I afraid they'd kill each other, I realized that I was really tired of people popping on and off of my property like it was a train station on the supernatural railroad.

Quinn's hands became clawed. A growl rumbled deep in his chest.

"No!" I said, willing them to listen to me. This was the day from hell.

"You're not even on the list, vampire," Quinn said, and his voice wasn't really his any longer. "You're the past."

"I will make you a rug on my floor," Bill said, and his voice was colder and smoother than ever, like ice on glass.

The two idiots launched themselves at each other.

I started to jump in to stop them, but the functioning part of my brain told me that would be suicidal. I thought, *My grass is going to get sprinkled by a little more blood this evening.* What I should have been thinking was, *I need to get the hell out of the way.* In fact, I should have run inside and locked the door and left them to it.

But that was hindsight. Actually, what I did was stand there for a moment, hands fluttering uselessly, trying to figure out how to separate them . . . and then the two grappling figures lurched and staggered. Quinn threw Bill away from him with all his strength. Bill cannoned into me with such force that I actually went up in the air an inch or two—and then, very decisively, down I came.

Chapter 10

Cold water trickled over my face and neck. I spluttered and choked as some trickled into my mouth.

"Too much?" asked a hard voice, and I pried open my eyes to see Eric. We were in my room, and only the bathroom light was on.

"Enough," I said. The mattress shifted as Eric got up to carry the washrag into my bathroom. In a second he was back with a hand towel, dabbing at my face and neck. My pillow was damp, but I decided not to worry about it. The house was cooling off now that the sun was gone, and I was lying there in my underwear. "Cold," I said. "Where are my clothes?"

"Stained," Eric said. There was a blanket at the end of the bed, and he pulled it up over me. He turned his back to me for a moment, and I heard his shoes hit the floor. Then he got under the blanket with me and propped himself up on an elbow. He was looking down at me. His back was to the light coming from the bathroom, so I couldn't discern his expression. "Do you love him?" he said.

"Are they alive?" No point in deciding if I loved Quinn or not if he was dead, right? Or maybe Eric meant Bill. I couldn't decide. I realized I felt a little odd.

"Quinn drove away with a few broken ribs and a broken jaw," Eric told me, his voice quite neutral. "Bill will heal tonight, if he hasn't already."

I considered that. "I guess you had something to do with Bill being here?"

"I knew when Quinn disobeyed our ruling. He was sighted within half an hour of crossing into my area. And Bill was the closest vampire to send to your house. His task was to make sure you weren't being harassed while I made my way here. He took his role a little too seriously. I'm sorry you were hurt," Eric said, his voice stiff. He wasn't used to making apologies, and I smiled in the darkness. It was almost impossible for me to feel anxious, I noticed in a distant kind of way. And yet surely I ought to be upset and angry?

"So they stopped fighting when I hit the ground, I hope."

"Yes, the collision ended the . . . scuffle."

"And Quinn left on his own?" I ran my tongue around my mouth, which tasted funny: kind of sharp and metallic.

"Yes, he did. I told him I would take care of you. He knew he'd crossed too many lines by coming to see you, since I'd told him not to enter my area. Bill was less accepting, but I made him return to his house."

Typical sheriff behavior. "Did you give me some of your blood?" I asked.

Eric nodded quite casually. "You had been knocked unconscious," he said. "And I know that is serious. I wanted you to feel well. It was my fault."

I sighed. "Mr. High-handed," I muttered.

"Explain. I don't know this term."

"It means someone who thinks he knows what's best for everyone. He makes decisions for them without asking them." Maybe I had put a personal spin on the term, but so what?

"Then I am high-handed," Eric said with no shame whatsoever. "I'm also very . . ." He dipped his head and kissed me slowly, leisurely.

"Horny," I said.

"Exactly," he said, and kissed me again. "I've worked with my new masters. I've shored up my authority. I can have my own life now. It's time I claimed what is mine."

I'd told myself I'd make up my own mind, no matter how Eric and I were tied by our blood exchanges. After all, I still had free will. But whether or not the inclination had been planted by Eric's blood donation, I found that my body was strongly in favor of returning the kiss and of trailing the palm of my hand down Eric's broad back. Through the fabric of his shirt, I could feel the muscles and tendons and the bones of his spine as they moved. My hands seemed to remember the map of Eric's topography even as my lips remembered the way he kissed. We went on this way very slowly for a few minutes as he reacquainted himself with me.

"Do you really remember?" I asked him. "Do you really remember staying with me before? Do you remember what it felt like?"

"Oh, yes," he said, "I remember." He had my bra unhooked before I'd even realized his hand was back there. "How could I forget these?" he said, his hair falling around his face as his mouth fastened on my breast. I felt the tiny sting of his fangs and the sharp pleasure of his mouth. I touched the fly of his jeans, brushed my hand against the bulge inside, and suddenly the moment for being tentative was over.

His jeans were off, and his shirt, too, and my panties vanished. His long cool body pressed full-length against my warm one. He kissed me over and over in a kind of frenzy. He made a hungry noise, and I echoed it. His fingers probed me, fluttering against the hard nub in a way that made me squirm.

"Eric," I said, trying to position myself underneath him. "Now."

He said, "Oh, yes." He slid inside as if he'd never been gone, as if we'd made love every night for the past year. "This is best," he whispered, and his voice had that accent I caught occasionally, that hint of a time and place that were so far distant I could not imagine them. "This is *best*," he said again. "This is *right*." He pulled out a little, and I made a choked noise.

"Not hurting?" he asked.

"Not hardly," I said.

"I am too big for some."

"Bring it on," I said.

He shoved forward.

"Omigod," I said through clenched teeth. My fingers were digging hard into the muscles of his arms. "Yes, again!" He was as deep inside me as he could get without an operation, and he glowed above me, his white skin shining in the darkness of the room. He said something in a language I didn't recognize; after a long moment, he repeated it. And then he began to move quicker and quicker until I thought I would be pounded into pieces, but I kept up. I kept up, until I saw his fangs glisten as he bent over me. When he bit my shoulder, I left my body for a minute. I'd never felt anything so good. I didn't have enough breath to scream or even speak. My arms were around Eric's back, and I felt him shudder all over as he had his own good minute.

I was so shaken I couldn't have talked if my life had depended on it. We lay in silence, exhausted. I didn't mind his weight on me. I felt safe.

He licked the bite mark in a lazy way, and I smiled into the darkness. I stroked his back as if I were soothing an animal. I felt better than I'd felt in months. It had been a while since I'd had sex, and this was like . . . *gourmet* sex. Even now I felt little jolts of pleasure ripple out from the epicenter of the orgasm.

"Will this change the blood bond?" I asked. I was careful not to sound like I was accusing him of something. But of course, I was.

"Felipe wanted you. The stronger our bond, the less chance there is he can maneuver you away."

I flinched. "I can't do that."

"You won't need to," Eric said, his voice flowing over me like a feather quilt. "We are pledged with the knife. We are bonded. He can't take you from me."

I could only be grateful I didn't have to go to Las Vegas. I didn't want to leave home. I couldn't imagine how it would feel to be surrounded by so much greed; well, yes, I could. It would be awful. Eric's big, cool hand cupped my breast, and he stroked with his long thumb.

"Bite me," Eric said, and he meant it literally.

"Why? You said you already gave me some."

"Because it makes me feel good," he said, and moved on top of me again. "Just . . . for that."

"You can't be . . ." But he *was* ready again.

"Would you like to be on top?" Eric asked.

"We could do that for a while," I said, trying not to sound too femme fatale. In fact, it was hard not to growl. Before I could even gather myself, we'd reversed positions. His eyes were intent on mine. His hands went up to my breasts, caressing and pinching gently, and his mouth followed after his hands.

I was afraid I was losing control of my leg muscles, I was so relaxed. I moved slowly, not very regularly. I felt the tension gradually beginning to build again. I began to focus, to move steadily.

"Slow," he said, and I reduced the pace. His hands found my hips and began to direct me.

"Oh," I said, as a sharper pleasure began to seep through me. He'd found my pleasure center with his thumb. I began to speed things up, and if he tried to slow me after that, I ignored it. I rose and fell faster and faster, and then I took his wrist, and I bit with all my strength, sucked on the wound. He yelled, an incoherent sound of release and relief. That was enough to finish me, and I collapsed on top of him. I licked his wrist lazily, though I didn't have the coagulant in my saliva that he possessed.

"Perfect," he said. "Perfect."

I started to tell him he couldn't possibly mean that, as many women as he'd had over the centuries, but I figured, *Why spoil the moment? Let it be.* In a rare moment of wisdom, I listened to my own advice.

"Can I tell you what happened today?" I asked after we'd drowsed for a few minutes.

"Of course, my lover." His eyes were half open. He was lying on his back beside me, and the room smelled of sex and vampire. "I'm all ears—for the moment, at least." He laughed.

This was the real treat, or at least one of the real treats—having someone with whom to share the day's events. Eric was a good listener, at least in his postcoital relaxed state. I told him about Andy and Lattesta's visit, about Diantha's appearance while I was sunbathing.

"I thought I tasted the sun on your skin," he said, stroking my side. "Go on."

So off I babbled like a brook in the spring, telling him about my rendezvous with Claude and Claudine and all they'd told me about Breandan and Dermot.

Eric was more alert when I was talking about the fairies. "I smelled fairies around the house," he said. "But in my overwhelming anger at seeing your tiger-striped suitor, I put the thought aside. Who came here?"

"Well, this bad fairy named Murry. But don't worry—I killed him," I said. If I'd ever doubted I had Eric's full attention, I didn't doubt it any longer.

"How did you do that, my lover?" he asked very gently.

I explained, and by the time I got to the part where my great-grandfather and Dillon showed up, Eric sat up, the blanket falling away. He was completely serious and alert.

"The body is gone?" he asked for the third time, and I said, "Yes, Eric, it is."

"It might be a good idea for you to stay in Shreveport," Eric said. "You could even stay in my house."

That was a first. I'd never been invited to Eric's house before. I had no idea where it was. I was astonished and sort of touched.

"I really appreciate that," I said, "but it would be awful hard for me to commute from Shreveport back here to work."

"You would be much safer if you left your job until this problem with the fairies is resolved." Eric cocked his head while he looked at me, his face quite expressionless.

"No, thanks," I said. "Nice of you to offer. But it would be really inconvenient for you, I bet, and I know it would be for me."

"Pam is the only other person I've invited to my home."

I said brightly, "Only blondes permitted, huh?"

"I honor you with the invitation." Still not a clue on his face. If I hadn't been so used to reading people's minds, maybe I could have interpreted his body language better. I was too accustomed to knowing what people *really* meant, no matter what words they spoke.

"Eric, I'm clueless," I said. "Cards on the table, okay? I can tell you're waiting for me to give you a certain reaction, but I have no idea what it is."

He looked baffled; that's what he looked.

"What are you after?" he asked me, shaking his head. The beautiful golden hair tumbled around his face in tangles. He was a total mess since we'd made love. He looked better than ever. Grossly unfair.

"What am I after?" He lay back down, and I turned on my side to face him. "I don't think I'm after anything," I said carefully. "I was after an orgasm, and I got plenty of those." I smiled at him, hoping that was the right answer.

"You don't want to quit your job?"

"Why would I quit my job? How would I live?" I asked blankly. Then, finally, I got it. "Did you think that since we made whoopee and you said I was yours, I'd want to quit work and keep house for you? Eat candy all day, let you eat me all night?"

Yep, that was it. His face confirmed it. I didn't know how

to feel. Hurt? Angry? No, I'd had enough of all that today. I couldn't pump another strong emotion to the surface if I had all night. "Eric, I like to work," I said mildly. "I need to get out of the house every day and mingle with people. If I stay away, it's like a deafening clamor when I get back. It's much better for me to deal with people, to stay used to keeping all those voices in the background." I wasn't explaining very well. "Plus, I like being at the bar. I like seeing everyone I work with. I guess giving people alcohol isn't exactly noble or a public service; maybe the opposite. But I'm good at what I do, and it suits me. Are you saying . . . What are you saying?"

Eric looked uncertain, an expression that sat oddly on his normally self-assured face. "This is what other women have wanted from me," he said. "I was trying to offer it before you asked for it."

"I'm not anyone else," I said. It was hard to shrug in my position on the bed, but I tried.

"You're mine," he said. Then he noticed my frown and amended his words hastily. "You're only my lover. Not Quinn's, not Sam's, not Bill's." There was a long pause. "Aren't you?" he said.

A relationship discussion initiated by the guy. This was different, if I went by the stories I'd heard from the other barmaids.

"I don't know if the—comfort—I feel with you is the blood exchange or a feeling I would've had naturally," I said, picking each word carefully. "I don't think I would have been so ready to have sex with you tonight if we didn't have a blood bond, because today has been one hell of a day. I can't say, 'Oh, Eric, I love you, carry me away,' because I don't know what's real and what's not. Until I'm sure, I have no intention of changing my life drastically."

Eric's brows began to draw together, a sure sign of displeasure.

"Am I happy when I'm with you?" I put my hand against his cheek. "Yes, I am. Do I think making love with you is the greatest thing ever? Yes, I do. Do I want to do it again? You bet, though not right now since I'm sleepy. But soon. And often. Am I having sex with anyone else? No. And I won't, unless I decide the bond is all we have."

He looked as if he were thinking of several different responses. Finally he said, "Do you regret Quinn?"

"Yes," I said, because I had to be honest. "Because we had the beginning of something good going, and I may have made a huge mistake sending him away. But I've never been seriously involved with two men at the same time, and I'm not starting now. Right now, that man is you."

"You love me," he said, and he nodded.

"I appreciate you," I said cautiously. "I have big lust for you. I enjoy your company."

"There's a difference," Eric said.

"Yes, there is. But you don't see me bugging you to spell out how you feel about me, right? Because I'm pretty damn sure I wouldn't like the answer. So maybe you better rein it in a little yourself."

"You don't want to know how I feel about you?" Eric looked incredulous. "I can't believe you're a human woman. Women *always* want to know how you feel about them."

"And I'll bet they're sorry when you tell them, huh?"

He lifted one eyebrow. "If I tell them the truth."

"That's supposed to put me in a confiding mood?"

"I always tell you the truth," he said. And there wasn't a trace of that smile left on his face. "I may not tell you everything I know, but what I tell you . . . it's true."

"Why?"

"The blood exchange has worked both ways," he said. "I've had the blood of many women. I've had almost utter control over them. But they never drank mine. It's been decades, maybe centuries since I gave any woman my blood. Maybe not since I turned Pam."

"Is this the general policy among vampires you know?" I wasn't quite sure how to ask what I wanted to know.

He hesitated, nodded. "For the most part. There are some vampires who like to take total control over a human . . . make that human their Renfield." He used the term with distaste.

"That's from *Dracula*, right?"

"Yes, Dracula's human servant. A degraded creature . . . Why someone of Dracula's eminence would want so debased a man as that . . ." Eric shook his head disgustedly. "But it does happen. The best of us look askance at a vampire who makes servant after servant. The human is lost when the vampire assumes too much control. When the human goes completely under, he isn't worth turning. He isn't worth anything at all. Sooner or later, he has to be killed."

"Killed! Why?"

"If the vampire who's assumed so much control abandons the Renfield, or if the vampire himself is killed . . . the Renfield's life is not worth living after that."

"They have to be put down," I said. Like a dog with rabies.

"Yes." Eric looked away.

"But that's not going to happen to me. And you won't ever turn me." I was absolutely serious.

"No. I won't ever force you into subservience. And I will never turn you, since you don't want it."

"Even if I'm going to die, don't turn me. I would hate that more than anything."

"I agree to that. No matter how much I may want to keep you."

Right after we'd met, Bill had not changed me when I had been close to death. I'd never realized he might have been tempted to do so. He'd saved my human life instead. I put that away to consider later. Tacky to think about one man when you're in bed with another.

"You saved me from being bonded to Andre," I said. "But it cost me."

"If he'd lived, it would have cost me, too. No matter how mild his reaction, Andre would have paid me back for my intervention."

"He seemed so calm about it that night," I said. Eric had persuaded Andre to let him be his proxy. I'd been very grateful at the time, since Andre gave me the creeps and he didn't give a damn about me, either. I remembered my talk with Tara. *If I'd let Andre share blood that night, I'd be free now, since he's dead.* I still couldn't decide how I felt about that—probably three different ways.

Tonight was turning out to be a huge one for realizations. They could just stop coming any old time now.

"Andre never forgot a challenge to his will," Eric said. "Do you know how he died, Sookie?"

Ah-oh.

"He got stuck in the chest with a big splinter of wood," I said, swallowing a little. Like Eric, I didn't always tell the whole truth. The splinter hadn't gotten in Andre's chest by accident. Quinn had done that.

Eric looked at me for what seemed like a very long time. He could feel my anxiety, of course. I waited to see if he'd push the issue. "I don't miss Andre," he said finally. "I regret Sophie-Anne, though. She was brave."

"I agree," I said, relieved. "By the way, how are you getting along with your new bosses?"

"So far, so good. They're very forward-thinking. I like that."

Since the end of October, Eric had had to learn the structure of a new and larger organization, the characters of the vampires who made it work, and how to liaise with the new sheriffs. Even for him, that was a big bite to chew.

"I bet the vamps you had with you before that night are extra glad they pledged loyalty to you, since they survived when so many of the other vamps in Louisiana died that night."

Eric smiled broadly. It would have been really scary if I hadn't seen the fang display before. "Yes," he said with a whole bunch of satisfaction. "They owe me their lives, and they know it."

He slid his arms around me and held me against his cool body. I was content and sated, and my fingers trailed through the happy trail of golden hair that led downward. I thought of the provocative picture of Eric as Mr. January in the "Vampires of Louisiana" calendar. I liked the one he'd given me even more. I wondered if I could get a poster-sized blowup.

He laughed when I asked him. "We should think of producing another calendar," he said. "It was a real earner for us. If I can have a picture of you in the same pose, I'll give you a poster of me."

I thought about it for twenty seconds. "I don't think I could do a nude picture," I said with some regret. "They always seem to show up to bite you in the ass."

Eric laughed again, low and husky. "You talk a lot about that," he said. "Shall I bite you in the ass?" This led to a lot of other things, wonderful and playful things. After those things had come to a happy completion, Eric glanced at the clock beside my bed.

"I have to go," he whispered.

"I know," I said. My eyes were heavy with sleep.

He began to dress for his return to Shreveport, and I pulled down the covers and snuggled into the bed properly. It was hard to keep my eyes open, though watching him move around my bedroom was a sweet sight.

He bent to kiss me, and I put my arms around his neck. For a second, I knew he was thinking of crawling back in the bed with me; I hoped it was his body language and his murmur of pleasure that cued me to his thoughts. Every now and then, I got a flash from a vampire mind, and it scared me to death. I didn't think I'd last long if vampires realized I could read their minds, no matter how seldom that occurred.

"I want you again," he said, sounding a little surprised. "But I have to go."

"I'll see you soon, I guess?" I was awake enough to feel uncertain.

"Yes," he said. His eyes were bright and his skin glowed. The mark on his wrist was gone. I touched where it had been. He leaned over to kiss the place on my neck where he'd bitten me, and I shivered all over. "Soon."

Then he was gone, and I heard the back door close quietly behind him. With the last bit of energy in my muscles, I rose and passed through the kitchen in the dark to shoot the dead bolt. I saw Amelia's car parked by mine; at some point, she'd returned home.

I went to the sink to get a drink of water. I knew the dark kitchen like the back of my hand, so I didn't need a light. I drank and realized how thirsty I was. As I turned to go back to bed, I saw something move at the edge of the woods. I froze, my heart pounding in a very unpleasant way.

Bill stepped out of the trees. I knew it was him, though I couldn't see his face clearly. He stood looking up, and I knew he must have watched Eric take flight. Bill had recovered from the fight with Quinn, then.

I expected to be angry that Bill was watching me, but the anger never rose. No matter what had happened between us, I could not rid myself of the feeling that Bill had not simply been spying on me—he had been watching over me.

Also—more practically—there was nothing to be done about it. I could hardly throw open the door and apologize for having male company. At this moment, I wasn't the least bit sorry I'd gone to bed with Eric. In fact, I felt as sated as if I'd had the Thanksgiving feast of sex. Eric didn't look anything like a turkey—but after I had a happy mental image of him lying on my kitchen table with some sweet potatoes and marshmallows, I was able to think only of my bed. I slid under the covers with a smile on my face, and almost as soon as my head hit the pillow, I was asleep.

Chapter 11

I should have known my brother would come to see me. I should only have felt surprised that he hadn't appeared earlier. When I got up the next day at noon, feeling as relaxed as a cat in a pool of sunshine, Jason was in the backyard on the chaise I'd used the day before. I thought it was smart of him not to come inside, considering we were at odds with each other.

Today wasn't going to be nearly as warm as the day before. It was cold and raw. Jason was bundled in a heavy camo jacket and a knit cap. He was staring up into the cloudless sky.

I remembered the twins' warning, and I looked at him carefully; but no, it was Jason. The feel of his mind was familiar, but maybe a fairy could impersonate even that. I listened in for a second. No, this was definitely my brother.

It was strange to see him sitting idle and even stranger to see him alone. Jason was always talking, drinking, flirting with women, working at his job, or working on his house;

and if he wasn't with a woman, he nearly always had a male shadow—Hoyt (until he'd been preempted by Holly) or Mel. Contemplation and solitude were not states I associated with my brother. Watching him stare at the sky as I sipped my mug of coffee, I thought, *Jason's a widower now.*

That was a strange new identity for Jason, a heavy one he might not be able to manage. He'd cared for Crystal more than she'd cared for him. That had been a new experience for Jason, too. Crystal—pretty, stupid, and faithless—had been his female counterpart. Maybe her infidelity had been an attempt to reassert her independence, to struggle against the pregnancy that had tied her more securely to Jason. Maybe she'd just been a bad woman. I'd never understood her, and now I never would.

I knew I'd have to go talk to my brother. Though I'd told Jason to stay away from me, he wasn't listening. When had he ever? Maybe he'd taken the temporary truce caused by Crystal's death as a sign of a new state of things.

I sighed and went out the back door. Since I'd slept so late, I'd showered before I'd even made my coffee. I grabbed my old quilted pink jacket off the rack by the back door and pulled it over my jeans and sweater.

I put a mug of coffee on the ground by Jason, and I sat on the upright folding chair close to him. He didn't turn his head, though he knew I was there. His eyes were hidden behind dark glasses.

"You forgiven me?" he asked after he'd taken a gulp of coffee. His voice sounded hoarse and thick. I thought he'd been crying.

"I expect that sooner or later I might," I said. "But I'll never feel the same about you again."

"God, you've gotten hard. You're all the family I've got

left." The dark glasses turned to face me. *You have to forgive me, because you're all I have who can forgive.*

I looked at him, feeling a little exasperated, a little sad. If I was getting harder, it was in response to the world around me. "If you need me so much, I guess you should have thought twice before you set me up like that." I rubbed my face with my free hand. He had some family he didn't know about, and I wasn't going to tell him. He would only try to use Niall, too.

"When will they release Crystal's body?" I asked.

"Maybe in a week," he said. "Then we can have the funeral. Will you come?"

"Yes. Where will it be?"

"There's a chapel out close to Hotshot," he said. "It doesn't look like much."

"The Tabernacle Holiness Church?" It was a peeling, white ramshackle building way out in the country.

He nodded. "Calvin said they do the burials for Hotshot from there. One of the guys in Hotshot is the pastor for it."

"Which one?"

"Marvin Norris."

Marvin was Calvin's uncle, though he was four years younger.

"I think I remember seeing a cemetery out back of the church."

"Yeah. The community digs the hole, one of them puts together the coffin, and one of them does the service. It's real homey and personal."

"You've been to a funeral there before?"

"Yeah, in October. One of the babies died."

There hadn't been an infant death listed in the Bon Temps paper in months. I had to wonder if the baby had been born in a hospital or in one of the houses in Hotshot; if any trace of its existence had ever been recorded.

"Jason, have the police been by any more?"

"Over and over. But I didn't do it, and nothing they say or ask can make that change. Plus, the alibi."

I couldn't argue that.

"How are you fixed as far as work goes?" I wondered if they would fire Jason. It wasn't the first time he'd been in trouble. And though Jason was never guilty of the worst crimes attributed to him, sooner or later his reputation as being a generally okay guy would simply crumple for good.

"Catfish said to take time off until the funeral. They're going to send a wreath to the funeral home when we get her body back."

"What about Hoyt?"

"He hasn't been around," Jason said, sounding puzzled and hurt.

Holly, his fiancée, wouldn't want him hanging around with Jason. I could understand that.

"Mel?" I asked.

"Yeah," Jason said, brightening. "Mel comes by. We worked on his truck yesterday, and this weekend we're going to paint my kitchen." Jason smiled at me, but it faded fast. "I like Mel," he said, "but I miss Hoyt."

That was one of the most honest things I'd ever heard Jason say.

"Haven't you heard anything about this, Sookie?" Jason asked me. "You know—the way you *hear* things? If you could steer the police in the right direction, they could find out who killed my wife and my baby, and I could get my life back."

I didn't think Jason was ever going to get his old life back.

I was sure he wouldn't understand, even if I spelled it out. But then I saw what was in his head in a moment of true clarity. Though Jason couldn't verbalize these ideas, he *did* understand, and he was pretending, pretending hard, that everything would be the same . . . if only he could get out from under the weight of Crystal's death.

"Or if you tell us," he said, "we'll take care of it, Calvin and me."

"I'll do my best," I said. What else could I say? I climbed out of Jason's head and swore to myself I wouldn't get inside again.

After a long silence, he got up. Maybe he'd been waiting to see if I'd offer to make lunch for him. "I guess I'll go back home, then," he said.

"Good-bye."

I heard his truck start up a moment later. I went back in, hanging the jacket back where I'd gotten it.

Amelia had left me a note stuck to the milk carton in the refrigerator. "Hey, roomie!" it said by way of opening. "Sounded like you had company last night. Did I smell a vampire? Heard someone shut the back door about three thirty. Listen, be sure and check the answering machine. You got messages."

Which Amelia had already listened to, because the light wasn't blinking anymore. I pressed the Play button.

"Sookie, this is Arlene. I'm sorry about everything. I wish you'd come by to talk. Give me a call."

I stared at the machine, not sure how I felt about this message. It had been a few days, and Arlene had had time to reconsider stomping out of the bar. Could she possibly mean she wanted to recant her Fellowship beliefs?

There was another message, this one from Sam. "Sookie, can you come in to work a little early today or give me a call? I need to talk to you."

I glanced at the clock. It was just one p.m., and I wasn't due at work until five. I called the bar. Sam picked up.

"Hey, it's Sookie," I said. "What's up? I just got your message."

"Arlene wants to come back to work," he said. "I don't know what to tell her. You got an opinion?"

"She left a message on my answering machine. She wants to talk to me," I said. "I don't know what to think. She's always on some new thing, isn't she? Do you think she could have dropped the Fellowship?"

"If Whit dropped her," he said, and I laughed.

I wasn't so sure I wanted to rebuild our friendship, and the longer I thought about it, the more doubtful I became. Arlene had said some hurtful and awful things to me. If she'd meant them, why would she want to mend fences with a terrible person like me? And if she hadn't meant them, why on earth had they passed her lips? But I felt a twinge when I thought of her children, Coby and Lisa. I'd kept them so many evenings, and I'd been so fond of them. I hadn't seen them in weeks. I found I wasn't too upset about the passing of my relationship with their mother—Arlene had been killing that friendship for some time now. But the kids, I did miss them. I said as much to Sam.

"You're too good, *cher*," he said. "I don't think I want her back here." He'd made up his mind. "I hope she can find another job, and I'll give her a reference for the sake of those kids. But she was causing trouble before this last blowup, and there's no point putting all of us through the wringer."

After I'd hung up, I realized that Sam's decision had

influenced me in favor of seeing my ex-friend. Since Arlene and I weren't going to get the opportunity to gradually make peace at the bar, I'd try to at least fix things so we could nod at each other if we passed in Wal-Mart.

She picked up on the first ring. "Arlene, it's Sookie," I said.

"Hey, hon, I'm glad you called back," she said. There was a moment of silence.

"I thought I'd come over to see you, just for a minute," I said awkwardly. "I'd like to see the kids and talk to you. If that's okay."

"Sure, come over. Give me a few minutes, so I can pick up the mess."

"You don't need to do that for me." I'd cleaned Arlene's trailer many a time in return for some favor she'd done me or because I didn't have anything else to do while she was out and I was there to babysit.

"I don't want to slide back into my old ways," she said cheerfully, sounding so affectionate that my heart lifted . . . for just a second.

But I didn't wait a few minutes.

I left immediately.

I couldn't explain to myself why I wasn't doing what she'd asked me to do. Maybe I'd caught something in Arlene's voice, even over the phone. Maybe I was recalling all the times Arlene had let me down, all the occasions she'd made me feel bad.

I don't think I'd let myself dwell on these incidents before, because they revealed such a colossal pitifulness on my part. I'd needed a friend so badly I'd clung to the meager scraps from Arlene's table, though she'd taken advantage of me time after time. When her dating wind had blown the other way,

she hadn't thought twice about discarding me to win favor
with her current flame.

In fact, the more I thought, the more I was inclined to
turn around and head back to my house. But didn't I owe
Coby and Lisa one more try to mend my relationship with
their mom? I remembered all the board games we'd played,
all the times I'd put them to bed and spent the night in the
trailer because Arlene had called to ask if she could spend the
night away.

What the hell was I doing? Why was I trusting Arlene *now*?

I wasn't, not completely. That was why I was going to
scope out the situation.

Arlene didn't live in a trailer park but on an acre of land a
little west of town that her dad had given her before he passed
away. Only a quarter acre had been cleared, just enough for
the trailer and a small yard. There was an old swing set in
the back that one of Arlene's former admirers had assembled
for the kids, and there were two bikes pushed up against the
back of the trailer.

I was looking at the trailer from the rear because I'd
pulled off the road and into the overgrown yard of a little
house that had stood next door until its bad wiring had
caused a fire a couple of months before. Since then, the frame
house had stood half-charred and forlorn, and the former
renters had found somewhere else to live. I was able to pull
behind the house, because the cold weather had kept the
weeds from taking over.

I picked a path through the fringe of high weeds and trees
that separated this house from Arlene's. Working through
the thickest growth, I made my way to a vantage point where
I could see part of the parking area in front of the trailer and

all of the backyard. Only Arlene's car was visible from the road, since it had been left in the front yard.

From my vantage point, I could see that behind the trailer was parked a black Ford Ranger pickup, maybe ten years old, and a red Buick Skylark of approximately the same vintage. The pickup was loaded down with pieces of wood, one long enough to protrude beyond the truck bed. They measured about four by four, I estimated.

As I watched, a woman I vaguely recognized came out of the back of the trailer onto the little deck. Her name was Helen Ellis, and she'd worked at Merlotte's about four years before. Though Helen was competent and so pretty she'd drawn the men in like flies, Sam had had to fire her for repeated lateness. Helen had been volcanically upset. Lisa and Coby followed Helen onto the deck. Arlene was framed in the doorway. She was wearing a leopard print top over brown stretch pants.

The kids looked so much older than the last time I'd seen them! They looked reluctant and a little unhappy, especially Coby. Helen smiled at them encouragingly and turned back to Arlene to say, "Just let me know when it's over!" There was a pause while Helen seemed to struggle with how to phrase something she didn't want the kids to understand. "She's only getting what she deserves." I could see Helen only in profile, but her cheerful smile made my stomach heave. I swallowed hard.

"Okay, Helen. I'll call you when you can bring 'em back," Arlene said. There was a man standing behind her. He was too far back in the interior for me to identify with certainty, but I thought he was the man I'd hit on the head with a tray a couple of months back, the man who'd been so ugly to Pam and Amelia. He was one of Arlene's new buddies.

Helen and the kids drove off in the Skylark.

Arlene had closed the back door against the chill of the day. I shut my eyes and located her inside the trailer. I found there were two men in there with her. What were they thinking about? I was a little far, but I stretched out with my extra sense.

They were thinking about doing awful things to me.

I crouched under a bare mimosa, feeling as bleak and miserable as I've ever felt. Granted, I'd known for some time that Arlene wasn't truly a good person or even a faithful person. Granted, I'd heard her rant and rave about the eradication of the supernaturals of the world. Granted, I'd come to realize that she'd slipped into regarding me as one of them. But I'd never let myself believe that whatever affection she'd ever felt for me had slipped away entirely, transmuted by the Fellowship's policy of hate.

I pulled my cell phone out of my pocket. I called Andy Bellefleur.

"Bellefleur," he said briskly.

We were hardly buddies, but I sure was glad to hear his voice.

"Andy, it's Sookie," I said, taking care to keep my voice quiet. "Listen, there are two guys in Arlene's trailer with her, and there're some long pieces of wood in the back of their pickup. They don't realize I know they're in the trailer with Arlene. They're planning on doing the same thing to me that was done to Crystal."

"You got anything I could take to court?" he asked cautiously. Andy had always been a closet believer in my telepathy, though that didn't mean he was necessarily a fan of mine.

"No," I said, "they're waiting for me to show up." I crept closer, hoping like hell they weren't looking out the back windows. There was a box of extra-long nails in the pickup bed, too. I had to close my eyes for second as the horror crawled all over me.

"I've got Weiss and Lattesta with me," Andy said. "Would you be willing to go in if we were there to back you up?"

"Sure," I said, feeling anything but. I simply knew I was going to have to do this. It could be the end of any lingering suspicion of Jason. It could mean recompense or at least retribution for the deaths of Crystal and the baby. It could put at least a few of the Fellowship fanatics behind bars and maybe serve as a good lesson to the rest. "Where are you?" I asked, shaking with fear.

"We were already in the car to go to the motel. We can be there in seven minutes," Andy said.

"I parked behind the Freer house," I said. "I gotta go. Someone's coming out the back of the trailer."

Whit Spradlin and his buddy, whose name I couldn't recall, came down the steps and unloaded the wood beams from the pickup. The pieces were already formed into the correct lengths. Whit turned to the trailer and called something, and Arlene opened the door and came down the back steps, her purse over one shoulder. She walked toward the cab of the pickup.

Dammit, she was going to get in and drive away, leaving her car parked in front as though she were there! Any lingering tenderness I'd harbored in my heart burned away at that moment. I looked at my watch. Maybe three more minutes until Andy arrived.

She kissed Whit and waved at the other man, and they went into the trailer to hide so I wouldn't see them. According to their plan, I'd come to the front, knock on the door, and one of them would fling it open and drag me in.

Game over.

Arlene opened the truck door, the keys in her hand.

She had to stay. She was the weak link. I knew this in every way I could know it—intellectually, emotionally, and with my other sense.

This was going to be awful. I braced myself.

"Hi, Arlene," I said, stepping out of my cover.

She shrieked and jumped. "Jesus Christ, Sookie, what are you doing in my backyard?" She made an elaborate fuss of collecting herself. Her head was a snarled tangle of anger and fear and guilt. And regret. There was some, I swear.

"I've been waiting to see you," I said. I had no idea what to do now, but I'd slowed her down a little. I might have to physically tackle her. The men inside hadn't noticed my abrupt appearance, but that wouldn't last long unless I got extremely lucky. And I hadn't had a run of luck, much less extreme luck, lately.

Arlene was standing still, keys in hand. It was easy to get inside her head and rummage around, reading the awful story in there.

"What you doing, getting ready to go, Arlene?" I asked, keeping my voice very quiet. "You're supposed to be inside, waiting for me to get here."

She saw everything, and her eyes closed. Guilty, guilty, guilty. She had tried to construct a bubble to keep the men's intent hidden from herself, to keep it from touching her heart. That hadn't worked—but it hadn't stopped her treachery today, either. Arlene stood exposed to herself.

I said, "You got in too deep." My own voice sounded detached and level. "No one will understand that or forgive it." Her eyes went wide with the knowledge that what I was saying was true.

But I was in for my own kind of shock. I knew, suddenly and surely, that she had not killed Crystal and neither had these men; they'd planned to crucify me in emulation of Crystal's death because it seemed like such a great idea, such an open statement of their opinion of the shapeshifters' announcement. I'd been selected as the sacrificial lamb, despite the fact that they knew for sure I wasn't a shapeshifter; in fact, they thought I wouldn't put up as much of a fight since I was only a shapeshifter sympathizer, not one of the two-natured. I wouldn't be as strong, in their opinion. I found this incredible.

"You're a poor excuse for a woman," I said to Arlene. I couldn't seem to stop, and I couldn't seem to sound anything but matter-of-fact. "You've never told the truth to yourself in your whole life, have you? You still see yourself as a pretty, young thing of twenty-five, and you still think some man will come along and recognize that in you. Someone will take care of you, let you quit working, send your kids to private schools where they'll never have to talk to anyone different from them. That's not gonna happen, Arlene. This is your life." And I swept an open hand at the trailer in its weedy yard, the old truck. It was the meanest thing I'd ever said, and every word of it was true.

And she screamed. She couldn't seem to stop screaming. I looked into her eyes. She kept trying to look away, but she couldn't seem to do that. "You witch!" she sobbed. "You're a witch. There are such things, and you're one of 'em!"

If she'd been right, I could have prevented what happened next.

At that moment, Andy pulled into the Freer yard, just as I had. For all he knew, there was still time to creep up on the trailer. I heard his car more or less at my back. My whole

attention was concentrated on Arlene and the rear door of the
trailer. Weiss, Lattesta, and Andy came up behind me just as
Whit and his friend burst from the back door of the trailer,
rifles in hands.

Arlene and I were standing between two armed camps. I
felt the sun on my arms. I felt a cold breeze pick up my hair
and toss a lock playfully across my face. Over Arlene's shoulder, I saw the face of Whit's friend, and I finally remembered
his name was Donny Boling. He'd had a recent haircut. I
could tell from the white half inch at the base of his neck. He
was wearing an Orville's Stump Grinding T-shirt. His eyes
were a muddy brown. He was aiming at Agent Weiss.

"She has children," I called. "Don't do it!"

His eyes widened with fright.

Donny swung the rifle toward me. He thought, *Shoot
HER.*

I flung myself to the ground as the rifle went off.

"Lay down your arms!" Lattesta screamed. "FBI!"

But they didn't. I don't think his words even registered.

So Lattesta fired. But you couldn't say he hadn't warned
them.

Chapter 12

In the moments following Special Agent Lattesta's demand that the two men lay down their arms, bullets flew through the air like pine pollen in the spring.

Though I was in an exposed position, none of them hit me, which I found absolutely amazing.

Arlene, who didn't dive as fast as I did, got a crease across her shoulder. Agent Weiss took the bullet—the same one that creased Arlene—in the upper right side of her chest. Andy shot Whit Spradlin. Special Agent Lattesta missed Donny Boling with his first shot, got him with his second. It took weeks to establish the sequence, but that was what happened.

And then the firing was over. Lattesta was calling 911 while I was still prone on the ground, counting my fingers and toes to make sure I was intact. Andy was equally quick calling the sheriff's department to report that shots had been fired and an officer and civilians were down.

Arlene was screaming over her little wound like she'd been gut shot.

Agent Weiss was lying in the weeds bleeding, her eyes wide with fear, her mouth clamped shut. The bullet had gone in under her raised arm. She was thinking of her children and her husband and of dying out here in the sticks, leaving them behind. Lattesta pulled off her vest and put pressure on her wound, and Andy ran over to secure the two shooters.

I slowly pushed up to a sitting position. There was no way I could stand. I sat there in the pine needles and dirt and looked at Donny Boling, who was dead. There was not the faintest trace of activity in his brain. Whit was still alive though not in good shape. After Andy gave Arlene a cursory examination and told her to shut up, she quit shrieking and settled down to cry.

I have had lots of things to blame myself about in the course of my life. I added this whole incident to the list as I watched the blood seeping into the dirt around Donny's left side. No one would have gotten shot if I'd just climbed back in my car and driven away. But no, I had to try to catch Crystal's killers. And I knew now—too late—that these idiots weren't even the culprits. I told myself that Andy had asked me to help, that Jason needed me to help . . . but right now, I couldn't foresee feeling okay about this for a long time.

For a brief moment I considered lying back down and wishing myself dead.

"Are you okay?" Andy called after he'd cuffed Whit and checked on Donny.

"Yeah," I said. "Andy, I'm sorry." But he'd run into the front yard to wave down the ambulance. Suddenly there were a lot more people around.

"Are you all right?" asked a woman wearing an EMT

uniform. Her sleeves were folded up neatly to show muscles I didn't know women could develop. You could see each one rippling under her mocha skin. "You look kind of out of it."

"I'm not used to seeing people get shot," I said. Which was mostly true.

"I think you better come sit on this chair over here," she said, and pointed to a folding yard chair that had seen better days. "After I tend to the ones that are bleeding, I'll check you out."

"Audrey!" called her partner, a man with a belly like a bay window. "I need another pair of hands here." Audrey hustled over to help, and another team of EMTs came running around the trailer. I had nearly the same dialogue with them.

Agent Weiss left for the hospital first, and I gathered that the plan was to stabilize her at the hospital in Clarice and then airlift her to Shreveport. Whit was loaded into the second ambulance. A third arrived for Arlene. The dead guy waited for the coroner to appear.

I waited for whatever would happen next.

Lattesta stood staring blankly into the pines. His hands were bloodstained from pressing on Weiss's wound. As I watched, he shook himself. The purpose flooded back into his face, and his thoughts began flowing once again. He and Andy began to consult.

By now the yard was teeming with law enforcement people, all of whom seemed to be very pumped. Officer-involved shootings are not that ordinary in Bon Temps or in Renard Parish. When the FBI is represented at the scene, the excitement and tension were practically quadrupled.

Several more people asked me if I was all right, but no one seemed to be anxious to tell me what to do or to suggest I remove myself, so I sat in the rickety chair with my hands in my lap. I watched all the activity, and I tried to keep my mind blank. That wasn't possible.

I was worried about Agent Weiss, and I was still feeling the ebbing power of the huge wave of guilt that had washed over me. I should have been upset that the Fellowship guy was dead, I suppose. But I wasn't.

After a while, it occurred to me that I was also going to be late for work if this elaborate process didn't get a move on. I knew that was a trivial consideration, when I was staring at the blood that had soaked into the ground, but I also knew it wouldn't be trivial to my boss.

I called Sam. I don't remember what I said, but I remember I had to talk him out of coming to get me. I told Sam there were plenty of people on-site and most of them were armed. After that, I had nothing to do but stare off into the woods. They were a tangle of fallen branches, leaves, and various shades of brown, broken up by little pines of various heights that had volunteered. The bright day made the patterns of shadow and shade fascinating.

As I looked into the depths of the woods, I became aware that something was looking back. Yards back within the tree line, a man was standing; no, not a man—a fairy. I can't read fairies at all clearly; they're not as blank as vampires, but they're the closest I've found.

It was easy to read the hostility in his stance, though. This fairy was not on my great-grandfather's side. This fairy would have been glad to see me lying on the ground bleeding. I sat up straighter, abruptly aware I had no idea whether all the police officers in the world could keep me safe from a fairy. My heart thudded once again with alarm, responding to the adrenaline in a sort of tired way. I wanted to tell someone that I was in danger, but I knew that if I pointed the fairy out to any one of the people present, not only would he fade back into the woods, but I might be endangering the human. I'd done enough of that this day.

As I half rose from the lawn chair with no very good plan in mind, the fairy turned his back on me and vanished.

Can't I have a moment's peace? At this thought, I had to bend over and cover my face with my hands because I was laughing, and it wasn't good laughter. Andy came over and squatted in front of me, tried to look into my face. "Sookie," he said, and for once his voice was gentle. "Hey, girl, get it together. You got to come talk to Sheriff Dearborn."

Not only did I talk to Bud Dearborn, I also had to talk to lots of other people. Later, I couldn't remember any of the conversations I had. I told the truth to whoever asked me questions.

I didn't mention seeing the fairy in the woods simply because no one asked me, "Did you see anyone else here this afternoon?" When I had a second of not feeling stunned and miserable, I wondered why he'd shown himself, why he'd come. Was he tracking me somehow? Was there some kind of supernatural bug planted on me?

"Sookie," Bud Dearborn said. I blinked.

"Yessir?" I stood up, and my muscles were trembling.

"You can go now, and we'll talk to you again later," he said.

"Thanks," I told him, hardly aware of what I was saying. I climbed into my car, feeling absolutely numb. I told myself to drive home and put on my waitress outfit and get to work. Hustling drinks would be better than sitting at home recycling the events of the day, if I could manage to stand up that long.

Amelia was at work, so I had the house to myself as I pulled on my working pants and my long-sleeved Merlotte's

T-shirt. I felt cold to the bone and wished for the first time that Sam had thought about stocking a Merlotte's sweatshirt. My reflection in the bathroom mirror was awful: I was white as a vampire, I had big circles under my eyes, and I guessed I looked exactly like someone who'd seen a lot of people bleeding that day.

The evening felt cold and still as I walked out to my car. Night would fall soon. Since Eric and I had bonded, I'd found myself thinking of him every day as the sky grew dark. Now that we'd slept together, my thoughts had turned into cravings. I tried to stuff him in the back of my mind on the drive to the bar, but he persisted in popping to the fore.

Maybe because the day had been such a nightmare, I discovered I would give my entire savings account to see Eric *right now*. I trudged toward the employee door, gripping the trowel stuffed in my shoulder bag. I thought I was ready for an attack, but I was so preoccupied I didn't send out my extra sense to detect another presence, and I didn't see Antoine in the shadow of the Dumpster until he stepped out to greet me. He was smoking a cigarette.

"Geez Louise, Antoine, you scared me to death."

"Sorry, Sookie. You planning on doing some planting?" He eyed the trowel I'd whipped out of my bag. "We ain't too busy this evening. I took me a minute to have a smoke."

"Everybody calm tonight?" I stuffed the trowel down into my purse without trying to explain. Maybe he would chalk it up to my general strangeness.

"Yeah, no one preaching to us; no one getting killed." He smiled. "D'Eriq's full of talk about some guy showing up earlier that D'Eriq thought was a fairy. D'Eriq's on the simple side, but he can see stuff no one else can. But—fairies?"

"Not fairy like gay, but fairy like Tinker Bell?" I'd thought

I didn't have enough remaining energy to be alarmed. I'd thought wrong. I glanced around the parking lot with considerable alarm.

"Sookie? It's true?" Antoine was staring at me.

I shrugged weakly. Busted.

"Shit," Antoine said. "Well, shit. This ain't the same world I was born into, is it?"

"No, Antoine. It isn't. If D'Eriq says anything else, please tell me. It's important." Could have been my great-grandfather watching over me, or his son Dillon. Or it could have been Mr. Hostile who'd been lurking in the woods. What had set the fae world off? For years, I'd never seen one. Now you couldn't throw a trowel without hitting a fairy.

Antoine eyed me doubtfully. "Sure, Sookie. You in any trouble I should know about?"

Hip-deep in alligators. "No, no. I'm just trying to avoid a problem," I said, because I didn't want Antoine to worry and I especially didn't want him to share that worry with Sam. Sam was sure to be worried enough.

Of course, Sam had heard several versions of the events at Arlene's trailer, and I had to give him a quick summary as I got ready to work. He was deeply upset about the intentions of Donny and Whit, and when I told him Donny was dead, he said, "Whit should have got killed, too."

I wasn't sure I was hearing him right. But when I looked into Sam's face, I could see he was really angry, really vengeful. "Sam, I think enough people have died," I said. "I haven't exactly forgiven them, and maybe that's not even something I can do, but I don't think they were the ones who killed Crystal."

Sam turned away with a snort and put a bottle of rum away with such force that I thought it might shatter.

Despite a measure of alarm, as it turned out I treasured that evening . . . because nothing happened.

No one suddenly announced that he was a gargoyle and wanted a place at the American table.

No one stomped out in a hissy. No one tried to kill me or warn me or lie to me; no one paid me any special attention at all. I was back to being part of the ambience at Merlotte's, a situation that used to make me bored. I remembered the evenings before I'd met Bill Compton, when I'd known there were vampires but hadn't actually met one or seen one in the flesh. I remembered how I'd longed to meet an actual vampire. I'd believed their press, which alleged that they were victims of a virus that left them allergic to various things (sunlight, garlic, food) and only able to survive by ingesting blood.

That part, at least, had been quite true.

As I worked, I thought about the fairies. They were different from the vampires and the weres. Fairies could escape and go to their very own world, however that happened. It was a world I had no desire to visit or see. Fairies had never been human. At least vampires might remember what being human was like, and weres were human most of the time, even if they had a different culture; being a were was like having dual citizenship, I figured. This was an important difference between the fairies and other supernaturals, and it made the fairies more frightening. As the evening wore on and I plodded from table to table, making an effort to get the orders right and to serve with a smile, I had times of wondering whether it would have been better if I'd never met my great-grandfather at all. There was a lot of attraction in that idea.

I served Jane Bodehouse her fourth drink and signaled to

Sam that we needed to cut her off. Jane would drink whether we served her or not. Her decision to quit drinking hadn't lasted a week, but I'd never imagined it would. She'd made such resolutions before, with the same result.

At least if Jane drank here, we would make sure she got home okay. *I killed a man yesterday.* Maybe her son would come get her; he was a nice guy who never took a sip with alcohol in it. *I saw a man get shot dead today.* I had to stand still for a minute because the room seemed to be a little lopsided.

After a second or two, I felt steadier. I wondered if I could make it through the evening. By dint of putting one foot in front of the other and blocking out the bad stuff (from past experience I was an expert at that), I made it through. I even remembered to ask Sam how his mother was doing.

"She's getting better," he said, closing out the cash register. "My stepdad's filed for divorce, too. He says she doesn't deserve any alimony because she didn't disclose her true nature when they got married."

Though I'd always be on Sam's side, whatever it was, I had to admit (strictly to myself) that I could see his stepdad's point.

"I'm sorry," I said inadequately. "I know this is a tough time for your mom, for your whole family."

"My brother's fiancée isn't too happy about it, either," Sam said.

"Oh, no, Sam. She's freaked-out by the fact that your mom—?"

"Yeah, and of course she knows about me now, too. My brother and sister are getting used to it. So they're okay—but Deidra doesn't feel that way. And I don't think her parents do, either."

I patted Sam's shoulder because I didn't know what to say.

He gave me a little smile and then a hug. He said, "You've been a rock, Sookie," and then he stiffened. Sam's nostrils flared. "You smell like—there's a trace of vampire," he said, and all the warmth had gone out of his voice. He released me and looked at me hard.

I'd really scrubbed myself and I'd used all my usual skin products afterward, but Sam's fine nose had picked up that trace of scent Eric had left behind.

"Well," I said, and then stopped dead. I tried to organize what I wanted to say, but the past forty hours had been so tiring. "Yes," I said, "Eric was over last night." I left it at that. My heart sank. I'd thought of trying to explain to Sam about my great-grandfather and the trouble we were in, but Sam had enough troubles of his own. Plus, the whole staff was feeling pretty miserable about Arlene and her arrest.

There was too much happening.

I had another moment of sickening dizziness, but it passed quickly, as it had before. Sam didn't even notice. He was lost in gloomy reflection, at least as far as I could read his twisty shapeshifter mind.

"Walk me to my car," I said impulsively. I needed to get home and get some sleep, and I had no idea if Eric would show up tonight or not. I didn't want anyone else to pop up and surprise me, as Murry had done. I didn't want anyone trying to lure me to my doom or shooting guns in my vicinity. No more betrayal by people I cared for, either.

I had a long list of requirements, and I knew that wasn't a good thing.

As I pulled my purse out of the drawer in Sam's office and called good night to Antoine, who was still cleaning in the kitchen, I realized that the height of my ambition was to get home and go to bed without talking to anyone else, and to sleep undisturbed all night.

I wondered if that was possible.

Sam didn't say anything else about Eric, and he seemed to attribute my asking him to escort me as an attack of nerves after the incident at the trailer. I could have stood just inside the bar door and looked out with my other sense, but it was best to be double careful; my telepathy and Sam's nose made a good combination. He was eager to check the parking lot. In fact, he sounded almost disappointed when he announced there was nothing out there but us.

As I drove away, in my rearview mirror I saw Sam leaning on the hood of his truck, which was parked in front of his trailer. He had his hands in his pockets, and he was glaring at the gravel on the ground as if he hated the sight of it. Just as I pulled around the corner of the bar, Sam patted the truck's hood in an absentminded way and walked back into the bar, his shoulders bowed.

Chapter 13

"Amelia, what works against fairies?" I asked. *I'd gotten* a full night's sleep, and I was feeling much better in consequence. Amelia's boss was out of town, so she had the afternoon off.

"You mean something that'll act as a fairy repellent?" she asked.

"Yeah, or cause fairy death even," I said. "That's preferable to me getting killed. I need to defend myself."

"I don't know too much about fairies, since they're so rare and secretive," she said. "I wasn't sure they still existed until I heard about your great-grandfather. You need something like Mace for fairies, huh?"

I had a sudden idea. "I've already got some, Amelia," I said, feeling happier than I had in days. I looked in the racks on the door of the refrigerator. Sure enough, there was a bottle of ReaLemon. "Now all I got to do is buy a water pistol at Wal-Mart," I said. "It's not summer, but surely they've got some over in the toy department."

"That works?"

"Yeah, a little-known supernatural fact. Just contact with it is fatal. I understand if it's ingested, the result's even quicker. If you could squirt it in a fairy's open mouth, that would be one dead fairy."

"Sounds like you're in big trouble, Sookie." Amelia had been reading, but now she laid her book on the table.

"Yeah, I am."

"You want to talk about it?"

"It's complicated. Hard to explain."

"I understand the definition of 'complicated.'"

"Sorry. Well, it might not be safe for you to learn the ins and outs of it. Can you help? Will your wards work against fairies?"

"I'll check my sources," Amelia said in that wise way she had when she didn't have a clue. "I'll call Octavia if I have to."

"I'd appreciate it. And if you need some kind of spell-casting ingredients, money is no object." I'd gotten a check in the mail that very morning from Sophie-Anne's estate. Mr. Cataliades had come through with the money she'd owed me. I was going to run it to the bank this afternoon, since the drive-through would be open.

Amelia took a deep breath, stalled. I waited. Since she's an exceptionally clear broadcaster, I knew what she wanted to talk about, but to keep our relationship on an even keel, I simply held out until she spoke out loud.

"I heard from Tray, who's got a couple friends on the police force—though not many—that Whit and Arlene are denying up and down that they killed Crystal. They . . . Arlene says they planned on making you an example of what happens to people who hang around with the supernatural; that it was Crystal's death that gave them the idea."

My good mood evaporated. I felt a profound depression settle on my shoulders. Hearing this spoken out loud made it seem even more horrible. I could think of no comment to offer. "What does Tray hear about what might happen to them?" I said finally.

"Depends on whose bullet hit Agent Weiss. If it was Donny's—well, he's dead. Whit can say he was being shot at, so he shot back. He can say he didn't know anything about a plan to harm you. He was visiting his girlfriend and happened to have some pieces of wood in the back of his pickup."

"What about Helen Ellis?"

"She told Andy Bellefleur she just came to the trailer to pick up the kids because they'd done really well on their report cards, and she'd promised to take them to the Sonic for an ice cream treat. Any more than that, she doesn't know diddly-squat." Amelia's face expressed extreme skepticism.

"So Arlene is the only one talking." I dried the baking sheet. I'd made biscuits that morning. Baking therapy, cheap and satisfying.

"Yeah, and she may recant any minute. She was real shaken up when she talked, but she'll wise up. Maybe too late. At least we can hope so."

I'd been right; Arlene *was* the weakest link. "She gotten a lawyer?"

"Yeah. She couldn't afford Sid Matt Lancaster, so she hired Melba Jennings."

"Good move," I said thoughtfully. Melba Jennings was only a couple of years older than me. She was the only African-American woman in Bon Temps who'd been to law school. She had a hard-as-nails facade and was confrontational in the extreme. Other lawyers had been known to take incredible detours to dodge Melba if they saw her coming. "Makes her look less of a bigot."

"I don't think it's going to fool anyone, but Melba's like a pit bull." Melba had been in Amelia's insurance agency on behalf of a couple of clients. "I better go make my bed," Amelia said, standing and stretching. "Hey, Tray and I are going to the movies in Clarice tonight. Want to come?"

"You've really been trying to include me on your dates. You're not getting bored with Tray already, I hope?"

"Not a bit," Amelia said, sounding faintly surprised. "In fact, I think he's great. Tray's buddy Drake has been pestering him, though. Drake's seen you in the bar, and he wants to get to know you."

"He a Were?"

"Just a guy. Thinks you're pretty."

"I don't do regular guys," I said, smiling. "It just doesn't work out very well." It "worked out" disastrously, as a matter of fact. Imagine knowing what your date thinks of you every single minute.

Plus, there was the issue of Eric and our undefined but intimate relationship.

"Keep the possibility on the back burner. He's really cute, and by cute, I mean hotter than a steam iron."

After Amelia had tromped up the stairs, I poured myself a glass of tea. I tried to read, but I found I couldn't concentrate on the book. Finally, I slid my paper bookmark in and stared into space, thinking about a lot of things.

I wondered where Arlene's children were now. With Arlene's old aunt, who lived over in Clarice? Or still with Helen Ellis? Did Helen like Arlene enough to keep Coby and Lisa?

I couldn't rid myself of a nagging feeling of responsibility for the kids' sad situation, but it was going to have to be one of those things I simply suffered. The person really responsible was Arlene. There was nothing I could do for them.

As if thinking of children had triggered a nerve in the universe, the phone rang. I got up and went to the wall-mounted unit in the kitchen. "Hello," I said without enthusiasm.

"Ms. Stackhouse? Sookie?"

"Yes, this is she," I said properly.

"This is Remy Savoy."

My dead cousin Hadley's ex, father of her child. "I'm glad you called. How's Hunter?" Hunter was a "gifted" child, God bless him. He'd been "gifted" the same way I had been.

"He's fine. Uh, about that thing."

"Sure." We were going to talk telepathy.

"He's going to need some guidance soon. He'll be starting kindergarten. They're going to notice. I mean, it'll take a while, but sooner or later . . ."

"Yeah, they'll notice, all right." I opened my mouth to suggest that Remy bring Hunter over on my next day off or that I could drive to Red Ditch. But then I remembered that I was the target of a group of homicidal fairies. Not a good time for a young 'un to come visiting, and who's to say they couldn't follow me to Remy's little house? So far none of them knew about Hunter. I hadn't even told my great-grandfather about Hunter's special talent. If Niall himself didn't know, maybe none of the hostiles had uncovered the information.

On the whole, better to take no risks.

"I really want to meet with him and get to know him. I promise I'll help him as much as I can," I said. "Right now, it just isn't possible. But since we have a little time to spare before kindergarten . . . maybe in a month or so?"

"Oh," Remy said in a nonplussed way. "I was hoping to bring him over on my day off."

"I have a little situation here that I have to resolve." If I was alive after it was resolved . . . but I wasn't going to imagine that. I tried to think of a palatable excuse, and of course, I did have one. "My sister-in-law just died," I told Remy. "Can I call you when I'm not so busy with the details of . . ." I couldn't think of a way to wrap up that sentence. "I promise it'll be soon. If you don't have a day off, maybe Kristen could bring him?" Kristen was Remy's girlfriend.

"Well, that's part of the problem," Remy said, and he sounded tired but also a little amused. "Hunter told Kristen that he knew she didn't really like him, and that she should stop thinking about his daddy without any clothes on."

I drew a deep breath, tried not to laugh, didn't manage it. "I *am* sorry," I said. "How did Kristen handle that?"

"She started crying. Then she told me she loved me but my kid was a freak, and she left."

"Worst possible scenario," I said. "Ah . . . do you think she'll tell other people?"

"Don't see why she wouldn't."

This sounded depressingly familiar: shades of my painful childhood. "Remy, I'm sorry," I said. Remy had seemed like a nice guy on our brief acquaintance, and I had been able to see he was devoted to his son. "If it makes you feel any better, I survived that somehow."

"But did your parents?" There was a trace of a smile in his voice, to his credit.

"No," I said. "However, it didn't have anything to do with me. They got caught by a flash flood when they were driving home one night. It was pouring rain, visibility was terrible, the water was black like the road, and they just drove down onto the bridge and got swept away." Something buzzed in my brain, some kind of signal that this thought was significant.

"I'm sorry. I was just joking," Remy was saying in a shocked voice.

"No, no problem. Just one of those things," I said, the way you do when you don't want the other person to fuss about your feelings.

We left it that I would call him when I had "some free time." (That actually meant "when no one's trying to kill me," but I didn't explain that to Remy.) I hung up and sat on the stool by the kitchen counter. I was thinking about my parents' deaths for the first time in a while. I had some sad memories, but that was the saddest of all. Jason had been ten, and I had been seven, so my recollection wasn't precise, but we'd talked about it over the years, of course, and my grand-mother had recounted the story many times, especially as she grew older. It never varied. The torrential rain, the road leading down into the little hollow where the creek ran, the black water . . . and they'd been swept away into the dark. The truck had been found the next day; their bodies, a day or two after that.

I got dressed for work automatically. I slicked my hair up in an extra-tight ponytail, making sure any stray hairs were gelled into place. As I was tying my shoes, Amelia dashed downstairs to tell me that she'd checked her witch reference books.

"The best way to kill fairies is with iron." Her face was lit with triumph. I hated to rain on her parade. Lemons were even better, but it was kind of hard to slip a fairy a lemon without the fairy realizing it.

"I knew that," I said, trying not to sound depressed. "I mean, I appreciate the effort, but I need to be able to knock

them out." So I could run away. I didn't know if I could stand
to have to hose down the driveway again.

Of course, killing the enemy beat the alternative: letting
them catch me and do what they wished with me.

Amelia was ready for her date with Tray. She was wearing high heels with her designer jeans, an unusual look for
Amelia.

"What's with the heels?" I asked, and Amelia grinned,
displaying her excellent white teeth.

"Tray likes 'em," she said. "With the jeans on *or* off. You
should see the lingerie I'm wearing!"

"I'll pass," I said.

"If you want to meet us after you get off work, I'm betting
Drake will be there. He's seriously interested in getting to
know you. And he's cute, though his looks may not exactly
appeal to you."

"Why? What's this Drake look like?" I asked, mildly
curious.

"That's the freaky part. He looks a lot like your brother."
Amelia looked at me doubtfully. "That might weird you out,
huh?"

I felt all the blood drain out of my face. I'd gotten to my
feet to leave, but I sat down abruptly.

"Sookie? What's the matter? Sookie?" Amelia was hover-
ing around me anxiously.

"Amelia," I croaked, "you got to avoid this guy. I mean it.
You and Tray get away from him. And for God's sake, don't
answer any questions about me!"

I could see from the guilt on her face she had already
answered quite a few. Though she was a clever witch, Amelia couldn't always tell when people weren't really *people*.

Evidently, neither could Tray—though the sweet smell of even a half fairy should have alerted a Were. Maybe Dermot had the same scent-masking ability that his father, my great-grandfather, did.

"Who is he?" Amelia asked. She was scared, which was good.

"He's . . ." I tried to formulate the best explanation. "He wants to kill me."

"Does this have something to do with Crystal's death?"

"I don't think so," I said. I tried to give the possibility some rational consideration, found my brain simply couldn't deal with the idea.

"I don't get it," Amelia said. "We have months—well, weeks—of nothing but plain old life, and then, all of a sudden, here we are!" She threw up her hands.

"You can move back to New Orleans if you want to," I said, my voice faltering. Of course, Amelia knew she could leave anytime she wanted, but I wanted to make it clear I wasn't sucking her into my problems unless she chose to be sucked. So to speak.

"No," she said firmly. "I like it here, and my house in New Orleans isn't ready, anyway."

She kept saying that. Not that I wanted her to leave, but I couldn't see what the delay was. After all, her dad was a builder.

"You don't miss New Orleans?"

"Of course I do," Amelia said. "But I like it here, and I like my little suite upstairs, and I like Tray, and I like my little jobs that keep me going. And I also like—a *hell* of a lot—being out of my dad's line of sight." She patted me on the shoulder. "You go off to work and don't worry. If I haven't thought of anything by morning, I'll call Octavia. Now that I know the deal about this Drake, I'll stonewall him. And Tray will, too. No one can stonewall like Tray."

"He's very dangerous, Amelia," I said. I couldn't impress that on my roommate emphatically enough.

"Yeah, yeah, I get that," she said. "But you know, I'm not any little honey myself, and Dawson can fight with the best of 'em."

We gave each other a hug, and I allowed myself to immerse in Amelia's mind. It was warm, busy, curious, and . . . forward-looking. No brooding on the past for Amelia Broadway. She gave me a pat on the back to signal she was letting go, and we stepped back from each other.

I ran by the bank, then I stopped at Wal-Mart. After a bit of searching, I found one little rack of water guns. I got a two-pack of the clear plastic version, one blue and one yellow. When I thought of the ferocity and strength of the fairy race, and the fact that it took all I had to open the damn blister pack and extricate the water pistols, my chosen method of defense seemed ludicrous. I'd be armed with a plastic water pistol and a trowel.

I tried to clear my mind of all the worries that were plaguing me. There was so much to think about. . . . Actually, there was so much to fear. It might be time to take a leaf from Amelia's book and look forward. What did I need to do *tonight*? Which one of my ongoing worries could I actually do something to solve? I could listen in the bar tonight for clues about Crystal's death, as Jason had asked me to do. (I would have done it anyway, but it seemed even more important to track down her killers now that danger seemed to be piling up from all directions.) I could arm myself against fairy attack. I could be alert for any more Fellowship gangs. And I could try to arrange some more defense.

After all, I was supposed to be under the protection of the Shreveport Were pack because I'd helped them out. I was also under the protection of the new vampire regime because I'd saved their leader's ass. Felipe de Castro would have been a pile of ash if not for me; for that matter, so would Eric. Wasn't this the best time in the world to call in those markers?

I got out of my car behind Merlotte's. I looked up at the sky, but it was cloudy. I thought it was only a week after the new moon. And it was definitely full dark. I pulled my cell phone out of my purse. I'd discovered Eric's cell number scrawled on the back of one of his business cards, tucked halfway under my bedside phone. He answered on the second ring.

"Yes," he said, and I was able to tell by that one word that he was with others.

A little shiver went down my spine at the sound of his voice.

"Eric," I said, and then wished I'd spent a little time framing my request. "The king said he owed me," I continued, realizing this was a little bald and bold. "I'm in real danger. I wonder what he could do about that."

"The threat involving your older kin?" Yes, he was definitely with other people.

"Yes. The, ah, enemy has been trying to get Amelia and Tray to introduce him to me. He doesn't seem to realize I would recognize him, or maybe he's very good at pretending. He's supposed to be on the anti-human side, but he's half human. I don't understand his behavior."

"I see," Eric said after an appreciable pause. "So protection is necessary."

"Yes."

"And you ask this as . . . ?"

If he'd been with his own underlings, he'd have told them to leave so he could talk to me frankly. Since he hadn't done that, he was probably with one of the Nevada vamps: Sandy Sechrest, Victor Madden, or Felipe de Castro himself, though that was unlikely. Castro's far more lucrative business ventures in Nevada required his presence most of the time. I finally realized Eric was trying to find out if I was asking as his bed buddy and "wife," or as someone he owed big-time.

"I ask this as someone who saved Felipe de Castro's life," I said.

"I'll present this petition to Victor, since he's here at the bar," Eric said smoothly. "I'll get back to you this night."

"Great." Mindful of vamps' extreme hearing, I added, "I appreciate that, Eric," as if we were friendly acquaintances.

Mentally dodging the question of what we actually were to each other, I tucked away the cell phone and went into work, hustling because I was a couple of minutes late. Now that I'd talked to Eric, I felt much more optimistic about my chances of survival.

Chapter 14

I kept my mental ears open that night, so it was a hard evening for me. After years of practice and some help from Bill, I'd learned to block out most of the thoughts of the humans around me. But tonight was just like the bad old days, when I'd smiled all the time to cover the confusion in my head caused by the constant bombardment of mental mutterings.

When I walked past the table where Bud Dearborn and his ancient crony Sid Matt Lancaster were having chicken baskets and beers, I heard, *Crystal's no great loss, but no one gets crucified in Renard Parish. . . . We gotta solve that case,* and *Got me some genuine werewolves for clients. I wish Elva Deane had lived to see this; she woulda loved it.* But mostly Sid Matt was thinking about his hemorrhoids and his spreading cancer.

Oh, gosh, I hadn't known. My next pass by his table, I patted the venerable lawyer on the shoulder. "Let me know if you need anything," I said, and met his turtlelike stare with a blank face. He could take it any way he chose, as long as he knew I was willing to help.

When you throw out your net that wide, you come up with a lot of trash. I found out over the course of the evening that Tanya thought she might be settling down permanently with Calvin, that Jane Bodehouse thought she had chlamydia and wondered who was responsible, and that Kevin and Kenya, police officers who always requested the same shift, were actually living together now. Since Kenya was black and Kevin couldn't be whiter, this was causing Kevin's folks some problems, but he was standing firm. Kenya's brother wasn't too happy about her living situation, either, but he wasn't going to beat up Kevin or anything like that. I gave them a big smile when I brought them bourbon and Cokes, and they smiled back. It was so rare to see Kenya crack a grin that I almost laughed. She looked about five years younger when she smiled.

Andy Bellefleur came in with his new wife, Halleigh. I liked Halleigh, and we hugged each other. Halleigh was thinking she might be pregnant, and it would be mighty early in the marriage for them to start a family, but Andy was quite a bit older than her. This maybe-pregnancy hadn't been planned, so she was pretty worried about how Andy would take the news. Since I was laying myself out there tonight, I tried something new. I sent my extra sense down into Halleigh's belly. If she really was pregnant, it was too soon for the little brain to be registering.

Andy was thinking Halleigh had been quiet the past couple of days, and he was worried something was wrong with her. He was also worried about the investigation of Crystal's death, and when he felt Bud Dearborn's eyes on him, he wished he'd picked any other place in Bon Temps for his evening out. The gunfight at Arlene's trailer was haunting his dreams.

Other people in the bar were thinking about typical stuff.

What are the all-time most popular thoughts? Well, they're really, really boring.

Most people think about their money problems, what they need from the store, what housework they have to do, how their jobs are going. They worry about their kids . . . a lot. They brood over issues with their bosses and their spouses and their coworkers and other members of their churches.

On the whole, 95 percent of what I hear is nothing anybody'd want to write down in her diary.

Every now and then the guys (less often, the women) think about sex with someone they see in the bar—but honestly, that's so common I can brush it aside, unless they're thinking about me. That's pretty disgusting. The sex ideas multiply with the drinks consumed; no surprise there.

The people thinking about Crystal and her death were the law enforcement people charged with finding out who'd killed her. If one of the culprits was in the bar, he was simply not thinking about what he'd done. And there had to be more than a single person involved. Setting up a cross was not something a man on his own could handle; at least not without a *lot* of preparation and some elaborate arrangement of pulleys. You'd have to be some kind of supernatural to pull it off by yourself.

This was Andy Bellefleur's train of thought while he waited for his crispy chicken salad.

I had to agree with him. I'd bet Calvin had already considered that scenario. Calvin had sniffed the body, and he hadn't said he'd smelled another wereanimal of any kind. But then I recalled that one of the two men who'd been wheeling the body out had been a supe.

As far as learning anything new, I was drawing a blank until Mel came in. Mel, who lived in one of Sam's rental duplexes, looked like a reject from the cast of *Robin Hood, the Musical* tonight. His longish light brown hair, neat mustache and beard, and tight pants gave him a theatrical air.

Mel surprised me by giving me a half hug before he sat down, as if I were a good buddy of his.

If this behavior was because he and my brother were both panthers . . . but that still didn't make a lot of sense. None of the other werepanthers got cozy with me because of Jason— far from it. The Hotshot community had been a lot warmer toward me when Calvin Norris had been thinking of asking me to be his mate. Did Mel have a secret yearning to go out with me? That would be . . . unpleasant and unwelcome.

I took a little trip into Mel's head, where I saw no lusty thoughts about me. If he'd been attracted, he'd have been thinking them, since I was right in front of him. Mel *was* thinking about the things Catfish Hennessy, Jason's boss, had been saying about Jason in Bon Temps Auto Parts that day. Catfish's tolerance balloon had burst, and he'd told Mel he was thinking about firing Jason.

Mel was plenty worried about my brother, bless his heart. I'd wondered my whole life how someone as selfish as my brother could attract such faithful friends. My great-grandfather had told me that people with a trace of fairy blood were more attractive to other humans, so maybe that explained it.

I went behind the bar to pour some more tea for Jane Bodehouse, who was trying to be sober today because she was trying to compile a list of the guys who might have given her chlamydia. A bar is a bad place to start a sobriety program—but Jane had hardly any chance of succeeding, anyway. I put a slice of lemon in the tea and carried it to Jane, watched her hands shake as she picked up the glass and drank from it.

"You want something to eat?" I asked, keeping my voice low and quiet. Just because I'd never seen a drunk reform in a bar, that didn't mean it couldn't happen.

Jane shook her head silently. Her dyed brown hair was already escaping the clip that held it back, and her heavy black sweater was covered with bits of this and that. Her makeup had been applied with a shaky hand. I could see the lipstick caked in the creases in her lips. Most of the area alcoholics might stop in Merlotte's every now and then, but they based themselves at the Bayou. Jane was our only "resident" alkie since old Willie Chenier had died. When Jane was in the bar, she always sat on the same stool. Hoyt had made a label for it when he'd had too much to drink one night, but Sam had made him take it off.

I looked in Jane's head for an awful minute or two, and I watched the slow shifting of thoughts behind her eyes, noticed the broken veins in her cheeks. The thought of becoming like Jane was enough to scare almost anyone sober.

I turned away to find Mel standing beside me. He was on his way to the men's room, because that's what was in his head when I looked.

"You know what they do in Hotshot with people like that?" he asked quietly, nodding his head toward Jane as if she couldn't see or hear him. (Actually, I thought he was right about that. Jane was turned so inward that she didn't seem to be acknowledging the world much today.)

"No," I said, startled.

"They let them die," he said. "They don't offer them food

or water or shelter, if the person can't seek it for himself or herself."

I'm sure my horror showed on my face.

"It's kindest in the end," he said. He drew a deep, shuddering breath. "Hotshot has its ways of getting rid of the weak."

He went on his way, his back stiff.

I patted Jane on the shoulder, but I'm afraid I wasn't really thinking about her. I was wondering what Mel had done to deserve his exile to a duplex in Bon Temps. If it had been me, I would have been happy to be rid of the multiple ties of kinship and the microscopic hierarchy of the little cluster of houses huddled around the old crossroads, but I could tell that wasn't the way Mel felt about it.

Mel's ex-wife had a margarita in Merlotte's from time to time. I thought I might do a little research on my brother's new buddy the next time Ginjer dropped by.

Sam asked me a couple of times if I was okay, and I was surprised by the strength of my desire to talk to him about everything that had happened lately. I was astonished to realize how often I confided in Sam, how much he knew about my secret life. But I knew that Sam had enough on his plate right now. He was on the phone with his sister and his brother several times during the evening, which was really unusual for him. He looked harassed and worried, and it would be selfish to add to that load of worry.

The cell phone in my apron pocket vibrated a couple of times, and when I had a free moment, I ducked into the ladies' room and checked my text messages. One from Eric. "Protection coming," it said. That was good. There was another message, and this one was from Alcide Herveaux, the Shreveport packleader. "Tray called. Trouble Ur way?" it read. "We owe U."

My chances of survival had risen considerably, and I felt much more cheerful as I finished out my shift.

It was good to have stockpiled favors with both vampires and werewolves. Maybe all the shit I'd gone through last fall would prove to have been worth it after all.

All in all, though, I had to say my project for the evening had been a washout. Sure, after asking Sam for permission, I'd filled both the plastic water guns with juice from the lemons in the refrigerator (intended for iced tea). I thought maybe real lemons would somehow be more potent than the bottled lemon juice at home. So I felt a little safer, but the sum total of my knowledge about the death of Crystal had not increased by one fact. Either the murderers hadn't come in the bar, weren't fretting over the evil thing they'd done, or weren't thinking about it at the moment I was looking inside their heads. *Or*, I thought, *all of the above.*

Chapter 15

I had vampire protection, of a sort, waiting for me after work. Bubba was standing by my car when I left Merlotte's. He grinned when he saw me, and I was glad to give him a hug. Most people wouldn't have been pleased to see a mentally defective vampire with a penchant for cat blood, but I'd become fond of Bubba.

"When did you get back in town?" I asked. Bubba had gotten caught in New Orleans during Katrina, and he'd required a long recovery. The vampires were willing to accommodate him, because he had been one of the most famous people in the world until he'd been brought over in a morgue in Memphis.

"'Bout a week ago. Good to see you, Miss Sookie." Bubba's fangs slid out to show me how glad. Just as quickly, they snicked back into concealment. Bubba still had talent. "I've been traveling. I've been staying with friends. But I was in Fangtasia tonight visiting Mr. Eric, and he asked if I'd like the job of keeping watch over you. I told him, 'Miss Sookie and me, we're real good friends, and that would suit me just fine.' Have you gotten another cat?"

"No, Bubba, I haven't." Thank God.

"Well, I got me some blood in a cooler in the back of my car." He nodded toward a huge old white Cadillac that had been restored with time and trouble and lots of cash.

"Oh, the car's beautiful," I said. I almost added, "Did you own it while you were alive?" But Bubba didn't like references to his former state of existence; they made him upset and confused. (If you put it very carefully, from time to time he'd sing for you. I'd heard him do "Blue Christmas." Unforgettable.)

"Russell give that to me," he said.

"Oh, Russell Edgington? The King of Mississippi?"

"Yeah, wasn't that nice? He said since he was king of my home state, he felt like giving me something special."

"How's he doing?" Russell and his new husband, Bart, had both survived the Rhodes hotel bombing.

"He's feeling real good now. He and Mr. Bart are both healed up."

"I'm so glad to hear it. So, are you supposed to follow me home?"

"Yes'm, that's the plan. If you'll leave your back door unlocked, close to morning I'll get into that hidey-hole in your guest bedroom; that's what Mr. Eric said."

Then it was doubly good that Octavia had moved out. I didn't know how she would have reacted if I'd told her that the Man from Memphis needed to sleep in her closet all day long.

When I got home, Bubba pulled in right behind me in his amazing car. I saw that Dawson's truck was there, too. I

wasn't surprised. Dawson worked as a bodyguard from time
to time, and he was in the area. Since Alcide had decided he
wanted to help, Tray Dawson was an obvious choice, regardless of his relationship with Amelia.

Tray himself was sitting at my kitchen table when Bubba
and I came in. For the first time since I'd known him, the big
man looked seriously startled. But he was smart enough not
to blurt anything out.

"Tray, this is my friend Bubba," I said. "Where's
Amelia?"

"She's upstairs. I got some business to talk with you."

"I figured. Bubba's here for the same reason. Bubba, this
is Tray Dawson."

"Hey, Tray!" Bubba shook hands, laughing because he'd
made a rhyme. He hadn't translated real well. The spark of
life had been so faint by the time a morgue attendant of the
fanged persuasion had gotten hold of him, and the drugs in
his system so pervasive, that Bubba had been lucky to survive
the bringing over as well as he had, which wasn't too well.

"Hey," Tray said cautiously. "How are you doing . . .
Bubba?"

I was relieved Tray'd picked up on the name.

"I'm real good, thank you. Got me some blood in the
cooler out there, and Miss Sookie keeps some TrueBlood in
the refrigerator, or at least she used to."

"Yes, I have some," I said. "You want to sit down,
Bubba?"

"No, ma'am. I think I'll just grab me a bottle and settle
down out in the woods. Bill still live across the cemetery?"

"Yes, he does."

"Always good to have friends close."

I wasn't sure I could call Bill my friend; our history was too complicated for that. But I was absolutely sure that he'd help me if I was in danger. "Yes," I said, "that's always good."

Bubba rummaged around in the refrigerator and came out with a couple of bottles. He raised them to me and Tray, and took his leave smiling.

"Good God Almighty," Tray said. "That who I think it is?"

I nodded and took a seat opposite him.

"Explains all the sightings," he said. "Well, listen, you got him out there and me in here. That okay with you?"

"Yes. I guess you've talked to Alcide?"

"Yeah. I'm not trying to get in your business, but it would have been better to hear all this from you directly. Especially since you talked to Amelia about this guy Drake, and Amelia's all upset because apparently she's been blabbing to the enemy. If we'd known about your troubles, she would have kept her mouth shut. I would have killed him when he first introduced himself. Saved all of us a lot of trouble. You think about that?"

Bluntness was the way to go with Tray. "I think you are kind of getting in my business, Tray. When you're here as my friend and Amelia's boyfriend, I tell you what I think I can without endangering you or Amelia. It never occurred to me that Niall's enemies would think of getting information through my roommate. And it was news to me that you couldn't tell a fairy from a human." Tray winced. "You may not want to be responsible for guarding me, with the personal complication of having your girlfriend under the same roof as the woman you're supposed to protect. Is this too big a conflict of interest for you?"

Tray regarded me steadily. "No, I want the job," he said, and even though he was a Were, I could tell that his real goal was keeping Amelia safe. Since she lived with me, he could kill two birds with one stone by getting paid for protecting me. "For one thing, I owe that Drake payback. I never knew he was a fairy, and I don't know how he managed that. I got a good nose."

Tray's pride had been bruised. I could understand that. "Drake's dad can mask his smell, even from vampires. Maybe Drake can, too. Also, he's not completely fae. He's half-human, and his real name is Dermot."

Tray absorbed this, nodded. I could tell he felt a little better. I was trying to figure out if I did.

I had misgivings about the arrangement. I thought of calling Alcide and explaining why Tray might be a less than perfect bodyguard, but I decided against it. Tray Dawson was a great fighter and would do his best for me . . . up to the point where he had to make a choice between Amelia and me.

"So?" he said, and I realized I'd been quiet for too long.

"The vampire can take the nights and you can take the days," I said. "I should be okay while I'm at the bar." I pushed back my chair and left the kitchen without saying anything else. I had to admit that instead of feeling relieved, I was even more worried. I'd thought I'd been so clever asking for an extra layer of protection; instead, now I was going to worry about the safety of the men providing that layer.

I got ready for bed slowly, finally admitting to myself that I was hoping Eric would put in an appearance. I'd love to have his brand of relaxation therapy to help me sleep. I expected to lie awake anticipating the next attack. As it turned out, I was so tired from the night before that I drifted off to sleep very quickly.

Instead of my usual boring dreams (customers calling me constantly while I hurried to catch up, mold growing in my bathroom), that night I dreamed of Eric. In my dream, he was human and we walked together under the sun. Oddly enough, he sold real estate.

When I looked at the clock the next morning, it was very early, at least for me: not quite eight o'clock. I woke up with a feeling of alarm. I wondered if I'd had another dream, one I didn't remember. I wondered if my telepathic sense had caught something even while I slept, something wrong, something askew.

I took a moment to scan my own house, not my favorite way to start the day. Amelia was gone, but Tray was here and in trouble.

I put on a bathrobe and slippers and stepped out into the hall. The moment I opened my door, I could hear him being sick in the hall bathroom.

There are some moments that should be completely private, and the moments when you're throwing up are at the top of that list. But werewolves are normally completely healthy, and this was the guy who'd been sent to guard me, and he was obviously (excuse me) sick as a dog.

I waited until a lull in the sound. I called, "Tray, is there anything I can do for you?"

"I've been poisoned," he said, choking and gagging.

"Should I call the doctor? A human one? Or Dr. Ludwig?"

"No." That sounded definite enough. "I'm trying to get rid of it," he gasped, after another bout of retching. "But it's too late."

"You know who gave it to you?"

"Yeah. That new girlfriend . . ." He faded out for a few seconds. "Out in the woods. Vampire Bill's new fuck."

I had an instinctive reaction. "He wasn't with her, right?" I called.

"No, she—" More awful noises. "She came from the direction of his house, said she was his . . ."

I knew, without a doubt, that Bill didn't have a new girlfriend. Though it embarrassed me to admit it to myself, I was so sure because I knew he wanted me back. I knew he wouldn't jeopardize that by taking someone else to his bed or by permitting such a woman to roam in the woods where I might encounter her.

"What was she?" I said, resting my forehead against the cool wood of the door. I was getting tired of yelling.

"She was some fangbanger." I felt Tray's brain shift around through the fog of sickness. "At least, she felt like a human."

"The same way Dermot felt human. And you drank something she handed you." It was kind of mean of me to sound incredulous, but honestly!

"I couldn't help it," he said very slowly. "I was so thirsty. I had to drink it."

"And what was it? The stuff you drank?"

"It tasted like wine." He groaned. "Goddammit, it must have been vampire blood! I can taste it in my mouth now!"

Vampire blood was still the hot drug on the underground marketplace, and human reactions to it varied so widely that drinking the blood was very much like playing Russian roulette, in more ways than one. Vampires hated the Drainers who collected the blood because the Drainers often left the vampire exposed to the day. So vampires also loathed the users of the blood, since they created the market. Some users became addicted to the ecstatic sensation that the blood could offer, and those users sometimes tried to take the blood right from the source in a kind of suicide attack. But every now and then, the user went berserk and killed other humans. Either way, it was all bad press for the vamps who were trying to mainstream.

"Why would you do that?" I asked, unable to keep the anger out of my voice.

"I couldn't help it," he said, and the bathroom door finally opened. I took a couple of steps back. Tray looked bad and smelled worse. He was wearing pajama pants and nothing else, and a vast expanse of chest hair was right at my eye level. It was covered in goose pimples.

"How come?"

"I couldn't . . . not drink it. Maybe I was under some kind of compulsion spell." He shook his head. "And then I came back here and got in bed with Amelia, and I tossed and turned all night. I was up when the K— when Bubba came in and went to bed in your closet. He said something about a woman talking to him, but I was feeling really bad by then, and I don't remember what he said. Did Bill send her over here? Does he hate you that bad?"

I looked up then and met his eyes. "Bill Compton loves me," I said. "He would never hurt me."

"Even now that you're screwing the big blond?"

Amelia couldn't keep her mouth shut.

"Even now that I'm screwing the big blond," I said.

"You can't read vampire minds, Amelia says."

"No, I can't. But some things you just know."

"Right." Though Tray didn't have enough energy to look skeptical, he gave it a good shot. "I have to go to bed, Sookie. I can't take care of you today."

I could see that. "Why don't you go back to your own

house and try to get some rest in your own bed?" I said. "I'm going to work today, and I'll be around someone."

"No, you gotta be covered."

"I'll call my brother," I said, surprising even myself. "He's not going to work now, and he's a panther. He should be able to watch my back."

"Okay." It was a measure of Tray's wretchedness that he didn't argue, though he wasn't a Jason fan by any means. "Amelia knows I'm not feeling good. If you talk to her before I do, tell her I'll call her tonight."

The werewolf staggered out to his truck. I hoped he was good to drive home, and I called after him to make sure, but he just waved a hand at me and drove down the driveway.

Feeling oddly numb, I watched him go. I'd done the prudent thing for once; I'd called in my markers and gotten protection. And it hadn't done me a bit of good. Someone who couldn't attack me in my home—because of Amelia's good magic, I had to assume—had arranged to attack me in other ways. Murry had turned up outside, and now some fairy had met up with Tray in the woods, compelling him to drink vampire blood. It might have sent him mad; he might have killed all of us. I guess, for the fairies, it was a win-win situation. Though he hadn't gone crazy and killed me or Amelia, he'd gotten so sick that he was effectively out of the bodyguard business for a while.

I walked down the hall to go into my room and pull on some clothes. Today was going to be a hard day, and I always felt better when I was dressed while handling a crisis. Something about putting on my underwear makes me feel more capable.

I got my second shock of the day when I was about to turn in to my room. There was a movement in the living room. I stopped dead and took a huge, ragged breath. My great-grandfather was sitting on the couch, but it took me an awful moment to recognize Niall. He got up, regarding me with some astonishment while I stood gasping, my hand over my heart.

"You look rough today," he said.

"Yeah, well, not expecting visitors," I said breathlessly. He wasn't looking so great himself, which was a first. His clothes were stained and torn, and unless I was much mistaken, he was sweating. My fairy prince great-grandfather was actually less than gorgeous for the very first time.

I moved into the living room and looked at him more closely. Though it was early, I had my second stab of anxiety for the day. "What's up?" I asked. "You look like you've been fighting."

He hesitated for a long moment, as if he was trying to pick among several items of news. "Breandan has retaliated for the death of Murry," Niall said.

"What has he done?" I scrubbed my dry hands across my face.

"He caught Enda last night, and now she is dead," he said. I could tell from his voice that her death had not been a quick one. "You didn't meet her; she was very shy of humans." He pushed back a long strand of his pale hair so blond it looked white.

"Breanden killed a fairy woman? There aren't that many fairy women, right? So doing that . . . Isn't that extra awful?"

"It was intended to be," Niall said. His voice was bleak.

For the first time, I noticed that my great-grandfather's slacks were soaked with blood around the knees, which was probably why he hadn't come closer to hug me.

"You need to get out of those clothes," I said. "Please, Niall, go climb in the shower, and I'll put your stuff in the washing machine."

"I have to go," he said, and I could tell my words hadn't registered. "I came here to warn you in person, so you would take the situation very seriously. Powerful magic surrounds this house. I could appear here only because I'd been in here before. Is it true that the vampires and the Weres are looking out for you? You have extra protection; I can feel it."

"I have a bodyguard night and day," I lied, because he didn't need to be worrying about me. He was hip-deep in alligators himself. "And you know that Amelia is a strong witch. Don't worry about me."

He stared at me, but I didn't think he was seeing me at all. "I have to go," he said abruptly. "I wanted to be sure of your well-being."

"Okay . . . thanks a lot." I was trying to think of an improvement on this limp response when Niall poofed right out of my living room.

I'd told Tray I was going to call Jason. I wasn't sure how sincere I'd been about that, but now I knew I had to. The way I saw it, Alcide's favor to me had expired; he'd asked Tray to help, and now Tray was out of commission in the course of duty. I sure wasn't going to request that Alcide himself come guard me, and I wasn't close to any of his pack members. I took a deep breath and called my brother.

"Jason," I said when he answered the phone.

"Sis. What's up?" He sounded oddly jazzed, as if he'd just experienced something exciting.

"Tray had to leave, and I think I need some protection today," I said. There was a long silence. He didn't rush into questioning me, which was strange. "I was hoping you could go around with me? What I plan on doing today," I began, and then tried to figure out what that was. It was hard to have a good crisis when real life kept asking to be lived. "Well, I need to go to the library. I need to pick up a pair of pants at the dry cleaners." I hadn't checked the label before that particular purchase. "I have to work the day shift at Merlotte's. I guess that's it."

"Okay," Jason said. "Though those errands don't sound exactly urgent." There was a long pause. Suddenly he said, "Are you okay?"

"Yeah," I said cautiously. "Should I not be?"

"The weirdest thing happened this morning. Mel slept at my place last night, since he was the worse for wear after he met me at the Bayou. So early this morning, there was a knock at the door. I answered it, and this guy was there, and he was, I don't know, nuts or something. The strangest part was, this guy looked a lot like me."

"Oh, no." I sat on the stool abruptly.

"He wasn't right, sis," Jason said. "I don't know what was wrong with him, but he wasn't right. He just started talking when Mel answered the door, like we knew who he was. He was saying crazy stuff. Mel tried to get between him and me, and he threw Mel clear across the room and called him a killer. Mel might've broken his neck if he hadn't landed on the couch."

"Mel's okay, then."

"Yeah, he's okay. Pretty mad, but you know . . ."

"Sure." Mel's feelings were not the most important issue here. "So what did he do next?"

"He said some shit about now that he was face-to-face with me he could see why my great-grandfather didn't want me around, and crossbreeds should all die, but I was clearly blood of his blood, and he'd decided I should know what's going on around me. He said I was ignorant. I didn't understand a lot of it, and I still don't get what he was. He wasn't a vamp, and I know he wasn't a shifter of any kind or I'd've smelled him."

"You're okay—that's the big thing, right?" Had I been wrong all along about keeping Jason out of the fairy loop?

"Yeah," he said, his voice abruptly going all cautious and wary. "You're not going to tell me what this is all about, are you?"

"Come over here, and we'll talk about it. Please, please, don't open the door unless you know who's there. This guy is bad, Jason, and he's not picky about who he hurts. I think you and Mel were real lucky."

"You got someone there with you?"

"Not since Tray left."

"I'm your brother. I'll come over if you need me," Jason said with unexpected dignity.

"I really appreciate that," I said.

I got two for the price of one. Mel came with Jason. This was awkward, because I had some family stuff to tell Jason, and I couldn't with Mel around. With unexpected tact, Mel told Jason that he had to run home and get an ice pack for his shoulder, which was badly bruised. While Mel was gone, I sat Jason down on the other side of the kitchen table, and I said, "I got some things to tell you."

"About Crystal?"

"No, I haven't heard anything about that yet. This is about us. This is about Gran. You're going to have a hard time believing this." I'd given him fair warning. I remembered how upset I'd been when my great-grandfather had told me about how my half-fairy grandfather, Fintan, had met my grandmother, and how she'd ended up having two children with him: our dad and our aunt Linda.

Now Fintan was dead—murdered—and our grandmother was dead, and our father and his sister were dead. But we were living, and just a small part fairy, and that made us a target for our great-grandfather's enemies.

"And one of those enemies," I said after I'd told him our family history, "is our half-human great-uncle, Fintan's brother, Dermot. He told Tray and Amelia that his name was Drake, I guess because it sounded more modern. Dermot looks like you, and he's the one who showed up at your house. I don't know what his deal is. He joined up with Breandan, Niall's big enemy, even though he's half-human himself and, therefore, exactly what Breandan hates. So when you said he was crazy, I guess there's your explanation. He seems to want to connect with you, but he hates you, too."

Jason sat staring at me. His face was completely vacant. His thoughts had gotten caught in a traffic jam. Finally he said, "You tell me he was trying to get Tray and Amelia to introduce you? And neither of them knew what he was?"

I nodded. There was some more silence.

"So why did he want to meet you? Did he want to kill you? Why'd he need to meet you first?"

Good question. "I don't know," I said. "Maybe he just wanted to see what I was like. Maybe he doesn't know what he really wants." I couldn't figure this out, and I wondered if Niall would come back to explain it to me. Probably not. He had a war on his hands, even if it was a war being fought mostly away from human view. "I don't get it," I said out loud. "Murry came right here to attack me, and he was all fairy. Why is Dermot, who's on the same side, being all . . . indirect?"

"Murry?" Jason asked, and I closed my eyes. Shit.

"He was a fairy," I said. "He tried to kill me. He's not a problem now."

Jason gave me an approving nod. "You go, Sookie," he said. "Okay, let me see if I'm getting this straight. My great-grandfather didn't want to meet me because I look a lot like Dermot, who's my . . . great-uncle, right?"

"Right."

"But Dermot apparently likes me a little better, because he actually came to my house and tried to talk to me."

Trust Jason to interpret the situation in those terms. "Right," I said.

Jason hopped to his feet and took a turn around the kitchen. "This is all the vampires' fault," he said. He glared at me.

"Why do you think so?" This was unexpected.

"If they hadn't come out, none of this would be happening. Look at what's happened since they went on TV. Look at how the world has changed. Now *we're* out. Next, the fucking fairies. And the fae are bad news, Sookie; Calvin warned me about 'em. You think they're all pretty and sweetness and light, but they're not. He's told me stories about them that would make your hair curl. Calvin's dad knew a fairy or two. From what he's said, it would be a good thing if they died out."

I couldn't decide if I was surprised or angry. "Why are you being so mean, Jason? I don't need you arguing with me or saying bad things about Niall. You don't know him. You don't . . . Hey, you're part fairy, remember!" I had an awful feeling that some of what he'd said was absolutely true, but it sure wasn't the time to have this discussion.

Jason looked grim, every plane of his face tense. "I'm not

claiming kin to any fairy," he said. "He don't want me; I don't want him. And if I see that crazy half-and-half again, I'll kill the son of a bitch."

I don't know what I would have said, but at that moment Mel came in without knocking, and we both turned to look at him.

"I'm sorry!" he said, obviously flustered and disturbed by Jason's anger. He seemed, for a second, to think Jason had been talking about him. When neither of us gave him a guilty reaction, he relaxed. "Excuse me, Sookie. I forgot my manners." He was carrying an ice bag in his hand, and he was moving a little slowly and painfully.

"I'm sorry you got hurt by Jason's surprise visitor," I said. You're always supposed to put your company at ease. I hadn't put a whole lot of thought into Mel, but right at that second I realized I would have been happier if Jason's former BFF, Hoyt, had been here instead of the werepanther. It wasn't that I disliked Mel, I thought. It was just that I didn't know him very well, and I didn't feel an automatic trust in him the way you feel about people from time to time. Mel was different. Even for a werepanther, he was hard to read, but that didn't mean he was impossible.

After offering Mel something to drink, which was only polite, I asked Jason if he was going to stay the day, run around on my errands with me. I had serious doubts he would say yes. Jason was feeling rejected (by a fairy great-grandfather he'd never met and didn't want to acknowledge), and that was a state of affairs Jason didn't handle well.

"I'll go around with you," he said, unsmiling and stiff. "First, let me run over to the house and check out my rifle. I'll need it, and it hasn't been sighted in a coon's age. Mel? You coming with me?" Jason simply wanted to be out of my presence to calm down. I could read it as easily as if he'd written it on the grocery list pad by the telephone.

Mel rose to go with Jason.

"Mel, what did you make of Jason's visitor this morning?" I asked.

"Aside from the fact that he could throw me across the room and looked enough like Jason to make me turn to make sure your brother was coming out of his bedroom? Not much," Mel said. Mel had managed to dress in his usual khakis and polo shirt, but the blue bruises on his arms kind of ruined his neat appearance. He shrugged on a jacket with great care.

"See you in a while, Sookie. Come around to get me," Jason said. Of course, he'd want to ride in my car and burn up my gas, since we were running my errands. "In the meantime, you got my cell number."

"Sure. I'll see you in an hour or so."

Since being alone hadn't been a normal state of affairs for me lately, I would have actually enjoyed the feeling of having the house to myself if I hadn't been worried that a supernatural killer was after me.

Nothing happened. I ate a bowl of cereal. Finally, I decided to risk taking a shower despite my *Psycho* memories. I made sure all the outside doors were locked, and I locked the bathroom door, too. I took the quickest shower on record.

Nobody had tried to kill me yet. I dried off, put on some makeup, and dressed for work.

When it was time to go, I stood on the back porch and eyeballed the distance between the steps and my car door, over and over. I figured I'd have to take ten steps. I took a few deep breaths and unlocked the screen door. I pushed it open and fairly leaped off the porch, bypassing the steps entirely. In an undignified scramble, I yanked open the car door, slid inside, and slammed and locked the door. I looked around me.

Nothing moved.

I laughed a little breathlessly. Silly me!

Being so tense was making all the scary movies I'd ever seen pop into my head. I was thinking of *Jurassic Park* and dinosaurs—maybe my thought link was that fairies were the dinosaurs of the supernatural world—and I half expected a piece of goat to fall on my windshield.

That didn't happen, either. Okay . . .

I inserted the key and turned it, and the motor turned over. I didn't blow up. There was no Tyrannosaurus in my rearview mirror.

So far, so good. I felt better once I'd begun going slowly down the driveway through the woods, but I was sure keeping my eyes busy. I felt a compulsion to get in touch with someone, to let someone know where I was and what I was doing.

I whipped my cell phone out of my purse and called Amelia. When she answered, I said, "I'm driving over to Jason's. Since Tray is so sick, Jason's going around with me today. Listen, you know Tray was spelled by a fairy into drinking rotten vampire blood?"

"I'm at work here," Amelia said, caution in her voice. "Yes, he called ten minutes ago, but he had to go throw up. Poor Tray. At least the house was okay."

Amelia's point was that her wards had held. Well, she had a right to be proud of that.

"You're great," I said.

"Thanks. Listen, I'm really worried about Tray. I tried calling him back after a few minutes, but he didn't answer. I hope he's just sleeping it off, but I'm going over there after I leave work. Why don't you meet me there? We can figure out what to do about getting you some more security."

"Okay," I said. "I'll come over right after I get off work, probably around five." Phone in my hand, I jumped out and grabbed the mail from my mailbox, which sat up on Hummingbird Road. Then I got back in my car quick as I could.

That had been stupid. I could have gone without checking the mail for one day. Habits are very hard to break, even when they're unimportant habits. "I really am lucky you live with me, Amelia," I said. That might have been spreading it on a little thick, but it was the absolute truth.

But Amelia had gone off on another mental path. "You're speaking to Jason again? You told him? About *things?*"

"Yeah, I had to. Great-grandfather can't have everything his own way. Stuff has happened."

"It always does, around you," Amelia said. She didn't sound angry, and she wasn't condemning me.

"Not always," I said after a sharp moment of doubt. *In fact,* I thought, as I turned left at the end of Hummingbird Road to go to my brother's, *that point Jason made about everything changing when the vamps came out . . . that just might have been something I really agree with.*

Prosaically, I realized my car was almost out of gas. I had to pull into Grabbit Quik. While I was pumping the liquid gold into my car, I fell back to puzzling over what Jason had told me. What would be urgent enough to bring a reclusive and human-hating half fairy to Jason's door? Why would he tell Jason . . . ? I shouldn't be thinking about this.

This was stupid, and I should be watching out for myself instead of trying to solve Jason's problems.

But after a few more seconds of turning the conversation

over in my head, I began to have a sneaking suspicion that I understood it a little better.

I called Calvin. At first he didn't get what I was saying, but then he agreed to meet me at Jason's house.

I caught a glimpse of Jason in the backyard when I pulled into the circular driveway of the neat, small house my dad had built when he and my mother were first married. It was out in the country, out farther west than Arlene's trailer, and though it was visible from the road, it had a pond and several acres lying behind it. My dad had loved to hunt and fish, and my brother did, too. Jason had recently put in a makeshift range, and I could hear the rifle.

I decided to come through the house, and I took care to yell when I was at the back door.

"Hey!" Jason called back. He had a 30-30 in his hands. It had been our father's. Mel was standing behind him, holding a box of ammo. "We decided we better get in some practice."

"Good idea. I wanted to be sure you didn't think I was your crazy caller, come back to yell some more."

Jason laughed. "I still don't understand what good Dermot thought he'd do, coming up to the front door like that."

"I think I do," I said.

Jason held out his hand without looking, and Mel gave him some bullets. Jason opened the rifle and began loading. I looked over at the sawhorse he'd set up, noted all the empty milk jugs lying on the ground. He'd filled them with water so they'd sit steady, and thanks to the bullet holes, the water was flowing out onto the ground.

"Good shooting," I said. I took a deep breath. "Hey, Mel, you want to tell me about Hotshot funerals? I haven't ever been to one, and Crystal's will take place as soon as the body comes back, I reckon."

Mel looked a little surprised. "You know I haven't lived out there for years," he protested. "It's just not for me." Except for the fading bruises, he didn't look like he'd been thrown across the room by anyone, much less a crazed half fairy.

"I wonder why that guy threw you around instead of Jason," I said, and felt Mel's thoughts ripple with fear. "Are you hurt?"

He moved his right shoulder a little. "I thought I'd broken something. But I guess it's just going to be sore. I wonder what he was. Not one of us."

He hadn't answered my question, I noticed.

Jason looked proud that he hadn't blabbed.

"He's not entirely human," I said.

Mel looked relieved. "Well, that's good to know," he said. "My pride was pretty much shot to hell when he threw me around. I mean, I'm a full-blood panther, and it was like I was kindling or something."

Jason laughed. "I thought he'd come on in and kill me then, thought I was a goner. But once Mel was down, this guy just started talking to me. Mel was playing possum, and here's this fella looks a lot like me, telling me what a favor he's done me. . . ."

"It was weird," Mel agreed, but he looked uncomfortable. "You know I'd've been on my feet if he'd started punching on you, but he really rang my bell, and I figured I might as well stay down once it looked like he wasn't going to go after you."

"Mel, I hope you're really okay." I made my voice concerned, and I moved a little closer. "Let me have a look at that shoulder." I extended my hand, and Jason's eyebrows knit together.

"Why do you need to . . . ?" An awful suspicion was creeping over his face. Without another word, he stepped behind his friend and held him firm, his hands gripping Mel on either side right below Mel's shoulders. Mel winced with pain, but he didn't say anything, not a word; he didn't even pretend to be indignant or surprised, and that was almost enough.

I put a hand on either side of Mel's face, and I closed my eyes, and I looked in his head. And this time Mel was thinking about Crystal, not Jason.

"He did it," I said. I opened my eyes and looked at my brother's face across Mel's shoulder. I nodded.

Jason screamed, and it wasn't a human sound. Mel's face seemed to melt, as if all the muscles and bones had shifted. He hardly looked human at all.

"Let me look at you," Mel pleaded.

Jason looked confused, since Mel *was* looking at me; he couldn't look anywhere else, the way Jason was holding him. Mel wasn't struggling, but I could see every muscle under his skin standing out, and I didn't think he'd be passive forever. I bent down and picked up the rifle, glad Jason had reloaded it.

"He wants to look at you, not me," I told my brother.

"Goddammit," Jason said. His breathing was heavy and ragged as if he'd been running, and his eyes were wide. "You have to tell me *why*."

I stepped back and raised the rifle. At this distance, even I couldn't miss. "Turn him around, since he wants to talk to you face-to-face."

They were in profile to me when Jason spun Mel around.

Jason's grip refastened on the werepanther, but now Jason's face was a foot from Mel's.

Calvin walked around the house. Crystal's sister, Dawn, was with him. There was also a boy of about fifteen trailing along. I remembered meeting the boy at the wedding. He was Jacky, Crystal's oldest first cousin. Adolescents practically reek of emotion and confusion, and Jacky was no exception. He was struggling to conceal the fact that he was both nervous and excited. Maintaining a cool demeanor was just killing him.

The three newcomers took in the scene. Calvin shook his head, his face solemn. "This is a bad day," he said quietly, and Mel jerked at the sound of his leader's voice.

Some of the tension leaked out of Jason when he saw the other werepanthers.

"Sookie says he did it," he said to Calvin.

"That's good enough for me," Calvin said. "But, Mel—you should tell us yourself, brother."

"I'm not your brother," Mel said bitterly. "I haven't lived with you for years."

"That was your own choice," Calvin said. He walked around so he could see Mel's face, and the other two followed him. Jacky was snarling; any pretense at being cool had vanished. The animal was showing through.

"There isn't anyone else in Hotshot like me. I would have been alone."

Jason looked blank. "There are lots of guys in Hotshot like you," he said.

"No, Jason," I said. "Mel's gay."

"We're not okay with that?" my brother asked Calvin. Jason hadn't yet gotten the party line on a few issues, apparently.

"We're okay with people doing what they want to do in bed

after they've done their duty to the clan," Calvin said. "Pure-bred males have to father a young 'un, no matter what."

"I couldn't do it," Mel said. "I just plain couldn't do it."

"But you were married once," I said, and wished I hadn't spoken. This was a matter for the clan now. I hadn't called Bud Dearborn; I'd called Calvin. My word was good enough for Calvin, not for court.

"Our marriage didn't work in that department," Mel said. His voice sounded almost normal. "Which was okay with her. She had her own fish to fry. We never had . . . conventional sex."

If I found this distressing, I could only imagine how hard it had been for Mel. But when I remembered what Crystal had looked like up on that cross, all my sympathy drained away in a hurry.

"Why did you do that to Crystal?" I asked. I could tell from the rage building in the brains around me that the time for talking was almost over.

Mel looked beyond me, past my brother, away from his leader, his victim's sister and cousin. He seemed to be focused on the winter-bare limbs of the trees around the still, brown pond. "I love Jason," he said. "I love him. And she abused him and his child. Then she taunted me. She came here that day. . . . I'd stopped off to get Jason to help me build some shelves at the shop, but he wasn't here. She drove up while I was out in the yard writing Jason a note. She began to say . . . She said awful things. Then she told me I had to have sex with her, that if I did, she'd tell them at Hotshot and I'd be able to go back to live there, and Jason could come live with me. She said, 'His baby's inside me; doesn't that get you all hot?' And it got worse and worse. The bed of the truck was down because the wood I'd bought was sticking out, and she kind of backed up to it and lay down, and I could see her. It was . . . She was . . . She kept telling me what a pussy I was and that Jason would never care about me . . . and I slapped her as hard as I could."

Dawn Norris turned to one side as though she was going to throw up. But she pressed her lips together in a hard line and straightened up. Jacky wasn't that tough.

"She wasn't dead, though." My brother forced the words between his clenched teeth. "She bled all down the cross. She lost the baby after she'd been hung up."

"I'm sorry about that," Mel said. His gaze returned from the pond and the trees and focused on my brother. "I thought the blow had killed her—I really did. I would never have left her to go in the house if I'd thought she was still alive. I would never have let someone else get her. What I did was bad enough, because I intended for her to die. But I didn't crucify her. Please believe me. No matter what you think of me for hurting her, I would never have done that. I thought if I took her somewhere else, no one would think you did it. I knew you were going out that night, and I figured if I put her somewhere else, you'd have an alibi. I figured you'd end up spending the night with Michele." Mel smiled at Jason, and it was such a tender look that my heart ached. "So I left her in the back of the truck, and I came in the house to have a drink. And when I came back out, she was gone. I couldn't believe it. I thought she'd gotten up and walked away. But there wasn't any blood, and the wood was gone, too."

"Why Merlotte's?" Calvin said, and his voice came out like a growl.

"I don't know, Calvin," Mel said. His face was almost sub-lime with his relief from the load of his guilt, with the release of confessing his crime and his love for my brother. "Calvin, I know I'm about to die, and I swear to you that I have no idea what happened to Crystal after I went into the house. I did not do that horrible thing to her."

"I don't know what to make of that," Calvin said. "But we have your confession, and we'll have to proceed."

"I accept that," Mel said. "Jason, I love you."

Dawn turned her head just a fraction so her eyes could meet mine. "You better go," she said. "We got things to do."

I walked off with the rifle, and I didn't turn to look even when the other panthers began to tear Mel apart. I could hear it, though.

He didn't scream after a second.

I left Jason's rifle on his back porch, and I drove to work. Somehow having a bodyguard didn't seem important anymore.

Chapter 16

As I served beers and daiquiris and vodka Collinses to the people stopping by on their way home from work, I stood back and eyed myself in amazement. I'd worked for hours, serving and smiling and hustling, and I'd never broken down at all. Sure, I'd had to ask four people to repeat their orders. And I'd walked past Sam twice, and he'd said something to me to which I hadn't responded—I knew this because he'd stopped me to tell me so. But I'd gotten the right plates and drinks to the right tables, and my tips were running about average, which meant I'd been agreeable and hadn't forgotten anything crucial.

You're doing so good, I told myself. *I'm so proud of you. You just have to get through this. You can go home in fifteen minutes.*

I wondered how many women had given themselves the same lecture: the girl who'd held her head up at a dance where her date was paying attention to another classmate; the woman who'd been passed by for promotion at her job; the woman who had listened to a dire diagnosis and yet kept her face together. I knew men must have days like this, too.

Well, maybe not too many people had days *exactly* like this.

Naturally, I'd been turning over in my head Mel's strange insistence that he was not responsible for Crystal's crucifixion, during which she'd actually died. His thoughts had had the ring of truth. And really, there was no reason why he would've balked at confessing everything when he'd already confessed so much, found peace doing so. Why would someone steal the half-dead Crystal and the wood, and do a deed so disgusting? It would've had to have been someone who'd hated Crystal an awful lot, or maybe someone who had hated Mel or Jason. It was an inhuman act, yet I found myself believing in Mel's dying assertion that he had not done it.

I was so glad to leave work that I began driving home on automatic pilot. When I'd gotten almost to the turnoff into my driveway, I remembered that I'd told Amelia hours before that I'd meet her at Tray's house.

I'd completely forgotten.

I could forgive myself, considering the day I'd had—if Amelia was okay. But when I remembered Tray's mean state and his ingestion of vampire blood, I felt a jolt of panic.

I looked at my watch and saw I was more than forty-five minutes late. Turning around in the next driveway, I drove back to town like a bat out of hell. I was trying to pretend to myself I wasn't scared. I wasn't doing a very good job.

There weren't any cars in front of the small house. Its windows were dark. I could see the bumper of Tray's truck peering out from the carport behind the house.

I drove right by and turned around on a county road about half a mile farther out. Confused and worried, I returned to park outside Tray's. His house and the adjacent workshop were outside the Bon Temps city limits but not isolated. Tray had maybe a half-acre lot; his little home and the large metal building housing his repair business were right next to a similar setup owned by Brock and Chessie Johnson, who had an upholstery shop. Obviously, Brock and Chessie had retreated to their house for the night. The living room lights were on; as I watched, Chessie pulled the curtains shut, which most people out here didn't bother to do.

The night was dark and quiet; the Johnsons' dog was barking, but that was the only sound. It was too cold for the chorus of bugs that often made the night come alive.

I thought of several scenarios that could explain the dead look of the house.

One. The vampire blood still had hold over Tray, and he'd killed Amelia. Right now, he was in his house, in the dark, thinking of ways to kill himself. Or maybe he was waiting for me to come, so he could kill me, too.

Two. Tray had recovered from his ingestion of vamp blood, and when Amelia had appeared on his doorstep, they'd decided to treat their free afternoon as a honeymoon. They wouldn't be at all happy if I interrupted them.

Three. Amelia had come by, found no one at home, and was now back at the house cooking supper for herself and me, because she expected me to drive up at any moment. At least that explanation accounted for the absence of Amelia's car.

I tried to think of an even better series of events, but I couldn't. I pulled out my cell phone and tried my home number. I heard my own voice on the answering machine. Next, I tried Amelia's cell. It went to voice mail after three rings. I was running out of happy options. Figuring that a phone call would be less intrusive than a knock at the door, I tried

Tray's number next. I could hear the faint ring of the phone inside . . . but no one answered it.

I called Bill. I didn't think about it for more than a second. I just did it.

"Bill Compton," said the familiar cool voice.

"Bill," I said, and then couldn't finish.

"Where are you?"

"I'm sitting in my car outside of Tray Dawson's house."

"The Were who owns the motorcycle repair shop."

"Right."

"I'm coming."

He was there in less than ten minutes. His car pulled up behind mine. I was pulled over on the shoulder, because I hadn't wanted to drive up onto the gravel in front of the house.

"I'm weak," I said, when he got in beside me. "I shouldn't have called you. But I swear to God, I didn't know what else to do."

"You didn't call Eric." It was a simple observation.

"Take too long," I said. I told him what I'd done. "I can't believe I forgot Amelia," I said, stricken by my self-centeredness.

"I think forgetting one thing after such a day is actually permissible, Sookie," Bill said.

"No, it isn't," I said. "It's just that . . . I can't go in there and find them dead. I just can't do it. My courage has just collapsed."

He leaned over and kissed me on the cheek. "What's one more dead person to me?" he said. And then he was out of the car and moving silently in the faint light peeking around the curtains of the house next door. He got to the front door, listened intently. He didn't hear anything, I knew, because he opened the door and stepped inside.

Just as he vanished, my cell phone rang. I jumped so hard I almost hit my head on the roof. I dropped the phone and had to grope for it.

"Hello?" I said, full of fear.

"Hey, did you call? I was in the shower," Amelia said, and I collapsed over the steering wheel, thinking, *Thank you God thank you God thank you thank you.*

"You okay?" Amelia asked.

"Yes," I said. "I'm okay. Where is Tray? Is he there with you?"

"Nope. I went to his house, but he wasn't there. I waited a while for you, but you didn't show, so I figured he'd gone to the doctor, and I decided you must have been held up at work or something. So I left. I just got home about thirty minutes ago. What's up?"

"I'll be there soon," I said. "Lock the doors and don't let anyone in."

"Doors are locked; no one's knocking," she said.

"Don't let me in," I said, "unless I give you the password."

"Sure, Sookie," she said, and I could tell she thought I'd gone over the edge. "What's the password?"

"Fairypants," I said, and how I came up with that I have no idea. It simply seemed super unlikely that anyone else in the world would say it.

"I got it," Amelia said. "Fairypants."

Bill was back at the car. "I've got to go," I said, and hung up. When he opened the door, the dome light showed his face. It looked grim.

"He's not there," he said immediately. "But there's been a fight."

"Blood?"

"Yes."

"Lots?"

"He could still be alive. From the way it smelled, I don't think it was all his."

My shoulders slumped. "I don't know what to do," I confessed, and it felt almost good to say it out loud. "I don't know where to go to find him or how to help him. He's supposed to be working as my bodyguard. But he went out in the woods last night and met up with a woman who said she was your new girlfriend. She gave him a drink. It was bad vampire blood, and it made him sick as the flu." I looked over at Bill. "Maybe she got it from Bubba. I haven't seen him to ask. I'm kind of worried about him." I knew Bill could see me far more clearly than I could see him. I spread my hands in query. Did he know this woman?

Bill looked at me. His mouth curved up in a rather bitter little smile. "I'm not dating anyone," he said.

I decided to completely ignore the emotional slant. I didn't have the time or the energy tonight. I'd been right when I'd discounted the mysterious woman's identity. "So this was someone who could pretend to be a fangbanger, someone convincing enough to overcome Tray's good sense, someone who could put him under a spell so he'd drink the blood."

"Bubba doesn't have much good sense at all," Bill said. "Even though some fairy magic doesn't work on vampires, I don't think he'd be hard to bespell."

"Have you seen him tonight?"

"He came over to my place to put drinks in his cooler,

but he seemed weak and disoriented. After he drank a couple of bottles of TrueBlood, he seemed to be better. The last I saw of him, he was walking across the cemetery toward your house."

"I guess we better go there next."

"I'll follow you." Bill went to his own car, and we set off to drive the short distance to my place. But Bill caught the light at the intersection of the highway and Hummingbird Road, and I was ahead of him by quite a few seconds. I pulled up in back of the house, which was well-lit. Amelia had never worried about an electric bill in her life; it just made me want to cry sometimes when I followed her around turning off switch after switch.

I got out of the car and hurried for the back steps, all ready to say, "Fairypants!" when Amelia came to the door. Bill would be there in less than a minute, and we could make a plan on how to find Tray. When Bill got there, he'd check on Bubba; I couldn't go out in the woods. I was proud of myself for not rushing into the trees to find the vampire.

I had so much to think about that I didn't think about the most obvious danger.

There's no excuse for my lack of attention to detail.

A woman by herself always has to be alert, and a woman who's had the experiences I've had has extra cause for alarm when blips are on her radar. The security light was still on at the house and and the backyard looked normal, it was true. I had even glimpsed Amelia in the kitchen through a window. I hurried to the back steps, my purse slung over my shoulder, my trowel and water guns inside it, my keys in my hand.

But anything can be hiding in the shadows, and it takes only a moment's inattention for a trap to spring.

I heard a few words in a language I didn't recognize, but for a second I thought, *He's mumbling,* and I couldn't imagine what a man behind me would be mumbling, and I was about to put my foot on the first step to the back porch.

And then I didn't know a thing.

Chapter 17

I thought I was in a cave. It felt like a cave: cool, damp. And the sound was funny.

My thoughts were anything but speedy. However, the sense of wrongness rose to the top of my consciousness with a kind of dismaying certainty. I was not where I was supposed to be, and I shouldn't be wherever I was. At the moment, these seemed like two separate and distinct thoughts.

Someone had bopped me on the head.

I thought about that. My head didn't feel sore, exactly: it felt thick, as if I had a bad cold and had taken a serious decongestant on top of that. So, I concluded (with all the speed of a turtle), I had been knocked out magically rather than physically. The result was about the same. I felt like hell, and I was scared to open my eyes. At the same time, I very much wanted to know who was in this space with me. I braced myself and made my eyelids open. I caught a glimpse of a lovely and indifferent face, and then my eyelids clamped shut again. They seemed to be operating on their own timetable.

"She's joining us," said someone.

"Good; we can have some fun," said another voice.

That didn't sound promising at all. I didn't think the fun was going to be anything I could enjoy, too.

I figured I could get rescued anytime now, and that would be just fine.

But the cavalry didn't ride in. I sighed and forced my eyes open again. This time the lids stayed apart, and by the light of a torch—a real, honest-to-God flaming wood torch—I examined my captors. One was a male fairy. He was as lovely as Claudine's brother Claude and just about as charming— which is to say, not at all. He had black hair, like Claude's, and handsome features and a buff body, like Claude's. But his face couldn't even simulate interest in me. Claude was at least able to fake it when circumstances required that.

I looked at Kidnapper Number Two. She hardly seemed more promising. She was a fairy, too, and therefore lovely, but she didn't appear to be any more lighthearted or fun-loving than her companion. Plus, she was wearing a body stocking, or something very like one, and she looked good in it, which in and of itself was enough to make me hate her.

"We have the right woman," Two said. "The vampire-loving whore. I think the one with short hair was a bit more attractive."

"As if any human can truly be lovely," said One.

It wasn't enough to be kidnapped; I had to be insulted, too. Though their words were the last thing in the world I needed to be worrying about, a little spark of anger lit in my chest. *Just keep that up, asshole,* I thought. *You just wait till my great-grandfather gets ahold of you.*

I hoped they hadn't hurt Amelia or Bubba.

I hoped Bill was all right.

I hoped he'd called Eric and my great-grandfather.

That was a lot of hoping. As long as I was in the wishful-thinking zone, I wished that Eric was tuned in to my very great distress and my very real fear. Could he track me by my emotions? That would be wonderful, because I was certainly full of them. This was the worst fix I'd ever been in. Years ago, when Bill and I had exchanged blood, he'd told me he'd be able to find me. I hoped he'd been telling the truth, and I hoped that ability hadn't faded with time. I was willing to be saved by just about anybody. Soon.

Kidnapper One slid his hands under my armpits and yanked me to a sitting position. For the first time, I realized my hands were numb. I looked down to see they were tied with a strip of leather. Now I was propped up against a wall, and I could see I was not actually in a cave. We were in an abandoned house. There was a hole in the roof, and I could see stars through it. The smell of mildew was strong, almost choking, and under it trailed the scents of rotting wood and wallpaper. There was nothing in the room but my purse, which had been tossed into a corner, and an old framed pho-tograph, which hung crookedly on the wall behind the two fairies. The picture had been taken outside, probably in the nineteen twenties or thirties, and it was of a black family dressed up for their picture-taking adventure. They looked like a farming family. At least I was still in my own world, I figured, though probably not for long.

While I could, I smiled at Thing One and Thing Two. "My great-grandfather is going to kill you," I said. I even managed to sound pretty happy about that. "You just wait."

One laughed, tossing his black hair behind him in a

male-modelly gesture. "He'll never find us. He'll yield and step down rather than see you killed in a slow and painful way. He *loooooves* humans."

Two said, "He should have gone to the Summerlands long ago. Consorting with humans will kill us off even faster than we are dying already. Breandan will seal us off. We'll be safe. Niall is out-of-date."

Like he'd expired on the shelves or something.

"Tell me you have a boss," I said. "Tell me you're not the brains of the operation." I was sort of aware that I was seriously addled, probably as a result of the spell that had knocked me out, but knowing I wasn't myself didn't seem to stop me talking, which was a pity.

"We owe allegiance to Breandan," One said proudly, as if that would make everything clear to me.

Instead of connecting their words with my great-grandfather's archenemy, I pictured the Brandon I'd gone to high school with, who'd been a running back on the football team. He'd gone to Louisiana Tech and then into the air force. "He got out of the service?" I said.

They stared at me with a total lack of comprehension. I couldn't really fault them for that. "Service of whom?" asked Two.

I was still blaming her for saying I was a skank, and I decided I wasn't speaking to her. "So, what's the program?" I asked One.

"We wait to hear from Niall, who will respond to Breandan's demands," he said. "Breandan will seal us all in Faery, and we will never have to deal with your like again."

At the moment, that seemed like an excellent plan, and I was temporarily on Breandan's side.

"So Niall doesn't want that to happen?" I said, trying to keep my voice steady.

"No, he wants to visit the likes of you. While Fintan hid the knowledge of you and your brother, Niall behaved himself, but when we removed Fintan—"

"Bit by bit!" said Two, and laughed.

"He was able to find enough information to track you down. And so did we. We found your brother's house one day, and there was a gift outside in a truck. We decided to have some fun with it. We followed your scent to where you work, and we left your brother's wife and the abomination outside for all to see. Now we're going to have some fun with you. Breandan has said we can do with you what we will, short of death."

Maybe my slow wits were speeding up a little. I understood that they were enforcers for my great-grandfather's enemy, and that they had killed my grandfather Fintan and crucified poor Crystal.

"I wouldn't, if I were you," I said, quite desperately. "Hurt me, that is. Because after all, what if this Breandan doesn't get what he wants? What if Niall wins?"

"In the first place, that's not likely," Thing Two said. She smiled. "We plan to win, and we plan to have a *lot* of fun. Especially if Niall wants to see you; surely he'll demand proof you're alive before he surrenders. We have to leave you breathing . . . but the more terrible your plight, the faster the war will be over." She had a mouthful of the longest, sharpest teeth I'd ever seen. Some of them were capped with gleaming silver points. It was a ghastly touch.

At the sight of those teeth, those awful shining teeth, I threw off the remnants of the magic they'd laid on me, which was a great pity.

I was completely and utterly lucid for the next hour, which was the longest of my life.

I found it bewildering—and utterly shocking—that I could feel such pain and not die of it.

I would have been glad to die.

I know a lot about humans, since I see into their minds every day, but I didn't know a lot about fairy culture. I had to believe Thing One and Thing Two were in a league of their own. I couldn't imagine that my great-grandfather would have laughed when I began to bleed. And I had to hope that he wouldn't enjoy cutting a human with a knife, either, as One and Two did.

I'd read books where a person being tortured went "somewhere else" during the ordeal. I did my best to find somewhere else to go mentally, but I remained right there in the room. I focused on the strong faces of the farming family in the photograph, and I wished it wasn't so dusty so I could see them clearly. I wished the picture was straight. I just knew that good family would have been horrifed at what they were witnessing now.

At moments when the fairy duo wasn't hurting me, it was very hard to believe I was awake and that this was really happening. I kept hoping I was suffering through a particularly horrible dream, and I would wake from it . . . sooner, rather than later. I'd known from a very early age that there was cruelty in the world—believe me, I'd learned that—but I was still shocked that the Things were *enjoying themselves*. I had no personhood to them—no identity. They were completely indifferent to the plans I'd had for my life, the pleasures I'd hoped to enjoy. I might have been a stray puppy or a frog they'd caught by the creek.

I myself would have thought doing these things to a puppy or a frog was horrible.

"Isn't this the daughter of the ones we killed?" One asked Two while I was screaming.

"Yes. They tried to drive through water during a flood," Two said in a tone of happy reminiscence. "Water! When the man had sky blood! They thought the iron can would protect them."

"The water spirits were glad to pull them under," One said.

My parents hadn't died in an accident. They'd been murdered. Even through my pain, I registered that, though at the moment it was beyond me to form a feeling about the knowledge.

I tried to talk to Eric in my head in the hope he could find me through our bond. I thought of the only other adult telepath I knew, Barry, and I sent him messages—though I knew damn good and well that we were too far away from each other to transmit our thoughts. To my everlasting shame, toward the end of that hour I even considered trying to contact my little cousin Hunter. I knew, though, that not only was Hunter too young to understand, but also . . . I really couldn't do that to a child.

I gave up hope, and I waited for death.

While they were having sex, I thought of Sam and how happy it would make me if I could see him now. I wanted to say the name of someone who loved me, but my throat was too hoarse from screaming.

I thought about vengeance. I wanted One and Two to die with a craving that burned through my gut. I hoped someone, any one of my supe friends—Claude and Claudine,

Niall, Alcide, Bill, Quinn, Tray, Pam, Eric, Calvin, Jason—would tear these two limb from limb. Perhaps the other fairies could take the same length of time with them that they were taking with me.

One and Two had said that Breandan wanted them to spare me, but it didn't take a telepath to realize they weren't going to be capable of holding off. They were going to get carried away with their fun, as they had with Fintan and Crystal, and there would be no repairing me.

I became sure I was going to die.

I began to hallucinate. I thought I saw Bill, which made no sense at all. He was in my backyard probably, wondering where I was. He was back in the world that *made sense*. But I could swear I saw him creeping up behind the creatures, who were enjoying working with a pair of razor blades. He had his finger over his mouth as if he were telling me to keep silent. Since he wasn't there, and my throat was too raw to speak anyway (I couldn't even produce a decent scream anymore), that was easy. There was a black shadow following him, a shadow topped with a pale flame.

Two jabbed me with a sharp knife she'd just pulled from her boot, a knife that shone like her teeth. They both leaned close to me to drink in my reaction. I could only make a raspy noise. My face was crusted with tears and blood.

"Little froggy croaking," One said.

"Listen to her. Croak, froggy. Croak for us."

I opened my eyes and looked into hers, meeting them squarely for the first time in many long minutes. I swallowed and summoned up all my remaining strength.

"You're going to die," I said with absolute certainty. But I'd said it before, and they didn't pay any more attention now than they had the first time.

I made my lips move up in a smile.

The male had just enough time to look startled before something gleaming flashed between his head and his shoulders. Then, to my intense pleasure, he was in two pieces and I was covered in a wash of fresh red blood. It ran over me, drenching the blood already dried on my skin. But my eyes were clear, so I could see a white hand gripped Two's neck, lifting her, spinning her around, and her shock was intensely gratifying as teeth almost as sharp as her own ripped into her long neck.

Chapter 18

I wasn't in a hospital.

But I was in a bed, not my own. And I was a little cleaner than I had been, and bandaged, and in a lot of pain; in fact, a dreadful amount of pain. The part where I was cleaner and bandaged—oh, a wholly desirable state. The other part, the pain—well, that was expected, understandable, and finite. At least no one was trying to hurt me any worse than I'd already been hurt. So I decided I was excellent.

I had a few holes in my memory. I couldn't remember what had happened between being in the decrepit shack and being here; I could recall flashes of action, the sound of voices, but I had no coherent narrative to connect them. I remembered One's head becoming detached, and I knew someone had bitten Two. I hoped she was as dead as One. But I wasn't sure. Had I really seen Bill? What about the shadow behind him?

I heard a *click, click, click*. I turned my head very slightly.

Claudine, my fairy godmother, was sitting by the bed, knitting.

The sight of Claudine knitting was just as surrealistic as the sight of Bill appearing in the cave. I decided to go back to sleep—a cowardly retreat, but I thought I was entitled.

"She's going to be all right," Dr. Ludwig said. Her head came up past the side of my bed, which told me for sure that I wasn't in a modern hospital bed.

Dr. Ludwig takes care of the cases who can't go to the regular human hospital because the staff would flee screaming at the sight of them or the lab wouldn't be able to analyze their blood. I could see Dr. Ludwig's coarse brown hair as she walked around the bed to the door. Dr. Ludwig had a deep voice. I suspected she was a hobbit—not really, but she sure did look like one. Though she wore shoes, right? I spent some moments trying to remember if I'd ever caught a glimpse of Dr. Ludwig's feet.

"Sookie," she said, her eyes appearing at my elbow. "Is the medicine working?"

I didn't know if this was a second visit of hers, or if I'd blanked out for a few moments. "I'm not hurting as much," I said, and my voice was very rough and whispery. "I'm starting to feel a little numb. That's just . . . excellent."

She nodded. "Yes," she said. "Considering you're human, you're very lucky."

Funny. I felt better than when I'd been in the shack, but I couldn't say I felt lucky. I tried to scrape together some appreciation of my good fortune. There wasn't any there to gather up. I was all out. My emotions were as crippled as my body.

"No," I said. I tried to shake my head, but even the

painkillers couldn't disguise the fact that my neck was too sore to twist. They'd choked me repeatedly.

"You're not dead," Dr. Ludwig pointed out.

But I'd come pretty damn close; I'd sort of stepped over the line. There'd been an optimum rescue time. If I'd been liberated before that time, I would have laughed all the way to the secret supernatural clinic, or wherever I was. But I'd looked at death too closely—close enough to see all the pores in Death's face—and I'd suffered too much. I wouldn't bounce back this time.

My emotional and physical state had been sliced and gouged and pinched and bitten to a rough, raw surface. I didn't know if I could spackle myself back into my pre-kidnap smoothness. I said this, in much simpler words, to Dr. Ludwig.

"They're dead, if that helps," she said.

Yes indeedy, that helped quite a bit. I'd been hoping I hadn't imagined that part; I'd been a little afraid their deaths had been a delightful fantasy.

"Your great-grandfather beheaded Lochlan," she said. So he'd been One. "And the vampire Bill Compton tore the throat out of Lochlan's sister, Neave." She'd been Two.

"Where's Niall now?" I said.

"Waging war," she said grimly. "There's no more negotiation, no more jockeying for advantage. There's only killing now."

"Bill?"

"He was badly hurt," the little doctor said. "She got him with her blade before she bled to death. And she bit him back. There was silver in her knife and silver caps on her teeth. It's in his system."

"He'll get better," I said.

She shrugged.

I thought my heart was going to plunge down out of my chest, through the bed. I could not look this misery in the face.

I struggled to think of something besides Bill. "And Tray? He's here?"

She regarded me silently for a moment. "Yes," she said finally.

"I need to see him. And Bill."

"No. You can't move. Bill's in his daytime sleep for now. Eric is coming tonight, actually in a couple of hours, and he'll bring at least one other vampire with him. That'll help. The Were is too badly wounded for you to disturb."

I didn't absorb that. My mind was racing ahead. It was a mighty slow race, but I was thinking a little more clearly. "Has someone told Sam, do you know?" How long had I been out? How much work had I missed?

Dr. Ludwig shrugged. "I don't know. I imagine so. He seems to hear everything."

"Good." I tried to shift positions, gasped. "I'm going to have to get up to use the bathroom," I warned her.

"Claudine," Dr. Ludwig said, and my cousin put away her knitting and rose from the rocking chair. For the first time, I registered that my beautiful fairy godmother looked like someone had tried to push her through a wood chipper. Her arms were bare and covered with scratches, scrapes, and cuts. Her face was a mess. She smiled at me, but it was painful.

When she lifted me in her arms, I could feel her effort. Normally Claudine could heft a large calf without any trouble if she chose to.

"I'm sorry," I said. "I can walk. I'm sure."

"Don't think of it," Claudine said. "See, we're already there."

When our mission was accomplished, she scooped me up and took me back to bed.

"What happened to you?" I asked her. Dr. Ludwig had departed without another word.

"I got ambushed," she said in her sweet voice. "Some stupid brownies and one fairy. Lee, his name was."

"I guess they were allied with this Breandan?"

She nodded, fished out her bundle of knitting. The item she was working on appeared to be a tiny sweater. I wondered if it was for an elf. "They were," she said. "They are bits of bone and flesh now." She sounded quite pleased.

Claudine would never become an angel at this rate. I wasn't quite sure how the progression worked, but reducing other beings to their component parts was probably not the route of choice. "Good," I said. The more of Breandan's followers who met their match, the better. "Have you seen Bill?"

"No," Claudine said, clearly not interested.

"Where is Claude?" I asked. "Is he safe?"

"He's with Grandfather," she said, and for the first time, she looked worried. "They're trying to find Breandan. Grandfather figures that if he takes out the source, Breandan's followers will have no choice but to stop the war and pledge an oath to him."

"Oh," I said. "And you didn't go, because . . . ?"

"I'm guarding you," she said simply. "And lest you think I chose the path of least danger, I'm sure Breandan is trying to find this place. He must be very angry. He's had to enter the human world, which he hates so much, now that his pet killers are dead. He loved Neave and Lochlan. They were with him for centuries, and both his lovers."

"Yuck," I said from the heart, or maybe from the pit of

my stomach. "Oh, *yuck*." I couldn't even think about what kind of "love" they would make. What I'd seen hadn't looked like love. "And I would never accuse you of taking the path of least danger," I said after I'd gotten over being nauseated. "This whole world is dangerous." Claudine gave me a sharp look. "What kind of name is Breandan?" I asked after a moment of watching her knitting needles flash with great speed and panache. I wasn't sure how the fuzzy green sweater would turn out, but the effect was good.

"Irish," she said. "All the oldest ones in this part of the world are Irish. Claude and I used to have Irish names. It seemed stupid to me. Why shouldn't we please ourselves? No one can spell those names or pronounce them correctly. My former name sounds like a cat coughing up a fur ball."

We sat in silence for a few minutes.

"Who's the little sweater for? Are you going to have a bundle of joy?" I asked in my wheezy, whispery new voice. I was trying to sound teasing, but instead, I just sounded creepy.

"Yes," she said, raising her head to look at me. Her eyes were glowing. "I'm going to have a baby. A pure fairy child."

I was startled, but I tried to cover that with the biggest smile I could paste on my face. "Oh. That's great!" I said. I wondered if it would be tacky to inquire as to the identity of the father. Probably.

"Yes," she said seriously. "It's wonderful. We're not really a very fertile race, and the huge amount of iron in the world has reduced our birthrate. Our numbers decline every century. I am very lucky. It's one of the reasons I never take humans to bed, though from time to time I would love to; they are so delicious, some of them. But I'd hate to waste a fertile cycle on a human."

I'd always assumed it was her desired ascension to angel

status that had kept Claudine from bedding any of her numerous admirers. "So, the dad's a fairy," I said, kind of pussyfooting around the topic of the paternal identity. "Did you date for a while?"

Claudine laughed. "I knew it was my fertile time. I knew he was a fertile male; we were not too closely related. We found each other desirable."

"Will he help you raise the baby?"

"Oh, yes, he'll be there to guard her during her early years."

"Can I meet him?" I asked. I was really delighted at Claudine's happiness, in an oddly remote way.

"Of course—if we win this war and passage between the worlds is still possible. He stays mostly in Faery," Claudine said. "He is not much for human companionship." She said this in much the same way she would say he was allergic to cats. "If Breandan has his way, Faery will be sealed off, and all we have built in this world will be gone. The wonderful things that humans have invented that we can use, the money we made to fund those inventions . . . that'll all be gone. It's so intoxicating being with humans. They give off so much energy, so much delicious emotion. They're simply . . . fun."

This new topic was a fine distraction, but my throat hurt, and when I couldn't respond, Claudine lost interest in talking. Though she returned to her knitting, I was alarmed to notice that after a few minutes she became increasingly tense and alert. I heard noises in the hall, as if people were moving around the building in a hurry. Claudine got up and went over to the room's narrow door to look out. After the third time she did this, she shut the door and she locked it. I asked her what she was expecting.

"Trouble," she said. "And Eric."

One and the same, I thought. "Are there other patients here? Is this, like, a hospital?"

"Yes," she said. "But Ludwig and her aide are evacuating the patients who can walk."

I'd assumed I'd had as much fear as I could handle, but my exhausted emotions began to revive as I absorbed some of her tension.

About thirty minutes later, she raised her head and I could tell she was listening. "Eric is coming," she said. "I'll have to leave you with him. I can't cover my scent like Grandfather can." She rose and unlocked the door. She swung it open.

Eric came in very quietly; one moment I was looking at the door, and the next minute, he filled it. Claudine gathered up her paraphernalia and left the room, keeping as far from Eric as the room permitted. His nostrils flared at the delicious scent of fairy. Then she was gone, and Eric was by the bed, looking down at me. I didn't feel happy or content, so I knew that even the bond was exhausted, at least temporarily. My face hurt so much when I changed expressions that I knew it was covered with bruises and cuts. The vision in my left eye was awfully blurry. I didn't need a mirror to tell me how terrible I looked. At the moment, I simply couldn't care.

Eric tried hard to keep the rage from his face, but it didn't work.

"Fucking *fairies*," he said, and his lip curled in a snarl.

I couldn't remember hearing Eric curse before.

"Dead now," I whispered, trying to keep my words to a minimum.

"Yes. A fast death was too good for them."

I nodded (as much as I could) in wholehearted agreement.

In fact, it would almost be worth bringing them back to life just to kill them again more slowly.

"I'm going to look at your wounds," Eric said. He didn't want to startle me.

"Okay," I whispered, but I knew the sight would be pretty gross. What I'd seen when I pulled up my gown in the bathroom had looked so awful I hadn't had any desire to examine myself further.

With a clinical neatness, Eric folded down the sheets and the blanket. I was wearing a classic hospital gown—you'd think a hospital for supes would come up with something more exotic—and of course, it was scooted up above my knees. There were bite marks all over my legs—deep bite marks. Some of the flesh was missing. Looking at my legs made me think of Shark Week on the Discovery Channel.

Ludwig had bandaged the worst ones, and I was sure there were stitches under the white gauze. Eric stood absolutely still for a long moment. "Pull up the gown," he said, but when he realized that my hands and arms were too weak to cooperate, he did it.

They'd enjoyed the soft spots the most, so this was really unpleasant, actually disgusting. I couldn't look after one quick glance. I kept my eyes shut, like a child who's wandered into a horror film. No wonder the pain was so bad. I would never be the same person again, physically or mentally.

After a long time, Eric covered me and said, "I'll be back in a minute," and I heard him leave the room. He was back quickly with a couple of bottles of TrueBlood. He put them on the floor by the bed.

"Move over," he said, and I glanced up at him, confused. "Move over," he said again with impatience. Then he realized

I couldn't, and he put an arm behind my back and another under my knees and shifted me easily to the other side of the bed. Fortunately, it was much larger than a real hospital bed, and I didn't have to turn on my side to make room for him.

Eric said, "I'm going to feed you."

"What?"

"I'm going to give you blood. You'll take weeks to heal otherwise. We don't have that kind of time."

He sounded so briskly matter-of-fact that I felt my shoulders finally relax. I hadn't realized how tightly wound I'd been. Eric bit into his wrist and put it in front of my mouth. "Here," he said, as if there was no question I'd take it.

He slid his free arm under my neck to raise my head. This was not going to be fun or erotic, like a nip during sex. And for a moment I wondered at my own unquestioning acquiescence. But he'd said we didn't have time. On one level I knew what that meant, but on another I was too weak to do more than consider the time factor as a fleeting and nearly irrelevant fact.

I opened my mouth and swallowed. I was in so much pain and I was so appalled by the damage done to my body that I didn't think more than once about the wisdom of what I was doing. I knew how quick the effects of ingesting vampire blood would be. His wrist healed once, and he reopened it.

"Are you sure you should do this?" I asked as he bit himself for the second time. My throat rippled with pain, and I regretted trying a whole sentence.

"Yes," he said. "I know how much is too much. And I fed well before I came here. You need to be able to move." He was behaving in such a practical way that I began to feel a little better. I couldn't have stood pity.

"Move?" The idea filled me with anxiety.

"Yes. At any moment, Breandan's followers may—will—find this place. They'll be tracking you by scent now. You smell of the fairies who hurt you, and they know now Niall loves you enough to kill his own kind for you. Hunting you down would make them very, very happy."

At the thought of any more trouble, I stopped drinking and began crying. Eric's hand stroked my face gently, but he said, "Stop that now. You must be strong. I'm very proud of you, you hear me?"

"Why?" I put my mouth on his wrist and drank again.

"You are still together; you are still a person. Lochlan and Neave have left vampires and fairies in rags—literally, rags . . . but you survived and your personality and soul are intact."

"I got rescued." I took a deep breath and bent back to his wrist.

"You would have survived much more." Eric leaned over to get the bottle of TrueBlood, and he drank it down quickly.

"I wouldn't have wanted to." I took another deep breath, aware that my throat was aching still but not as sharply. "I hardly wanted to live after . . ."

He kissed my forehead. "But you did live. And they died. And you are mine, and you will be mine. They will not get you."

"You really think they're coming?"

"Yes. Breandan's remaining forces will find this place sooner or later, if not Breandan himself. He has nothing to lose, and his pride to retain. I'm afraid they'll find us shortly. Ludwig has removed almost all the other patients." He turned a little, as if he were listening. "Yes, most of them are gone."

"Who else is here?"

"Bill is in the next room. He's been getting blood from Clancy."

"Were you not going to give him any?"

"If you were irreparable . . . no, I would have let him rot."

"Why?" I asked. "He actually came to rescue me. Why get mad at him? Where were you?" Rage bubbled up my throat.

Eric flinched almost a half inch, a big reaction from a vampire his age. He looked away. I could not believe I was saying these things.

"It's not like you were obliged to come find me," I said, "but I hoped the whole time—I hoped you would come, I prayed you would come, I thought over and over you might hear me. . . ."

"You're killing me," he said. "You're killing me." He shuddered beside me, as if he could scarcely endure my words. "I'll explain," he said in a muted voice. "I will. You will understand. But now, we don't have enough time. Are you healing yet?"

I thought about it. I didn't feel as miserable as I had before the blood. The holes in my flesh were itching almost intolerably, which meant they were healing. "I'm beginning to feel like I'll be better sometime," I said carefully. "Oh, is Tray Dawson still here?"

He looked at me with a very serious expression. "Yes; he can't be moved."

"Why not? Why didn't Dr. Ludwig take him?"

"He would not survive being moved."

"No," I said, shocked even after all that I'd been through.

"Bill told me about the vampire blood he ingested. They hoped he'd go crazy enough to hurt you, but his leaving you alone was good enough. Lochlan and Neave were delayed; a pair of Niall's warriors found them, attacked them, and they had to fight. Afterward, they decided to stake out your house. They wanted to be sure Dawson wouldn't come to help you. Bill called me to tell me that you and he went to Dawson's house. By that time, they already had Dawson. They had fun with him before they had . . . before they caught you."

"Dawson's that hurt? I thought the effects of the bad vamp blood would wear off by now." I couldn't imagine the big man, the toughest Were I knew, being defeated.

"The vampire blood they used was just a vehicle for the poison. They'd never tried it on a Were, I suppose, because it took a long time to act. And then they practiced their arts on him. Can you rise?"

I tried to gather my muscles to make the effort. "Maybe not yet."

"I'll carry you."

"Where?"

"Bill wants to talk to you. You have to be brave."

"My purse," I said. "I need something from it."

Wordlessly Eric put the soft cloth purse, now spoiled and stained, on the bed beside me. With great concentration, I was able to open it and slide my hand inside. Eric raised his eyebrows when he saw what I'd pulled out of the purse, but he heard something outside that made him looked alarmed. Eric was up and sliding his arms under me, and then he straightened as easily as if I'd been a plate of spaghetti. At the door he paused, and I managed to turn the knob for him. He used his foot to push it open, and out we went into the corridor. I was able to see that we were in an old building, some kind of small business that had been converted to its present purpose. There were doors up and down the hall, and there was a glass-enclosed control room of some kind about midway down. Through the glass on its opposite side, I could see a gloomy warehouse. There were a few lights on in it, just enough to disclose that it was empty except for some discards, like dilapidated shelving and machine parts.

We turned right to enter the room at the end of the hall. Again, I performed the honors with the knob, and this time it wasn't quite as agonizing to grip the knob and turn it.

There were two beds inside this room.

Bill was in the right-hand bed, and Clancy was sitting in a plastic chair pulled up right against the side. He was feeding Bill the same way Eric had fed me. Bill's skin was gray. His cheeks had caved in. He looked like death.

Tray Dawson was in the next bed. If Bill looked like he was dying, Tray looked like he was already dead. His face was bruised blue. One of his ears had been bitten off. His eyes were swollen shut. There was crusted blood everywhere. And this was just what I could see of his face. His arms were lying on top of the sheet, and they were both splinted.

Eric laid me down beside Bill. Bill's eyes opened, and at least they were the same: dark brown, fathomless. He stopped drinking from Clancy, but he didn't move or look better.

"The silver is in his system," Clancy said quietly. "Its poison has traveled to every part of his body. He'll need more and more blood to drive it out."

I wanted to say, "Will he get better?" But I couldn't, not with Bill lying there. Clancy rose from beside the bed, and he and Eric began having a whispered conversation—a very unpleasant one, if Eric's expression was any indication.

Bill said, "How are you, Sookie? Will you heal?" His voice faltered.

"Exactly what I want to ask you," I said. Neither of us had the strength or energy to hedge our conversation.

"You will live," he said, satisfied. "I can smell that Eric has given you blood. You would have healed anyway, but that will help the scarring. I'm sorry I didn't get there faster."

"You saved my life."

"I saw them take you," he said.

"What?"

"I saw them take you."

"You . . ." I wanted to say, "You didn't stop them?" But that seemed too horrendously cruel.

"I knew I couldn't defeat the two of them together," he said simply. "If I'd tried to take them on and they'd killed me, you would have been as good as dead. I know very little about fairies, but even I had heard of Neave and her brother." These few sentences seemed to exhaust Bill. He tried to turn his head on the pillow so he could look directly into my face, but he managed to turn only an inch. His dark hair looked lank and lusterless, and his skin no longer had the shine that had seemed so beautiful to me when I'd seen it the first time.

"So you called Niall?" I asked.

"Yes," he said, his lips barely moving. "Or at least, I called Eric, told him what I'd seen, told him to call Niall."

"Where was the old house?" I asked.

"North of here, in Arkansas," he said. "It took a while to track you. If they'd gotten in a car . . . but they moved through the fae world, and with my sense of smell and Niall's knowledge of fae magic, we were able to find you. Finally. At least your life was saved. I think it was too late for the Were."

I hadn't known Tray was in the shack. Not that the

knowledge would have made any difference, but maybe I would have felt a little less lonely.

Of course, that was probably why the two fairies hadn't let me see him. I was willing to bet there wasn't much about the psychology of torture that Neave and Lochlan hadn't known.

"Are you sure he's . . ."

"Sweetheart, look at him."

"I haven't passed yet," Tray mumbled.

I tried to get up, to go over to him. That was still a little out of my reach, but I turned on my side to face him. The beds were so close together that I could hear him easily. I think he could sort of see where I was.

"Tray," I said, "I'm so sorry."

He shook his head wordlessly. "My fault. I should have known . . . the woman in the woods . . . wasn't right."

"You did your best. If you had resisted her, you would have been killed."

"Dying now," he said. He made himself try to open his eyes. He almost managed to look right at me. "My own damn fault," he said.

I couldn't stop crying. He seemed to fall unconscious. I slowly rolled over to face Bill. His color was a little better.

"I would not, for anything, have had them hurt you," he said. "Her dagger was silver, and she had silver caps on her teeth. . . . I managed to rip her throat out, but she didn't die fast enough. . . . She fought to the end."

"Clancy's given you blood," I said. "You'll get better."

"Maybe," he said, and his voice was as cool and calm as it had always been. "I'm feeling some strength now. It will get me through the fight. That will be time enough."

I was shocked almost beyond speech. Vampires died only

from staking, decapitation, or from a rare severe case of Sino-AIDS. Silver poisoning?

"Bill," I said urgently, thinking of so many things I wanted to say to him. He'd closed his eyes, but now he opened them to look at me.

"They're coming," Eric said, and all those words died in my throat.

"Breandan's people?" I said.

"Yes," Clancy said briefly. "They've found your scent." He was scornful even now, as if I'd been weak in leaving a scent to track.

Eric drew a long, long knife from a sheath on his thigh. "Iron," he said, smiling.

And Bill smiled, too, and it wasn't a pleasant smile. "Kill as many as you can," he said in a stronger voice. "Clancy, help me up."

"No," I said.

"Sweetheart," Bill said, very formally, "I have always loved you, and I will be proud to die in your service. When I'm gone, say a prayer for me in a real church."

Clancy bent to help Bill out of the bed, giving me a very unfriendly look while he did so. Bill swayed on his feet. He was as weak as a human. He threw off the hospital gown to stand there clad only in drawstring pajama pants.

I didn't want to die in a hospital gown, either.

"Eric, have you a knife to spare for me?" Bill asked, and without turning from the door, Eric passed Bill a shorter version of his own knife, which was halfway to being a sword, according to me. Clancy was also armed.

No one said a word about trying to shift Tray. When I glanced over at him, I thought he might have already died.

Eric's cell phone rang, which made me jump a couple of

inches. He answered it with a curt, "Yes?" He listened and then clicked it shut. I almost laughed, the idea of the supes communicating by cell phones seemed so funny. But when I looked at Bill, gray in the face, leaning against the wall, I didn't think anything in the world would ever be funny again.

"Niall and his fae are on the way," Eric told us, his voice as calm and steady as if he were reading us a story about the stock market. "Breandan's blocked all the other portals to the fae land. There is only one opening now. Whether they'll come in time, I don't know."

"If I live through this," Clancy said, "I'll ask you to release me from my vow, Eric, and I'll seek another master. I find the idea of dying in the defense of a human woman to be disgusting, no matter what her connection to you is."

"If you die," Eric said, "you'll die because I, your sheriff, ordered you into battle. The reason is not pertinent."

Clancy nodded. "Yes, my lord."

"But I will release you, if you should live."

"Thank you, Eric."

Geez Louise. I hoped they were happy now they'd gotten that settled.

Bill was swaying on his feet, but neither Eric nor Clancy regarded him with anything but approval. I couldn't hear what they were hearing, but the tension in the room mounted almost unbearably as our enemies came closer.

As I watched Bill, waiting with apparent calm for death to come to him, I had a flash of him as I'd known him: the first vampire I'd ever met, the first man I'd ever gone to bed with, the first suitor I'd ever loved. Everything that followed had tainted those memories, but for one moment I saw him clearly, and I loved him again.

Then the door splintered, and I saw the gleam of an ax

blade, and I heard high-pitched shouts of encouragement from the other fairies to the ax wielder.

I resolved to get up myself, because I'd rather perish on my feet than in a bed. I had at least that much courage left in me. Maybe, since I'd had Eric's blood, I was feeling the heat of his battle rage. Nothing got Eric going like the prospect of a good fight. I struggled to my feet. I found I could walk, at least a little bit. There were some wooden crutches leaning against the wall. I couldn't remember ever seeing wooden crutches, but none of the equipment at this hospital was standard human-hospital issue.

I took a crutch by the bottom, hefted it a little to see if I could swing it. The answer was "Probably not." There was a good chance I'd fall over when I did, but active was better than passive. In the meantime, I had the weapons in my hand that I'd retrieved from my purse, and at least the crutch would hold me up.

All this happened quicker than I can tell you about it. Then the door was splintering, and the fairies were yanking hanging bits of wood away. Finally the gap was large enough to admit one, a tall, thin male with gossamer hair, his green eyes glowing with the joy of the fight. He struck at Eric with a sword, and Eric parried and managed to slash his opponent's abdomen. The fairy shrieked and doubled over, and Clancy's blow caught him on the back of the neck and severed his head.

I pressed my back against the wall and tucked the crutch under one arm. I gripped my weapons, one in each hand. Bill and I were side by side, and then he slowly and deliberately stepped in front of me. Bill threw his knife at the next fairy through the door, and the point went right into the fairy's throat. Bill reached back and took my grandmother's trowel.

The door was almost demolished by now, and the assault-ing fairies seemed to move back. Another male stepped in through the splinters and over the body of the first fae, and I knew this must be Breandan. His reddish hair was pulled back in a braid and his sword slung a spray of blood from its blade as he raised it to swing at Eric.

Eric was the taller, but Breandan had a longer sword. Breandan was already wounded, for his shirt was drenched with blood on one side. I saw something bright, a knitting needle, protruding from Breandan's shoulder, and I was sure the blood on his sword was Claudine's. A rage went through me, and that held me up when I would have collapsed.

Breandan leaped sideways, despite Eric's attempts to keep him engaged, and a very tall female warrior jumped into the spot Breandan had occupied and swung a mace—a mace, for God's sake—at Eric. Eric ducked, and the mace continued its path and hit Clancy in the side of the head. Instantly his red hair was even redder, and he went down like a bag of sand. Breandan leaped over Clancy to face Bill, his sword slicing off Clancy's head as he cleared the body. Breandan's grin grew brighter. "You're the one," he said. "The one who killed Neave."

"I took out her throat," Bill said, and his voice seemed as strong as it ever had been. But he swayed on his feet.

"I see she's killed you, too," Breandan said, and smiled, his guard relaxing slightly. "I'll only be the one to make you realize it."

Behind him, forgotten on the corner bed, Tray Dawson made a superhuman effort and gripped the fairy's shirt. With a negligent gesture, Breandan twisted slightly and brought the gleaming sword down on the defenseless Were, and when he pulled the sword back, it was freshly coated with red. But in the moment it took Breandan to do this, Bill thrust my trowel under Breandan's raised arm. When Breandan turned back, his expression was startled. He looked down at the hilt as if he couldn't imagine how it came to be sticking out of his side, and then blood ran from the corner of his mouth.

Bill began to fall.

Everything stood still for a moment, but only in my mind. The space in front of me was clear, and the woman abandoned her fight with Eric and leaped on top of the body of her prince. She screamed, long and loud, and since Bill was falling she aimed the thrust of her sword at me.

I squirted her with the lemon juice in my water pistol.

She screamed again, but this time in pain. The juice had fallen on her in a spray, across her chest and upper arms, and where the lemon had touched her, smoke began to rise from her skin. A drop had hit her eyelid, I realized, because she used her free hand to rub at the burning eye. And while she did that, Eric swung his long knife and severed her arm, and then he stabbed her.

Then Niall filled the doorway of the room, and my eyes hurt to see him. He wasn't wearing the black suit he wore when he met me in the human world but a sort of long tunic and loose pants tucked into boots. Everything about him was white, and he shone . . . except where he was splashed with blood.

Then there was a long silence. There was no one left to kill.

I slid to the floor, my legs as weak as Jell-O. I found myself slumped against the wall by Bill. I couldn't tell if he was alive or dead. I was too shocked to weep and too horrified to scream. Some of my cuts had reopened, and the scent of the blood and the reek of fairy lured Eric, pumped full of the excitement of battle. Before Niall could reach me, Eric was on his knees beside me, licking the blood from a slice on my cheek. I didn't mind; he'd given me his. He was recycling.

"Off her, vampire," said my great-grandfather in a very soft voice.

Eric raised his head, his eyes shut with pleasure, and shuddered all over. But then he collapsed beside me. He stared at Clancy's body. All the exultation drained from his face and a red tear made its way down his cheek.

"Is Bill alive?" I asked.

"I don't know," he said. He looked down at his arm. He'd been wounded, too: a bad slash on his left forearm. I hadn't even seen it happen. Through the torn sleeve, I watched the cut begin to heal.

My great-grandfather squatted in front of me.

"Niall," I said, my lips and mouth working with great effort. "Niall, I didn't think you would come in time."

Truthfully, I was so stunned I hardly knew what I was saying or even which crisis I was referring to. For the first time, keeping on living seemed so difficult I wasn't sure it was worth the trouble.

My great-grandfather took me in his arms. "You are safe now," he said. "I am the only living prince. No one can take that away from me. Almost all of my enemies are dead."

"Look around," I said, though I lay my head on his shoulder. "Niall, look at all that's been taken." Tray Dawson's blood trickled slowly down the soaked sheet to patter on the floor. Bill was crumpled against my right thigh. As my great-grandfather held me close and stroked my hair, I looked past his arm at Bill. He'd lived for so many years, survived by hook or by crook. He'd been ready to die for me. There is no female—human, fairy, vamp, Were—who wouldn't be affected by that. I thought of the nights we'd spent together, the times we'd talked lying together in bed—and I cried, though I felt almost too tired to produce tears.

My great-grandfather sat back on his heels and looked at me. "You need to go home," he said.

"Claudine?"

"She's in the Summerlands."

I couldn't stand any more bad news.

"Fairy, I leave cleaning this place to you," Eric said. "Your great-granddaughter is my woman, mine and mine alone. I'll take her to her home."

Niall glared at Eric. "Not all the bodies are fae," Niall said with a pointed glance at Clancy. "And what must we do with that one?" He jerked his head toward Tray.

"*That one* needs to go back into his house," I said. "He has to be given a proper burial. He can't just vanish." I had no idea what Tray would have wanted, but I couldn't let the fairies shovel his body into a pit somewhere. He deserved far better than that. And there was Amelia to tell. Oh, God. I tried to pull my legs up preparatory to standing, but my stitches yanked and pain shot through me. "*Ahh,*" I said, and clenched my teeth.

I stared down at the floor while I got my breath back. And while I was staring, one of Bill's fingers twitched.

"He's alive, Eric," I said, and though it hurt like the dickens, I could smile about that. "Bill's alive."

"That's good," Eric said, though he sounded too calm. He flipped open his cell phone and speed-dialed someone. "Pam," he said. "Pam, Sookie lives. Yes, and Bill, too. Not Clancy. Bring the van."

Though I lost a little time somewhere in there, eventually Pam arrived with a huge van. It had a mattress in the back, and Bill and I were loaded in by Pam and Maxwell Lee, a black businessman who just happened to be a vampire. At least, that was the impression Maxwell always gave. Even on this night of violence and conflict, Maxwell looked neat and unruffled. Though he was taller than Pam, they got us into the back with gentleness and grace, and I appreciated it very much. Pam even forewent making any jokes, which was a welcome change.

As we drove back to Bon Temps, I could hear the vampires talking quietly about the end of the fairy war.

"It will be too bad if they leave this world," Pam said. "I love them so much. They're so hard to catch."

Maxwell Lee said, "I never had a fairy."

"Yum," Pam said, and it was the most eloquent "yum" I've ever heard.

"Be quiet," Eric said, and they both shut up.

Bill's fingers found mine, gripped them.

"Clancy lives on in Bill," Eric told the other two.

They received this news in a silence that seemed respectful to me.

"As you live on in Sookie," Pam said very quietly.

My great-grandfather came to see me two days later. After she let him in, Amelia went upstairs to cry some more. She knew the truth, of course, though the rest of our community was shocked that someone had broken into Tray's house and tortured him. Popular opinion said that his assailants must have believed Tray was a drug dealer, though there was absolutely no drug paraphernalia found in an intensive search of his house and shop. Tray's ex-wife and his son were making the funeral arrangements, and Tray would be buried at

Immaculate Conception Catholic Church. I was going to try to go to support Amelia. I had another day to get better, but today I was content to lie on my bed, dressed in a nightgown. Eric couldn't give me any more blood to complete my healing. For one thing, in the past few days he'd already given me blood twice, to say nothing of the nips we'd exchanged during lovemaking, and he said we were dangerously close to some undefined limit. For another thing, Eric needed all his blood to heal himself, and he took some of Pam's, too. So I itched and healed, and saw that the vampire blood had filled in the bitten-out flesh of my legs.

That made my explanation of my injuries (a car accident; I'd been hit by a stranger who'd driven away) just feasible if not too many people examined the wounds. Of course, Sam had known right away that wasn't the truth. I had ended up telling him what had happened the first time he came to see me. The patrons of Merlotte's were very sympathetic, he reported when he came the second time. He had brought me daisies and a chicken basket from Dairy Queen. When he'd thought I wasn't watching, Sam had looked at me with grim eyes.

After Niall pulled a chair close to the bed, he took my hand. Maybe the events of the past few days had made the fine wrinkles in his skin a fraction deeper. Maybe he looked a little sad. But my royal great-grandfather was still beautiful, still regal, still strange, and now that I knew what his race could do . . . he looked frightening.

"Did you know Lochlan and Neave killed my parents?" I asked.

Niall nodded after a perceptible pause. "I suspected," he said. "When you told me your parents had drowned, I had to consider it possible. They all had an affinity to water, Breandan's people."

"I'm glad they're dead," I said.

"Yes, I am, too," he said simply. "And most of Breandan's followers are dead, as well. I spared two females, since we need them so much, and though one of them was the mother of Breandan's child, I let her live."

He seemed to want my praise for that. "What about the child?" I asked.

Niall shook his head, and the sheet of pale hair moved with the gesture.

He loved me, but he was from a world even more savage than mine.

As if he had heard my thoughts, Niall said, "I'm going to finish blocking the passage to our land."

"But that's what the war was over," I said, bewildered. "That was what Breandan wanted."

"I have come to think that he was right, though for the wrong reason. It isn't the fae who need to be protected from the human world. It's the humans who need to be protected from us."

"What will that mean? What are the consequences?"

"Those of us who've been living among the humans will have to choose."

"Like Claude."

"Yes. He'll have to cut his ties with our secret land, if he wants to live out here."

"And the rest? The ones who live there already?"

"We won't be coming out anymore." His face was luminous with grief.

"I won't get to see you?"

"No, dear heart. It's better not."

I tried to summon up a protest, to tell him that it was *not* better, it was awful, since I had so few relatives, that I would not talk to him again. But I just couldn't make the words come out of my mouth. "What about Dermot?" I said instead.

"We can't find him," Niall said. "If he's dead, he went to ash somewhere we haven't discovered. If he's here, he's being very clever and very quiet. We'll keep trying until the door closes."

I hoped devoutly that Dermot was on the fairy side of that door.

At that moment, Jason came in.

My great-grandfather—*our* great-grandfather—leaped to his feet. But after a moment, he relaxed. "You must be Jason," he said.

My brother stared at him blankly. Jason had not been himself since the death of Mel. The same edition of our local paper that had carried the story about the awful discovery of the body of Tray Dawson had carried another story about the disappearance of Mel Hart. There was wide conjecture that maybe the two events were connected somehow.

I didn't know how the werepanthers had covered up the scene in back of Jason's house, and I didn't want to know. I didn't know where Mel's body was, either. Maybe it had been eaten. Maybe it was at the bottom of Jason's pond. Maybe it lay in the woods somewhere.

The last was what I suspected. Jason and Calvin had told the police that Mel had said he was going hunting by himself, and Mel's truck was found parked at a hunting preserve where he had a share. There were some bloodstains discovered in the back of the truck that made police suspect Mel might know something about Crystal Stackhouse's awful death, and now Andy Bellefleur had been heard to say he wouldn't be surprised if old Mel hadn't killed himself out in the woods.

"Yeah, I'm Jason," my brother said heavily. "You must be . . . my great-grandfather?"

Niall inclined his head. "I am. I've come to bid your sister good-bye."

"But not me, huh? I'm not good enough."

"You are too much like Dermot."

"Well, crap." Jason threw himself down on the foot of the bed. "Dermot didn't seem too bad to me, *Great-grandfather*. Least, he came to warn me about Mel, let me know that Mel had killed my wife."

"Yes," Niall said remotely. "Dermot may have been partial to you because of the resemblance. I suppose you know that he helped to kill your parents?"

We both stared at Niall.

"Yes, the water fae who followed Breandan had pushed the truck into the stream, as I hear it, but only Dermot was able to touch the door and pull your parents out. Then the water nymphs held them underwater."

I shuddered.

"Ask me, I'm glad you're saying good-bye," Jason said. "I'm glad you're leaving. I hope you never come back, not a one of you."

Pain flitted over Niall's face. "I can't dispute your feeling," he said. "I only wanted to know my great-granddaughter. But I've brought Sookie nothing but grief."

I opened my mouth to protest, and then I realized he was telling the truth. Just not all the truth.

"You brought me the reassurance that I had family who loved me," I said, and Jason made a choking sound. "You sent Claudine to save my life, and she did, more than once. I'll miss you, Niall."

"The vampire is not a bad man, and he loves you," Niall

said. He rose. "Good-bye." He bent and kissed my cheek. There was power in his touch, and I suddenly felt better. Before Jason could gather himself to object, Niall kissed his forehead, and Jason's tense muscles relaxed.

Then my great-grandfather was gone before I could ask him which vampire he meant.

Turn the page for an excerpt from
the next novel in Charlaine Harris's
Sookie Stackhouse series

DEAD IN THE FAMILY

Available now from Ace Books!

MARCH—THE FIRST WEEK

"I feel bad that I'm leaving you like this," Amelia said. Her eyes were puffy and red. They'd been that way, off and on, ever since Tray Dawson's funeral.

"You have to do what you have to do," I said, giving her a very bright smile. I could read the guilt and shame and ever-present grief roiling around Amelia's mind in a ball of darkness. "I'm lots better," I reassured her. I could hear myself babbling cheerfully along, but I couldn't seem to stop. "I'm walking okay, and the holes all filled in. See how much better?" I pulled down my jeans waistband to show her a spot that had been bitten out. The teeth marks were hardly perceptible, though the skin wasn't quite smooth and was visibly paler than the surrounding flesh. If I hadn't had a huge dose of vampire blood, the scar would've looked like a shark had bitten me.

Amelia glanced down and hastily away, as if she couldn't bear to see the evidence of the attack. "It's just that Octavia keeps e-mailing me and telling me I need to come home and accept my judgment from the witches' council, or what's left of it," she said in a rush. "And I need to check all the repairs to my house. And since there are a few tourists again, and people returning and rebuilding, the magic store's reopened. I can work there part-time. Plus, as much as I love you and I love living here, since Tray died . . ."

"Believe me, I understand." We'd gone over this a few times.

"It's not that I blame you," Amelia said, trying to catch my eyes.

She really didn't blame me. Since I could read her mind, I knew she was telling me the truth.

Even *I* didn't totally blame myself, somewhat to my surprise.

It was true that Tray Dawson, Amelia's lover and a Were, had been killed while acting as my bodyguard. It was true that I'd requested a bodyguard from the Were pack nearest me because they owed me a favor and my life needed guarding. However, I'd been present at the death of Tray Dawson at the hands of a sword-wielding fairy, and I knew who was responsible.

So I didn't feel guilty, exactly. But I felt heartsick about losing Tray, on top of all the other horrors. My cousin Claudine, a full-blooded fairy, had also died in the Fae War, and since she'd been my real, true fairy godmother, I missed her in a lot of ways. And she'd been pregnant.

I had a lot of pain and regret of all kinds, physical and mental. While Amelia carried an armful of clothes downstairs, I stood in her bedroom, gathering myself. Then I braced my shoulders and lifted a box of bathroom odds and ends. I descended the stairs carefully and slowly, and I made my way out to her car. She turned from depositing the clothes across the boxes already stowed in her trunk. "You shouldn't be doing that!" she said, all anxious concern. "You're not healed yet."

"I'm fine."

"Not hardly. You always jump when someone comes into the room and surprises you, and I can tell your wrists hurt," she said. She grabbed the box and slid it into the backseat. "You still favor that left leg, and you still ache when it rains. Despite all that vamp blood."

"The jumpiness'll get better. As time passes, it won't be so fresh and at the front of my mind," I told Amelia. (If telepathy had taught me anything, it was that people could bury the most serious and painful of memories, if you gave them enough time and distraction.) "The blood is not just any vampire's. It's Eric's blood. It's strong stuff. And my wrists are a lot better." I didn't mention that the nerves were jumping around in them like hot snakes just at this moment, a result of their having been tied together tightly for several hours. Dr. Ludwig, physician to the supernatural, had told me the nerves—and the wrists—would be back to normal— eventually.

"Yeah, speaking of the blood . . ." Amelia took a deep breath and steeled herself to say something she knew I wouldn't like. Since I heard it before she actually voiced it, I was able to brace myself. "Had you thought about . . . Sookie, you didn't ask me, but I think you better not have any more of Eric's blood. I mean, I know he's your man, but you got to think about the consequences. Sometimes people get flipped by accident. It's not like it's a math equation."

Though I appreciated Amelia's concern, she'd trespassed into private territory. "We don't swap," I said. *Much.* "He just has a sip from me at, you know . . . the happy moment." These days Eric was having a lot more happy moments than I was, sadly. I kept hoping the bedroom magic would return; if any male could perform sexual healing, that male would be Eric.

Amelia smiled, which was what I'd been aiming for. "At least . . ." She turned away without finishing the sentence, but she was thinking, *At least you feel like having sex.*

I didn't so much feel like having sex as I felt like I ought to keep trying to enjoy it, but I definitely didn't want to discuss that. My ability to cast aside control, which is the key to good sex, had been pinched out of existence during the torture. I'd been absolutely helpless. I could only hope that I'd recover in that area, too. I knew Eric could feel my lack of completion. He'd asked me several times if I was sure I wanted to engage in sex. Nearly every time, I said yes, operating on the bicycle theory. Yes, I'd fallen off. But I was always willing to try to ride it again.

"So, how's the relationship doing?" she said. "Aside from the whoopee." Every last thing was in Amelia's car. She was stalling, dreading the moment when she actually got into her car and drove away.

It was only pride that was keeping me from bawling all over her.

"I think we're getting along pretty well," I said with a great effort at sounding cheerful. "I'm still not sure what I feel as opposed to what the bond is making me feel." It was kind of nice to be able to talk about my supernatural connection to Eric, as well as my regular old man-woman attraction. Even before my injuries during the Fae War, Eric and I had established what the vampires called a blood bond, since we'd exchanged blood several times. I could sense Eric's general location and his mood, and he could feel the same things about me. He was always faintly present in the back of my mind—sort of like turning on a fan or an air filter to provide a little buzz of noise that would help you get to sleep. (It was good for me that Eric slept all day, because I could be by myself at least part of the time. Maybe he felt the same way after I went to bed at night?) It wasn't like I heard voices in my head or anything—at least no more than usual. But if I felt happy, I had to check to make sure it was me and not Eric who felt happy. Likewise for anger; Eric was big on anger, controlled and carefully banked anger, especially lately. Maybe he was getting that from me. I was pretty full of anger myself these days.

I'd forgotten all about Amelia. I'd stepped right into my own trough of depression.

She snapped me out of it. "That's just a big fat excuse," she said tartly. "Come on, Sookie. You love him, or you don't. Don't keep putting off thinking about it by blaming everything on your bond. Wah, wah, wah. If you hate the bond so much, why haven't you explored how you can get free of it?" She took in the expression on my face, and the irritation faded out of her own. "Do you want me to ask Octavia?" she asked in a milder voice. "If anyone would know, she would."

"Yes, I'd like to find out," I said, after a moment. I took a deep breath. "You're right, I guess. I've been so depressed I've put off making any decisions, or acting on the ones I've already made. Eric's one of a kind. But I find him . . . a little overwhelming." He was a strong personality, and he was used to being the big fish in the pond. He also knew he had infinite time ahead of him.

I did not.

He hadn't brought that up yet, but sooner or later, he would.

"Overwhelming or not, I love him," I continued. I'd never said it out loud. "And I guess that's the bottom line."

"I guess it is." Amelia tried to smile at me, but it was a woeful attempt. "Listen, you keep that up, the self-knowledge thing." She stood for a moment, her expression frozen into the half smile. "Well, Sook, I better get on the road. My dad's expecting me. He'll be all up in my business the minute I get back to New Orleans."

Amelia's dad was rich, powerful, and had no belief in Amelia's power at all. He was very wrong not to respect her witchcraft. Amelia had been born with the potential for the power in her, as every true witch is. Once Amelia had some more training and discipline, she was going to be really scary—scary on purpose, rather than because of the drastic nature of her mistakes. I hoped her mentor, Octavia, had a program in place to develop and train Amelia's talent.

After I waved Amelia down the driveway, the broad smile dropped from my face. I sat on the porch steps and cried. It didn't take much for me to be in tears these days, and my friend's departure was just the trigger now. There was so much to weep about.

My sister-in-law, Crystal, had been murdered. My brother's friend Mel had been executed. Tray and Claudine and Clancy the vampire had been killed in the line of duty. Since Crystal, like Claudine, had been pregnant, that added two more deaths to the list.

Probably that should have made me long for peace above all else. But instead of turning into the Bon Temps Gandhi, in my heart I held the knowledge that there were plenty of people I wanted dead. I wasn't directly responsible for most of the deaths that were scattered in my wake, but I was haunted by the feeling that none of them would have happened if it weren't for me. In my darkest moments—and this was one of them—I wondered if my life was worth the price that had been paid for it.

MARCH—THE END OF THE FIRST WEEK

My cousin Claude was sitting on the front porch when I got up on a cloudy, brisk morning a few days after Amelia's departure. Claude wasn't as skilled at masking his presence as my great-grandfather Niall had been. Because Claude was fae, I couldn't read his mind—but I could tell his mind was there, if that isn't too obscure a way to put it. I carried my coffee out to the porch, though the air was nippy, because drinking that first cup on the porch had been one of my favorite things to do before I . . . before the Fae War.

I hadn't seen my cousin in weeks. I hadn't seen him during the Fae War, and he hadn't contacted me since the death of Claudine.

I'd brought an extra mug for Claude, and I handed it to him. He accepted it silently. I'd considered the possibility he might throw it in my face. His unexpected presence had thrown me off course. I had no idea what to expect. The breeze lifted his long black hair, tossed it around like rippling ebony ribbons. His caramel eyes were red-rimmed.

"How did she die?" he said.

I sat on the top step. "I didn't see it," I said, hunching over my knees. "We were in that old building Dr. Ludwig was using as a hospital. I think Claudine was trying to stop the other fairies from coming down the corridor to get into the room where I was holed up with Bill and Eric and Tray." I looked over at Claude to make sure he knew the place, and he nodded. "I'm pretty sure that it was Breandan who killed her, because one of her knitting needles was stuck in his shoulder when he busted into our room."

Breandan, my great-grandfather's enemy, had also been a prince of the fae. Breandan had believed that humans and the fae should not consort. He'd believed that to the point of fanaticism. He'd wanted the fae to completely abstain from their forays into the human world, despite the fae's large financial stake in mundane commerce and the products it had produced . . . products that helped them blend into the modern world. Breandan had especially hated the occasional taking of human lovers, a fae indulgence, and he'd hated the children born as a result of such liaisons. He'd wanted the fae separate, walled away into their own world, consorting only with their own kind.

Oddly enough, that's what my great-grandfather had decided to do after defeating the fairy who believed in this apartheid policy. After all the bloodshed, Niall concluded that peace among the fae and safety for humans could be reached only if the fae blocked themselves into their world. Breandan had achieved his ends by his own death. In my worst moments, I thought that Niall's final decision had made the whole war unnecessary.

"She was defending you," Claude said, pulling me back into the moment. There was nothing in his voice. Not blame, not anger, not a question.

"Yeah." That had been part of her job, defending me, by Niall's orders.

I took a long sip of coffee. Claude's sat untouched on the arm of the porch swing. Maybe Claude was wondering if he should kill me. Claudine had been his last surviving sibling.

"You knew about the pregnancy," he said finally.

"She told me right before she was killed." I put down my mug and wrapped my arms around my knees. I waited for the blow to fall. At first I didn't mind all that much, which was even more horrible.

Claude said, "I understand Neave and Lochlan had hold of you. Is that why you're limping?" The change of subject caught me off guard.

"Yeah," I said. "They had me for a couple of hours. Niall and Bill Compton killed them. Just so you know—it was Bill who killed Breandan, with my grandmother's iron trowel." Though the trowel had been in my family's toolshed for decades, I associated it with Gran.

Claude sat, beautiful and unreadable, for a long time. He never looked at me directly nor drank his coffee. When he'd reached some inner conclusion, he rose and left, walking down the driveway toward Hummingbird Road. I don't know where his car was parked. For all I knew, he'd walked all the way from Monroe, or flown over on a magic carpet. I went into the house, sank to my knees right inside the door, and cried. My hands were shaking. My wrists ached.

The whole time we'd been talking, I'd been waiting for him to make his move.

I realized I wanted to live.

MARCH—THE SECOND WEEK

JB said, "Raise your arm all the way up, Sookie!" His handsome face was creased with concentration. Holding the five-pound weight, I slowly lifted my left arm. Geez Louise, it hurt. Same with the right.

"Okay, now the legs," JB said, when my arms were shaking

with strain. JB wasn't a licensed physical therapist, but he was a personal trainer, so he'd had practical experience helping people get over various injuries. Maybe he'd never faced an assortment like mine, since I'd been bitten, cut, and tortured. But I hadn't had to explain the details to JB, and he wouldn't notice that my injuries were far from typical from those incurred in a car accident. I didn't want any speculation going around Bon Temps about my physical problems—so I made the occasional visits to Dr. Amy Ludwig, who looked suspiciously like a hobbit, and I enlisted the help of JB du Rone, who was a good trainer but dumb as a box of rocks.

JB's wife, my friend Tara, was sitting on one of the weight benches. She was reading *What to Expect When You're Expecting*. Tara, almost five months pregnant, was determined to be the best mother she could possibly be. Since JB was willing but not bright, Tara was assuming the role of Most Responsible Parent. She'd earned her high school spending money as a babysitter, which gave her some experience in child care. She was frowning as she turned the pages, a look familiar to me from our school years.

"Have you picked a doctor yet?" I said, after I'd finished my leg lifts. My quads were screaming, particularly the damaged one in my left leg. We were in the gym where JB worked, and it was after hours, because I wasn't a member. JB's boss had okayed the temporary arrangement to keep JB happy. JB was a huge asset to the gym; since he'd started working, new female clients had increased by a noticeable percentage.

"I think so," said Tara. "There were four choices in this area, and we interviewed all of them. I've had my first appointment with Dr. Dinwiddie, here in Clarice. I know it's a little hospital, but I'm not high-risk, and it's so close."

Clarice was just a few miles from Bon Temps, where we all

lived. You could get from my house to the gym in less than twenty minutes.

"I hear good things about him," I said, the pain in my quads making stuff start to slide around inside my head. My forehead broke out in a clammy sweat. I was used to thinking of myself as a fit woman, and mostly I'd been a happy one. There were days now when it was all I could do to get out of bed and get in to work.

"Sook," JB said, "look at the weight on here." He was grinning at me.

For the first time, I registered that I'd done ten extensions with ten more pounds than I'd been using.

I smiled back at him. It didn't last long, but I knew I'd done something good.

"Maybe you'll babysit for us sometime," Tara said. "We'll teach the baby to call you Aunt Sookie."

I'd be a courtesy aunt. I'd get to take care of a baby. They trusted me. I found myself planning on a future.

THE SAME WEEK

I spent the next night with Eric. As I did at least three or four times a week, I woke up panting, filled with terror, completely at sea. I held on to him as if the storm would sweep me away unless he was my anchor. I was already crying when I woke. It wasn't the first time this had happened, but this time he wept with me, bloody tears that streaked the whiteness of his face in a startling way.

"Don't," I begged him. I had been trying so hard to act like my old self when I was with him. Of course, he knew differently. Tonight I could feel his resolve. Eric had something to say to me, and he was going to tell me whether I wanted to listen or not.

"I could feel your fear and your pain that night," he said, in a choked voice. "But I couldn't come to you."

Finally, he was telling me something I had been waiting to learn.

"Why not?" I said, trying very hard to keep my voice level. This may seem incredible, but I had been in such shaky condition I hadn't dared to ask him.

"Victor wouldn't let me leave," he said. Victor Madden was Eric's boss; he'd been appointed by Felipe de Castro, King of Nevada, to oversee the conquered kingdom of Louisiana.

My initial reaction to Eric's explanation was bitter disappointment. I'd heard this story before. *A vampire more powerful than me made me do it:* Bill's excuse for going back to his maker, Lorena, revisited. "Sure," I said. I turned over and lay with my back to him. I felt the cold, creeping misery of disillusionment. I decided to pull my clothes on, to drive back to Bon Temps, as soon as I gathered the energy. The tension, the frustration, the rage in Eric was sapping me.

"Victor's people chained me with silver," Eric said behind me. "It burned me everywhere."

"Literally." I tried not to sound as skeptical as I felt.

"Yes, literally. I knew something was happening with you. Victor was at Fangtasia that night, as if he knew ahead of time he should be there. When Bill called to tell me you'd been taken, I managed to call Niall before three of Victor's people chained me to the wall. When I—protested—Victor said he couldn't *allow* me to take sides in the Fae War. He said that no matter what happened to you, I couldn't get involved."

Rage made Eric fall silent for a long moment. It poured

through me like a burning, icy stream. He resumed his story in a choked voice.

"Pam was also seized and isolated by Victor's people, though they didn't chain her." Pam was Eric's second in command. "Since Bill was in Bon Temps, he was able to ignore Victor's phone messages. Niall met Bill at your house to track you. Bill had heard of Lochlan and Neave. We all had. We knew time would run out for you." I still had my back to Eric, but I was listening to more than his voice. Grief, anger, desperation.

"How did you get out of the chains?" I asked the dark.

"I reminded Victor that Felipe had promised you protection, promised it to you *personally*. Victor pretended not to believe me." I could feel the bed move as Eric threw himself back against the pillows. "Some of the vampires were strong and honorable enough to remember they were pledged to Felipe, not Victor. Though they wouldn't defy Victor to his face, behind his back they let Pam call our new king. When she had Felipe on the line, she explained to him that you and I had married. Then she demanded Victor take the telephone and talk to Felipe. Victor didn't dare to refuse. Felipe ordered Victor to let me go." A few weeks ago, Felipe de Castro had become the king of Nevada, Louisiana, *and* Arkansas. He was powerful, old, and very crafty. And he owed me big-time.

"Did Felipe punish Victor?" Hope springs eternal.

"There's the rub," Eric said. Somewhere along the line, my Viking honey had read Shakespeare. "Victor claimed he'd temporarily forgotten our marriage." Even if I sometimes tried to forget it myself, that made me angry. Victor had been sitting right there in Eric's office when I'd handed the ceremonial knife to Eric—in complete ignorance that my action constituted a marriage, vampire-style. I might have been ignorant, but Victor certainly wasn't. "Victor told our king that I was

lying in an attempt to save my human lover from the fae. He
said vampire lives must not be lost in the rescue of a human.
He told Felipe that he hadn't believed Pam and me when we
told him Felipe had promised you protection after you saved
him from Sigebert."

I rolled over to face Eric, and the bit of moonlight coming
in the window painted him in shades of dark and silver. In my
brief experience of the powerful vampire who'd maneuvered
himself into a position of great power, Felipe was absolutely
no fool. "Incredible. Why didn't Felipe kill Victor?" I asked.

"I've given that a lot of thought, of course. I think Felipe
has to pretend he believes Victor. I think Felipe realizes that
in making Victor his lieutenant in charge of the whole state
of Louisiana, he has inflated Victor's ambitions to the point
of indecency."

It was possible to look at Eric objectively, I discovered,
while I was thinking over what he'd said. My trust had gotten me burned in the past, and I wasn't going to get too close
to the fire this time without careful consideration. It was one
thing to enjoy laughing with Eric, or to look forward to the
times when we twined together in the dark. It was another
thing to trust him with more fragile emotions. I was really
not into trust right now.

"You were upset when you came to the hospital," I said
indirectly. When I'd wakened in the old factory Dr. Ludwig
was using as a field hospital, my injuries had been so painful
I'd thought dying might prove easier than living. Bill, who
had saved me, had been poisoned with a bite from Neave's
silver teeth. His survival had been up in the air. The mortally
wounded Tray Dawson, Amelia's werewolf lover, had hung
on long enough to die by the sword when Breandan's forces
stormed the hospital.

"While you were with Neave and Lochlan, I suffered with you," he said, meeting my eyes directly. "I hurt with you. I bled with you—not only because we're bonded, but because of the love I have for you."

I raised a skeptical eyebrow. I couldn't help it, though I could feel that he meant what he was saying. I was just willing to believe that Eric would have come to my help much faster, if he could have. I was willing to believe that he'd heard the echo of the horror of my time with the fae torturers.

But my pain and blood and terror had been my own. He might have felt them, but from a separate place. "I believe you would have been there if you could have," I said, knowing my voice was too calm. "I really do believe that. I know you would have killed them." Eric leaned over on one elbow, and his big hand pressed my face to his chest.

I couldn't deny that I felt better since he'd brought himself to tell me. Yet I didn't feel as much better as I'd hoped, though now I knew why he hadn't come when I'd been screaming for him. I could even understand why it had taken so long for him to tell me. Helplessness was a state Eric didn't often encounter. Eric was supernatural, and he was incredibly strong, and he was a great fighter. But he was not a superhero, and he couldn't overcome several determined members of his own race. And I realized he'd given me a lot of blood when he himself was healing from the silver chains.

Finally, something inside me relaxed at the logic of his story. I believed him in my heart, not just in my head.

A red tear fell on my bare shoulder and coursed down. I swept it up on my finger, putting my finger to his lips— offering his pain back to him. I had plenty of my own.

COMING IN JUNE
TO DVD, BLU-RAY™
AND DIGITAL DOWNLOAD

EDITED BY
#1 *NEW YORK TIMES* BESTSELLING AUTHOR

CHARLAINE HARRIS
&
TONI L. P. KELNER

HOME IMPROVEMENT: UNDEAD EDITION

There's nothing quite like a home renovation for finding
skeletons in the closet—or witches in the attic. And if the
home in question belongs to a vampire, a wizard, a
ghost or even a demon, the possibility of DIY
going bad is very, very high...

ALL-NEW ORIGINAL TALES
OF HAUNTED HOME REPAIR BY

CHARLAINE HARRIS
PATRICIA BRIGGS
VICTOR GISCHLER
JAMES GRADY
HEATHER GRAHAM
SIMON R. GREEN
STACIA KANE
TONI L. P. KELNER
E. E. KNIGHT
ROCHELLE KRICH
MELISSA MARR
SEANAN McGUIRE
SUZANNE McLEOD
S. J. ROZAN

Coming August 2011 from Ace Books

Includes a never-before-published
SOOKIE STACKHOUSE story!

penguin.com

M808T1110